MINA

Warrior in the Shadows Series
Book 1

By Deborah Cullins Smith

www.YeOldeDragonBooks.com

Ye Olde Dragon Books
P.O. Box 30802
Middleburg Hts., OH 44130

www.YeOldeDragonBooks.com

2OldeDragons@gmail.com

ISBN 13: 978-1-952345-57-9

Published in the United States of America
Publication Date: December 1, 2021

Cover Art Copyright Kaitlyn Emery 2021

CHAPTER 1

LONDON, 1871

Shadows lengthened and trash blew across cobblestone streets in the dying light over London. Mina Harker gripped her cloak closer and hastened her footsteps. Professor Van Helsing's lab lay just ahead, and she longed for the comforting fire, a warm cup of tea, and the reassurance the old man would apply liberally to her spirit.

The wind picked up, and Mina's pulse rate responded likewise. Her eyes darted from side to side, and like lightning, she spun and half-crouched, ready for an attack. No one appeared in the darkened street. Lamplighters were about a block away, by the flickers of light she could see in the misty twilight. But Mina's eyes were sharp. She sensed the presence, though she still did not see it. She was not foolish enough to dismiss the prickly sensation that told her she was being stalked by a predator. She knew too well what that sensation meant, and she would not be caught unaware. Only a few more doors.

She rose from the crouch and turned —

To see a tall man standing inches from her face. His skin was pale, and he sported a short, dark beard and thin mustache. His clothes were impeccable, the evening coat of a gentleman, with a silk scarf draped around his neck. His top hat perched above round, dark glasses and his smile showed the glimmer of even white teeth. *Dark glasses at this time of night?*

"Not a good neighborhood for a lady of your ... gentility," he said with a smile that held no mirth.

"Not your concern, sir," Mina said, stepping backward in measured steps that held her fear in check and revealed no consternation at his sudden appearance.

He tilted his head, and his brow creased ever so slightly. Obviously, he had expected her to swoon or scream. Most women would in this year of 1871. He certainly didn't expect her to stand her ground. His eyes were hidden behind the darkened lenses of the glasses, so it was difficult to tell. But then, Count Dracula had often worn glasses like that, Mina reminded herself. Her eyes narrowed and she remained wary of his every move.

"But you should have an escort, miss," he said, stepping closer. "I would be happy to accommodate."

She took another step backward and realized he had purposefully maneuvered her back to the mouth of an alley. With that last step, his breath hit her in the face and she smelled it—the odor of death, of blood. Vampire. Mina gripped her small purse firmly in her left hand, and with her right, she yanked a silver-bladed dagger from the sheath sewn into its side. Lunging forward, she stabbed toward his heart, but he sidestepped her easily, knocking the blade from her grip.

"Now that's not very nice, when I've tried to be so helpful to you." He bared his fangs and grabbed her shoulders firmly with both hands.

"*No!*" she shouted, as she flung him backward with a force that surprised them both.

"How did you do that?" he snarled as he scrambled to his feet. "Who are you?"

He slammed into her, forcing her backward against the bricks. Bits of mortar chewed into the back of her head as her hat fell off and landed in a pile of trash. She scratched at his pale face and one metal frame broke on his glasses, leaving them hanging from his right ear. There! His eyes held the preternatural gleam of an undead creature.

As he jerked backward away from her fingernails, Mina kicked viciously, and landed a solid blow to his kneecap. She heard the bones snap and the creature howled. Stumbling backward, he cursed her. But she'd found her handbag in the dark alley and pulled more weapons from it. Holding it high in her left hand so the light of the rising moon caught in it and reflected in the shining surface. The man screamed again as the shadow of a silver cross fell upon his broken form. With her right hand, she dashed a small glass bottle on the ground near him. It shattered and splashed him with holy water. He cursed her in a voice of harsh, guttural tones.

"Get away from me!" she screamed.

Just then, a door opened and an elderly man stood poised on his doorstep with a gun in one hand. "Mina?" His silver hair glistened like a halo in the dim light from his open doorway, but his posture was ramrod stiff, his eyes alert.

The vampire turned and whirled away so quickly it almost

seemed as though he disappeared into the foggy night. Mina sagged for a moment, panting in relief, then retrieved her knife and purse, and hastened across the street to join Van Helsing.

"Who was that?" Van Helsing demanded.

"I don't know who he was, but I know *what* he was," she said, returning the cross and the dagger to her purse.

"Are you harmed?" he asked.

"No, I'm all right." She patted her head tentatively and winced. "Though I will have a bruised head, and I fear my hat is gone for good." Her fingers came away sticky with blood.

"Tea." He stated it, then took another look at her face. "On second thought, perhaps a brandy."

Mina smiled, her dark eyes sparkling ever so slightly. "Tea would be fine, Professor. And perhaps a bandage."

Safely seated before the fireplace with a cup of tea, Mina submitted to the ministrations of the good doctor as he cleaned the abrasion on her head. She winced as a healthy splash of whisky sloshed into her dark, curly hair.

"To kill the germs, *ja?*" The doctor patted her arm, reassuring her as the stinging gradually reduced to a dull ache. He carefully applied a sterile dressing to the area, then wrapped linen around her head to hold it in place. Standing back, he frowned. "*Nein*... that will attract attention. One moment." He left the room briskly, and Mina slumped in her chair.

Mina sipped her tea, wrinkling her nose a bit as the taste bit her tongue. A smile curved her lips and she shook her head. Professor Van Helsing had spiked her tea with a dab of brandy after all! How like him. For her own good, he would insist. Well, maybe he was right after all. She did need it. The encounter had left her shaken. She'd been feeling uneasy of late, almost waiting for the other shoe to fall. Now she knew. Dracula was not the only monster roaming the streets. She and Van Helsing and their friends had defeated Dracula, but others still walked the night.

It wasn't over.

She leaned back in the stiff wingback chair, weariness overtaking her. Mother would scold. A lady's spine should never touch the back of any chair. 'Sit up straight, Wilhelmina,' came the ghostly voice. But Mina didn't have the strength or the will to obey.

"This should do..." Professor Van Helsing returned with a simple scarf in his hands, but stopped in his tracks. His eyes took in her slumped form, the glaze in her eyes. He nodded slowly, silently acknowledging her thoughts.

"So. My little friend, you have realized it." His words were softly spoken, but they hit Mina like a thunderbolt.

"You knew, didn't you?" she said, sitting up so suddenly the room spun ever so slightly. She gripped the arms of the chair, and her empty tea cup clattered to the floor.

Van Helsing retrieved it, placing it carefully on the small table nearby. He sighed. "Yes, I knew."

"Why didn't you tell us? Why didn't you tell me?" she asked.

"We had won a battle. A terrible battle. After battle, soldiers need to regroup, to recover, to regain their bearings." He sighed again. "I had hoped for more of a respite before we had to enter the fray once again. For you, I had hoped perhaps it was over. That you and your Jonathan could live out your days in peace."

"But that creature tonight—" Mina said. "He asked me what I was. Like I'm not quite human anymore. And I threw him across the alley! How did I do that, Professor? What am I?" Her voice rose in panic.

The professor's hands patted the air in a calming motion, which did little to placate Mina. He stared into her eyes for long moments, gauging, weighing. Abruptly, he rose and paced the room. Mina took a deep breath and willed herself to calm down and wait for him to formulate a plan. She'd seen him react this way before, when dealing with the Nosferatu, the monster who had deceived and beguiled her. He had pulled her back from the brink of destruction and set her back on the path to God again. If there was any hope to be found in this situation, Van Helsing would know where to look.

"First, we test your blood," he said. She began to roll up her sleeve, but he stopped her. "*Nein, mein liebling.* Not tonight. Too much trauma tonight. For now, you will rest. But soon, we will get answers. You partook of Dracula's blood, Mina. Perhaps you retain some of his power, but you belong to God now. You are His. He can use you, even if you have this strength. But we should see just what you have been given in this exchange."

Mina nodded, suddenly very tired.

"Then I want you to do something else as well." Professor Van Helsing hesitated, his brilliant blue eyes piercing her own dark ones. "I wish you to begin instruction with Father Michael Gallagher. I will arrange it tomorrow and let you know when."

"What kind of instruction?" Mina's brow furrowed in confusion.

"That I will discuss with Father Gallagher first," Van Helsing said, looking away. "Now, I must assume that you were coming to my domicile for more tonic for Jonathan, *ja*? I will get a fresh supply and we must get you home before your husband becomes concerned for your safety."

He walked briskly from the room before she could formulate more questions. She had indeed come for more tonic. Jonathan's own encounter with Dracula had been almost as bad as her own. Leaving him locked in his castle with his three brides — vicious, blood-sucking creatures of the night — had weakened Jonathan's body and aged him beyond his twenty-six years.

But never once did Jonathan give in to infecting himself by drinking from them, Mina reminded herself, beating herself once again for her own weakness in the face of the Count's magnetic personality. *Not like I did.*

Now, the professor provided a tonic to build up the blood Jonathan had lost, vitamins and minerals, and iron. His law firm paid them handsomely, even when Jonathan was unable to work for long periods of time. After all, they had sent him to that obscure country in the middle of Eastern Europe to meet with a reclusive count who wanted to buy up property in London. How could they have known that they were dealing with a murderous maniac? A lunatic that would keep him prisoner for months? It was a miracle that Jonathan had escaped at all, but the result was devastating to his physical and mental health. He was better, but still weak and gaunt.

And vulnerable.

Mina's breath caught in her throat at the thought of Jonathan at the mercy of these beasts of the night. They were no longer men and women, but beasts, creatures… monsters.

She looked up and saw Van Helsing watching her from the doorway. How did he always seem to see right through her? But there was never anger or judgment in his eyes. Only compassion. Understanding.

"Come, Mina." He placed two large bottles in a large cloth bag and moved to tie the scarf around her head, covering the bandage. When he finished, he gripped her shoulders and stared into her eyes. "Be ever on guard. You stand between your Jonathan and danger, but you must remember this always — you do not stand alone. Go with God."

He led her outside to where a carriage waited. He gave the address to the driver and paid him generously.

"Professor, this is quite unnecessary," Mina protested as the coins passed hands. "It's not far."

"No, no," Van Helsing said. "I will brook no argument. There is danger in the air tonight. You will be delivered home safely, Mina. But still—be on your guard." He shook a finger at her, then closed the carriage door and motioned for the driver to go.

CHAPTER 2

When Mina arrived home, Betsy met her at the door as soon as she stepped inside.

"Oh, Missus! The master's been right worried," she said, fluttering about. She reached for the hat that would usually be placed in her hands by now, and did a double-take as she noted the simple headscarf of a peasant woman in place of the ladies' hat that Mina had left wearing. "Ma'am, your hat…"

"I lost it, Betsy," Mina said, smoothing her dress and trying to calm herself before she entered Jonathan's study.

"Oh, Mrs. Harker, your new hat…" the girl moaned. Her fingers twisted in her apron, a nervous gesture that Mina somehow found particularly irritating this evening. Betsy was young, a mere sixteen years of age. She was teachable, true, but this was only her second post as a maid, a rise in position from her last job as a scullery maid. When the master of the house had been unable to keep his teen-aged son from trying to visit her in the night, Mrs. Hardman had asked if the Harkers might be able to make use of Betsy in their own household. Mina had agreed immediately.

"Don't fuss, Betsy." Mina tried to be patient, but the girl's agitation was adding to her own tension. "It's only a hat. It was an accident."

"You were in an accident, Miss?" Betsy's voice rose.

"No!" Mina let out an exasperated sigh. "It simply blew off and I couldn't find it in the dark, Betsy. Please calm down. We don't want to upset Mr. Harker, do we?"

Betsy shrank in shame, and Mina tried to squeeze her arm reassuringly. "Can you please ask Mrs. Hardman to bring us some tea?"

"She just brought some to Mr. Harker a few minutes ago," Betsy whispered, her head tucked.

"Wonderful," Mina said, attempting to infuse her voice with approval. "That'll be all for now, Betsy."

Betsy curtseyed and darted down the hall toward the kitchen.

She was a trial, but she worked hard and she really did try to please. Mina was fond of her, even when she hovered a little too much. She took a deep breath to steady herself, then opened the door to the study and breezed in.

Jonathan paced in front of the fireplace, his face gaunt in the dim light. He had always maintained a fine carriage, a firm body of well-toned muscle, but since his imprisonment in eastern Europe, he was too thin, his cheekbones jutting sharply against translucent skin.

"Goodness, Jonathan! Why didn't you light a few of the gas lamps?" she asked lightly. She twisted the keys on the sides of the chambers and lights flared in the room. Jonathan flinched, but said nothing until she reached for one closer to his chair by the fire.

"No, Mina. That's quite enough."

She looked at him more closely and saw the pain in his eyes. Another headache. They were the bane of his existence since his experience, and light made them worse. That explained the darkened room. She felt terrible. She didn't even think to ask.

"I'm so sorry, Jonathan." She bit her lip. "Should I turn them down? Or off?"

"No, just don't turn on any more lights." He rubbed his head. "Where were you, Mina? I was worried."

"I went to see Professor Van Helsing for your tonic," she said, pulling the bottles from her bag. She looked at him quizzically. Where did he think she was? But he was staring at her head. Oh dear…

"What in God's name are you wearing?" he asked.

She winced. Since the battle, she had become more and more sensitive to any form of using the Lord's name in vain. But Jonathan was not deterred. His jaw stiffened when she didn't reply immediately. Did he still doubt her? Well, of course. Why wouldn't he?

"I simply lost my hat on the way to the professor's house, and he gave me something to cover my head," she said lamely. She reached for the tea pot and poured a cup of tea. She turned to see him still staring at her and knew it would come out sooner or later. With a sigh, she set her tea cup down. Motioning him to take a seat by the fire, she sat with him on the small divan and took his hands.

"All right, Jonathan. There was an … incident tonight just outside the professor's house." Jonathan started to rise, but she held him in place. "Please listen to me. Please, my dearest. I'm fine. The professor is fine, and no one was injured."

She took a deep breath and described her encounter with the vampire in the alley, ending by removing the scarf. The wound had seeped through Van Helsing's bandage and Jonathan's face paled further at the sight of the blood. He reached up and lifted one edge of the bandage to view the abrasion below. Gently, he repositioned the bandage to cover the wound.

"Dear God," he murmured. "There are more of them?"

"Yes," Mina admitted. "Evidently there are."

"And Van Helsing knew this?"

Mina hesitated. "Yes, he did."

"Why didn't he tell us?"

"You were so ill, Jonathan. And I was … broken. Poor Arthur still mourned beloved Lucy, and we had lost Quincy. None of us was in any shape to face the fact that we might have to ever face these monsters again."

Lord Arthur Holmwood had been engaged to Mina's best friend from childhood, Lucy Westenra. Precious, innocent Lucy was one of Dracula's first victims. After he turned her into an undead creature like himself, Van Helsing had helped Arthur destroy her and behead her to keep her from passing the curse to others. Quincy Morris was an American who had courted Lucy before Arthur won her heart, but he stayed on to hunt the evil that had destroyed her life, though it cost his own. Dracula killed him in the mountains of Carpathia. Jack Seward, their friend, had cared for Jonathan's predecessor in the firm, R.M. Renfield, who had been thought to be mad. As it turned out, he was simply under Dracula's thrall too. While the men had hunted Dracula, he had slipped into the hospital and killed Renfield before coming to Mina's room and finishing his seduction of her innocence. But how did one explain that a vampire came through the bars, the windows, as a mist to murder a man he'd enslaved by drinking his blood? Dr. Seward was in an untenable situation with a dead patient and no explanations.

Dracula had led her to believe he had answers, that he could make her pain and confusion go away, but all he held out was death and more death for all eternity. He was evil.

He was the devil.

"He should have warned us." Jonathan's fist slammed down on the arm of the divan.

"He would have, my dear," Mina said, tears gathering in her

eyes. "This just happened faster than he thought it would. He thought we would have a little time to regroup before they started appearing." She tried to put her thoughts into words because Van Helsing hadn't really given her reasons. But she understood so much more than he ever said to her. There was an unspoken language between them. "I think he expected them to be afraid to show themselves right away. If we could kill one as old and as powerful as Dracula, they might not be so eager to take on humanity." She took a shaky breath.

Jonathan turned to her, taking her hands in his own. "Mina, you must not take further chances. I cannot lose you. You must not go out alone at night. Promise me that."

"But, Jonathan—" she started to protest.

"No, Mina, I am the man of the house, and I want you to listen to me," he insisted. "You are used to doing as you've pleased, and that has gotten us into deeper waters than we ever knew existed in this world. I want to be able to protect you, but I can't do that if I don't even know where you are."

Mina felt a frown forming between her eyes. "Jonathan, you knew where I was. I told you I was going to Professor Van Helsing's. I didn't go anywhere else."

"Yes, and you were attacked!"

"Yes, and I fought back!"

They faced one another, suddenly standing almost toe to toe. White-faced. Shaking.

"It's my duty as your husband to protect you, Mina," Jonathan said, his voice strained and his words tight with emotion. "And I would remind you that it's your duty before God to obey me."

She stared at him, not believing this was her Jonathan, her beloved. She had always known he was a very traditional Victorian man, but she would have never expected him to become her jailer.

"I'm going to bed," he said abruptly, leaving the room and slamming the door behind him.

Mina sank to the divan and watched the fire burn down to embers.

"God, what am I supposed to do now?"

CHAPTER 3

Breakfast was subdued. Jonathan had awakened to find Mina's side of the bed undisturbed. As he was shaving, Mina entered the room and took fresh clothing from her wardrobe. When he had finished in the bathroom, he returned to the bedroom to dress for the day, and wordlessly, she took her clothes to the bathroom to do her own morning ablutions.

When she entered the dining room, Jonathan looked up from his newspaper. She refilled his tea cup, then poured her own. Mrs. Hardman entered with a platter of eggs and toast. Sensing the somber mood, she served in silence, glancing from one to the other, her bright eyes missing little though she never gossiped about the young missus and master. Her black dress swished softly, and her pigeon-shaped body departed as swiftly as she had come, drifting forward in smooth, graceful steps.

"Mina, I'm sorry about last night," Jonathan began.

Mina set her tea cup down and stared at him.

"But I'm so very worried about you." He flipped the newspaper open to the second page.

The article read, ***Mutilated body found by docks; Police suspect wild dogs.*** Mina took the paper and scanned it. Very little blood at the scene, though the neck was torn and slashed. Looked like an animal attack. Animals could have licked up the blood. Yes, this fit the bill for a vampire. Or it could be an animal attack, just like the paper said.

"Jonathan, I understand why you're worried," she began, trying not to undermine him. "But I can't become a prisoner in our home either. How can you expect that of me?"

"How can you expect me to let you run around London with those foul creatures out there?" Jonathan's voice held anguish, but there was a note of anger too.

"I'm hardly running around London, Jonathan," she objected. "We've both stayed home since..." She couldn't continue. What? Since Lucy's death? Since Jonathan's return from Carpathia, an old man before his time? Since the battle with Dracula that was so dramatic, so horrible? Did he even understand what that had cost her?

Betsy appeared at the door. "'scuse me, but—"

"Not now, Betsy!" Jonathan snapped.

"But, sir, Professor Van Helsing is here, sir," Betsy said quickly. "'e's in the study."

"Thank you, Betsy," Mina said, quickly. She rose, dropping her napkin beside her untouched breakfast. "He'll be here to check that bandage." She patted her head gently.

Betsy gasped at the sight of the reddened bandage, which she hadn't seen the night before because of the scarf. Mina realized that was probably what had struck Mrs. Hardman so speechless too, but she was too good a servant to ever say a word to her young mistress.

Jonathan sighed, exasperation clearly written on his face as he shoved away from the table forcefully and threw his napkin on the table. Betsy stared after them and looked at the uneaten breakfasts. Mrs. Hardman would not be pleased. She hurriedly cleared the dishes and headed for the kitchen.

~~~

Van Helsing stared out the windows to the street. The hustle and bustle seemed very normal, but beneath the everyday flow ran a current that felt 'other.' Were the Harkers being observed already?

He turned when Mina and Jonathan entered and he smiled warmly, holding one hand out to shake Jonathan's hand, though his face suggested his reluctance, and that other to half-embrace Mina.

"I thought I should make a house call this time, *ja*?" he said jovially. He motioned to the divan and stood behind her to remove the dressing. Other than a tiny scar, no signs remained of the abrasion.

"But I saw it!" Jonathan exclaimed. "I lifted but a corner of the bandage. The skin was scraped raw!"

"Yes," Van Helsing mused. "Incredible healing power of the body, is it not?"

Mina's fingers probed the area and found nothing, no scabs, no raw tissue, no blood. She whirled to face the professor. "What does this mean, professor? Does this mean..." Her face paled. "Am I turning after all?"

"No, *mein liebling*, not at all," he said, returning to his medical bag, which he had deposited on Jonathan's desk. He removed a
~~~

needle and several vials. "I think we go ahead and take that blood now, yes? I run my tests, then we will know for sure."

"Know what?" Jonathan demanded.

"What changes have been wrought in Miss Mina's blood." Van Helsing's piercing blue eyes turned on Jonathan. "She may well be something … very extraordinary."

Jonathan stared at Van Helsing, then at Mina, before sitting very suddenly. His face was paler than normal as he dropped his head to his hands.

So much for our normal life together, Mina thought with a sigh.

CHAPTER 4

Two days passed before Van Helsing visited them again. In the meantime, Jonathan left for work, and Mina rattled about the house, shaken and jittery. She tried to write in her diary, but couldn't find the words to express her doubts, her fears. She tried to pray, but didn't even know where to begin.

Lady Westenra invited her for tea, but she cried the entire time, and Mina felt like a limp handkerchief by the time she arrived home. Her head ached from the pain of reliving the loss of her dearest friend, as well as from all the things she still could not truly explain to Lady Westenra. How do you tell a woman that her daughter became a monster? You can't. That must never be spoken. She must never know that her daughter's head was severed to keep her from rising from the grave to murder innocents. Arthur Holmwood had been present as well, but had finally excused himself when the tears became more than he could stand. Mina had forced herself to stay out of love for Lucy, but now a headache pounded her skull unmercifully.

"Mina!" Jonathan stood in the door to the study. Taking one look at her face, his voice softened. "Are you all right? What has happened?"

"I'm fine, Jonathan. Why are you home so early?" she asked. His face was worn, and she could see the pain creasing his brow, radiating around his eyes. They were sending him home more and more often. How long would he be able to keep working with headaches this severe?

"I brought some contracts home to work on." He waved a hand dismissively. "You went out today?"

Mina sighed. "Jonathan, I told you at breakfast that Lady Westenra had asked me to come to tea today. Remember? Arthur was there as well."

Jonathan sighed and nodded. "I'm sorry, Mina. I had forgotten. Yes, dearest. You did tell me that. Was it as bad as it seems?"

"Worse," she said, removing her hat and handing it to Betsy, who curtseyed and hastily moved away from them as they wandered into the study. "She's devastated, Jonathan. And I could do nothing to comfort her."

"I'm sure just your presence was comfort enough, Mina," Jonathan said, patting her arm and guiding her to the divan. They sat together, and Jonathan pulled her into his arms. She leaned back, heedless of decorum, and enjoyed the moment of intimacy. Jonathan's heartbeat thumped against her cheek, and Mina knew a moment of peace.

She would remember that moment for a long time to come.

~~~

The next morning, Van Helsing showed up on their doorstep before they'd even made it down for breakfast. Jonathan and Mina hastened to the study where Betsy had left the Professor, at his request. Once again, he stood by the window.

"Mina, come," he motioned, "but softly. No sudden movements."

She eased around the room and inched to his side to gaze out the window. "What is happening, Professor?"

"That man across the street, does he look familiar to you?"

Mina followed the Professor's gaze and gasped. A tall, pale man sporting a top hat and dark eyeglasses appeared to be watching their home. The dark beard and mustache — it was the man from the alley, right down to the silk scarf around his neck!

"That's him!" she exclaimed. "That's the creature who attacked me in the alley."

Jonathan bolted to the window. "Where?"

The vampire smiled when he saw Jonathan pull back the curtain, tipped his hat, and vanished into the crowd.

"Come. Sit, my friends," Van Helsing said, as he ushered them toward the divan. He remained standing, ever the professor in lecture mode. The lines in his face had deepened this morning, though, and Mina noticed a definite thinning in his beard and sideburns. The professor was aging. Then she noticed the newspaper in his hands.

"I thought I saw him outside when I was here the other day, but I was not sure," he began. "I don't know whether he followed me here or perhaps followed Mina home from my house the night of the attack. I suspect the latter."

"Why?" asked Jonathan.
~~~

"Curiosity." The Professor never minded questions, but today he seemed to welcome them. He was definitely bringing them news he did not want to deliver. "Mina fought back. She matched his strength, or at least held her own. He did not expect that. I think he wanted to know what or who she was. So of course, he would follow and watch.

"Which brings me to the reason for my visit. I have the results of Mina's tests. Her blood shows significant changes in certain enzymes and cells. Her white cells attack germs and decimate them almost instantly. That accounts for her own regenerative abilities. Her blood count itself has almost doubled."

"Then I'm no longer human," Mina said, her voice dropping.

"Not at all, Mina!" Van Helsing exclaimed. "You are human, but you are also more than human. We do not yet know how much more. That is why I wish you to do some more tests."

"What kind of tests, Professor?" Jonathan asked.

"Strength, agility, eyesight, hearing. I think we will find that Miss Mina has significantly more power and ability in these areas than we ever realized might be possible."

"I don't want my wife becoming some sort of lab experiment!" Jonathan exclaimed. "She's my wife, not a—a—a circus oddity. I won't have her put on display."

"Of course not! What an idea!" Van Helsing's shock was enough to placate them only slightly. "This is a private matter. *Ja?* Only we would know. But it is important to find out."

Jonathan's head shot up. "You want to use her as a weapon, don't you? To fight *them?*" He pointed toward the window. "Creatures like that … thing that attacked her the other night? I won't allow it! I won't allow you to put my wife at risk like that. We've been through enough. *She's* been through enough."

The professor looked away from them and studied the newspaper he still held clutched in his hands. Mina realized he'd been holding it the entire time they'd been talking. He'd been nattering on about her blood, distracting them from the creature who had been tracking her, following her…

A wave of dizziness passed over Mina and she clutched Jonathan's hands until her knuckles whitened.

"Professor, what has he done?" Mina asked, her voice low. Tears gathered in the corners of her eyes. Jonathan looked at her in surprise, then at the newspaper, finally catching on. He gripped her hands tightly and stared at Van Helsing.

"Tell us." His voice was strained.

Van Helsing unrolled the paper. The front-page headline told it all.

Lady Westenra Murdered

Mina shrieked one long, "Noooooooooo…" before hitting the floor in a dead faint.

CHAPTER 5

Lord Arthur Holmwood sipped tea in the Harkers' parlor, his black mourning suit at odds with his fair complexion. Greys and linens had always been his preferred colors and it seemed odd to see him wearing only black these days. In the old days, black was reserved for formal wear. Now it was his only attire. Grey hair appeared in his mustache and at his temples too, and new lines appeared around his eyes. Lord Holmwood obviously slept about as well as Mina did these days.

"It's my fault, you know," Mina said. "I led him right to her. I could kick myself for being so careless." She sipped her tea, then set it aside. Mrs. Hardwood had made a lovely sponge cake and smothered it in fresh strawberries and cream, but they both picked at the offering, having little appetite.

"You can't think of it that way, Mina," Arthur scolded. "She loved you like a daughter. She would have been crushed if you had turned her down for tea. You were all she talked about over dinner that night. How much she loved seeing you, how well you looked, how much you reminded her of the good times you and Lucy had together as girls. She cherished every minute of your time together. I'm just glad you gave her that gift before she died."

"But Arthur…"

"No buts, Mina," Arthur said firmly. "Besides…" He hesitated. He cleared his throat, then leaned forward. "Look, Mina, we both know she wouldn't have lived long. Grief had swallowed the woman whole. And her doctor…" He paused again. "No one else had been told, but Lady Westenra had been putting her affairs in order. Cancer. She wouldn't have lived much longer anyway. It was monstrous what happened to her, but in reality, he spared her a long illness with a lot of indignity and a painful death."

He stood and leaned against the fireplace for a moment. "Personally, I can't wait to offer my thanks — with my silver-coated sword right through his lifeless heart."

"Only if you beat me to it," Mina murmured, sipping her tea.

"So, Van Helsing knew they were out there."

"Yes," she said with a sigh. It was becoming a familiar refrain. They'd all felt the same way — betrayed, angry, but the professor had truly been acting in their best interests at the time.

"It would have been nice to know, but I suppose I can understand. I think I might have slit my own wrists if I thought the supply of monsters was going to be never-ending after the battle with Dracula." Arthur's smile was bitter.

"Arthur." Mina fought for the right words. "Lucy wouldn't want you to grieve forever. She would want you to go on with your life and be happy."

"Would she really?" His voice was strange.

Mina frowned.

"Yes, Arthur, I believe she would."

"I wonder..." he mused.

"What do you wonder, Arthur?"

He turned to look her full in the face, his eyes full of anguish. "Did you really know her at all, Mina? Lucy wanted all of a man. She would never want to see me with another woman! She wanted a man, body, soul, and spirit. And not just one man. She played so many of us at one time. And then Dracula came along, and she danced willingly to his tune. Why did she do that?"

Mina stared at him, her face draining of color.

"And you, Mina. You love Jonathan, yet you fell for Dracula too. Can you explain that to me please? I would really like to understand it. Because I don't, you see. I don't understand." He sat and dropped his head to his hands.

Mina was frozen. She opened her mouth and closed it over and over as she tried to find words to say.

"Arthur, it was ... like... a dream... where nothing is real... and you think that when you wake up, it will all be gone, so what harm can there be? It doesn't seem wrong at the time, because it's not real. None of it was real. Lucy being dead, then alive, then Van Helsing taking her head — I kept thinking 'I'm going to wake up and Lucy is going to laugh at me over this ridiculous nightmare.' But it just kept getting worse and worse. Dracula said he could make it all go away. I don't know what he promised Lucy. She never told me. But I know that, if she could have seen her death, and your sorrow, she would have never done the things she did." Mina paused as Arthur looked up into her eyes. "She loved you, Arthur. More than anything. And she wanted to marry you. It was all she talked about."

Arthur nodded. He reached over and took her hand, raised it to his lips and kissed her fingertips gently. "Thank you, Mina." Then he stood and walked to the fireplace once again to take a moment to compose himself.

Mina needed that moment herself. She was shaken to her core. These were things she hadn't sorted out for herself yet. But she wondered if she had been totally truthful with Lord Arthur Holmwood. Lucy had been flirty and flighty, but she had been good-hearted, hadn't she? Or had Dracula found his way in because she was wayward with men, an inconstant woman? If so, what did that say about Mina herself?

"Arthur!" Jonathan entered the room and deposited his briefcase on his desk before crossing the room to clasp his friend by the arms. "So very sorry about Lady Westenra. Mina and I were both horrified to hear the news."

Mina rose to fetch another cup, but Betsy was already at her elbow with one. Mrs. Hardman was working wonders with her. Mina smiled her thanks and excused the girl, who curtseyed and left before the men realized she'd even been there. Mina poured Jonathan a cup of tea, which he accepted gratefully as he sank into a chair and visited with their guest. Mina passed Jonathan her untouched sponge cake and he managed a few bites, exclaiming that it was one of Mrs. Hardman's best. With such acclaim, Arthur finally tried his own and choked down a few bites before taking his leave.

"Thank you again, Mina," he said, kissing her cheek gently. The sadness in his eyes hurt her to the core, but she locked away those feelings, hoping for time to process them later.

CHAPTER 6

Mina awakened from a deep sleep. Was it a cry? A whimper? She drew her wrapper over her gown and hurried to the bedroom window. Jonathan turned in his sleep, but didn't awaken. Something stirred in the alley across the street, then she heard another cry, a shriek. She ran from the room and bolted down the stairs. Grabbing a cloak from the hook by the door, she flung it around herself and unlocked the door.

A shadow flitted across the edge of the alley, and Mina took a step back, wary and alert. She heard a low chuckle.

"We meet again, Mina Harker." The voice slithered around her like silk, and she recognized the timber, an echo of the devil himself, Dracula, though not the same. So, Mr. Top Hat had learned her name. Mina's expression grew cold. Then she realized she had run out here with no weapon at all. No knife, no cross, nothing but rage that he might be hurting someone else.

She saw a foot, a woman's shoe, in the alley. Tentatively, listening, senses alert, Mina approached. A woman, no — a girl. The vampire jerked the girl's body back into his arms, her neck gushing blood. Hidden in the shadows of the alley, he now allowed Mina to see him, as he cradled the child in his arms.

"Miss…. Please…" the child gurgled.

The vampire lowered bloody fangs to her neck and with one violent rip, tore her throat open.

"Nooooooo!" shrieked Mina, as she charged forward. The vampire flung the girl at her with enough force to knock her to the cobblestone pavement. The wind left Mina's lungs as the weight of the girl pinned her to the street. Her blood seeped into Mina's cloak. Down the street, a policeman's whistle blew the alarm and one by one lights came on as the residents woke.

A policeman knelt by Mina's side, lifting the dead girl off of her. "You all right, Missus?"

"Yes," Mina murmured. "I'm fine. But that man…"

"What man, Missus?"

"The man… the one who did this…" Mina looked at the girl, her eyes glazed, her neck broken and mangled.

"A man did this?" the policeman asked. "Missus, you sure about this?"

"I saw him," she insisted. "I saw him right there in the alley."

"You sure you're not hurt, Missus?"

"Mina?" Jonathan's voice drifted over the street. "Mina? Mina!" Footsteps ran toward her, but policemen intercepted him.

"That's my wife! I demand you let me through." Jonathan was every inch the lawyer now. A man of standing and position, and the policemen finally gave way.

"Inspector is going to want to talk to you, Missus," the policeman said, as Jonathan attempted to lead Mina away.

"Harker. Mrs. Jonathan Harker." Jonathan's voice was sharp. "We live in that house right there." He pointed it out. "He's welcome to come over at his convenience. But I need to take my wife home."

"Really shouldn't be wandering around alone at night, you know," the policeman called after them.

"Really?" Jonathan said sharply. "We'll take that under advisement. Thank you, officer. You may return to your more pressing duties, like getting that poor girl off the street."

Jonathan bundled Mina into their home. Mrs. Hardman and Betsy met them at the door in their nightgowns with shawls around their shoulders. Betsy shrieked at the sight of the blood on the cloak. Jonathan ripped the cloak away and handed it to Mrs. Hardman. "Do you think you can get the blood out of that thing? Betsy, stop screaming and go run a bath for Mrs. Harker, please."

Betsy ran up the stairs ahead of them as Mrs. Hardman headed toward the kitchen with the cloak held at arm's length. Jonathan and Betsy helped Mina out of her gown and wrapper, both of which were soaked with blood.

"Just burn those." Jonathan said, tersely. "We'll send out for new ones in the morning. There will be no way to get them clean enough to wear again." He grimaced as Betsy carried them gingerly from the room. Mina remained in the tub, wordlessly watching the blood swirl away from her body, as Betsy brought jug after jug of warm water upstairs to fill the tub.

He did it to get my attention, she thought. *Well. You have my attention now, you little twit. It's time to fight back.*

"Mina, you shouldn't have run out in the street like that,"

Jonathan began. "What were you thinking? You could have been killed."

Mina stared at him, her dark eyes unblinking.

"Darling, this is not your fault. You can't keep throwing yourself in harm's way like this." He brushed the dark curls away from her face, his eyes focused on her. Worry radiated from him in waves. "Mina, please promise me you'll be more careful."

"Yes, Jonathan," she spoke at last. He hugged her wet body close to his own. "I promise to be very careful," she whispered into the shoulder of his dressing gown.

CHAPTER 7

Jonathan did not leave for work until the next afternoon. They spent the entire morning with an inspector from the London police, who seemed more intent on finding that this was an animal attack and that Mrs. Harker only imagined a man in the alley. But Mina was not shaken in her testimony. When she finally suggested that perhaps she should repeat her story to his superior since he didn't appear to understand the Queen's English, he left with his nose distinctly out of joint.

At the door, Jonathan added a final note on the matter. "By the way, Inspector. Should you be inclined to embellish on my wife's account, please keep in mind that I am a lawyer myself and I will be checking the records to see exactly what you write up. Mrs. Harker is not given to flights of fancy. If my wife's account is not exactly as she has given it, I will be discussing it further with whomever I need to in order to correct the records and ensure that the truth comes out in this matter."

The inspector grimly touched the brim of his hat and stalked off down the street.

Once they had closed the door, Mina held Jonathan close, breathing in the scent of him. These moments were fleeting, and she was never more aware of it than now.

"Thank you for speaking up for me, my love."

"I'm not sure I did either of us any favors," he said wryly, as he held her close and leaned his head on her hair. "It would be better to let them believe it was a wild animal. In a way, it is. These creatures aren't human any longer. They can't be classed as 'men', can they?"

"No, but if people are looking for animals, they won't suspect a man when one walks up and begins to talk to them, either. Maybe the description I've given will help them to at least be wary of the man." She sighed.

"This one," Jonathan said. "If Van Helsing is right, there are many of these foul beings. Where will it all end?"

"We have to try," Mina said, burying her face in his shirt. "I don't want to either, Jonathan, but we can't ignore it. We have to try."

He sighed. "Mina, what are you planning to do?"

"I'm just going to go see the professor for now," she said. "That won't be dangerous."

"The last time you went…"

"I'll take a carriage," she interrupted.

Jonathan peeled some money from his wallet and put it in her hand. "Make sure you do." He kissed her gently.

~~~

"So, now this vampire kills on your very doorstep," Van Helsing muttered after Mina had recounted the events of the previous night. "Interesting. I wonder why he does this. Is it to draw you out? To engage you in some way? To antagonize you? If he knows you killed Dracula, why does he paint the target on his back, as they say? If he does not know this, why does he bother with you? I wonder…"

"I'm not sure I care why anymore, Professor," Mina said, defiance in the tilt of her chin. "I'm going to make sure he stops. I'll not have him making a game out of killing children right in front of me. That girl couldn't have been more than fourteen or fifteen at the most. And he ended her life like that." She snapped her fingers.

"But I care," Van Helsing said, sharp blue eyes piercing her. "Even the vampires kill with purpose. They think, they plan, they plot. This one, he has a reason for stalking you. I want to know what that reason is." He rose from his armchair, clapping his hands energetically. She stood, a bit less certainly. He seemed to be preparing for battle, though what he had planned, Mina had no clue.

"But first we see what you can do!" He pulled her toward the basement.

"What was that?" Mina pulled up sharply. Her eyes searched the upper floors, senses on alert.

"What was what?" Van Helsing asked.

"There was a thump," she said, heading for the stairs.

"You are sure?"

"Yes, someone is upstairs. In the attic, I think."

Van Helsing's eyes widened. "Wait here. Don't move, Mina!" He charged up the stairs. He was gone for several minutes, and Mina was ready to follow him up the steps, when she heard his measured tread returning. He smiled widely as he held up a book triumphantly.

"You were right, *mein liebling*! A book fell from the shelf. You
~~~

heard that all the way down here? Remarkable!"

Mina's ears picked up a rattle and another thunk.

"Professor, what's going on? Are you going to tell me that books are suddenly just randomly falling from shelves up there?"

He threw back his head and laughed. A small head peered over the banister.

"That oright, gov'ner?" the lad asked in a thick cockney accent.

"*Ja*, Freddy, that was perfect," Van Helsing crowed. "Freddy is helping to bring down some of my books and research materials from the attic today. When you heard that tiny noise, which I myself did not even hear, I decided to test you one more time. So, he rattles the window, then drops a much smaller book. Still you hear it. Magnificent!"

Mina looked doubtfully up at the smiling face beaming over the railing.

"*Ja*! Is good, Mina. Is very good. I had not devised a hearing test, but you come up with one of your own. I couldn't have done better myself. Come." Van Helsing led the way to the cellar, still chucking. Freddy gave her a wave, which she returned with a grin and a wry shake of her head.

Van Helsing's lab was rudimentary at best, but sufficient. He tested her eyesight and found she could see farther and with more accuracy than he thought possible, so he took her to the top floor of the house and out onto the balcony. They looked over the city of London and he asked her to look the farthest in each direction and describe what she saw. He could only make out the dim outlines of buildings she saw in great details. She even saw birds nesting in specific sections of the church spires of St. Mary's Church.

"Fascinating," Van Helsing muttered. "I must check with the good Father at the church. He can direct me to all the nests in the spires, I'm sure." He caught the look Mina gave him and he laughed as he patted her arm gently. "Not that I disbelieve you, dear Mina. But that is the scientist in me. I must have the proof to corroborate the claim. Do you see? It is not enough for a scientist to say, 'I believe this is true.' He must also set out to find the absolute proof that says, 'Yes, this is so!' Come! We will have our tea now."

He led the way to his sitting room.

"I wonder, Mina, can you help an old man with this table? I would like to move it over to the fireplace by the chairs."

Mina found the request odd, that a gentleman would ask a lady to help him move furniture, but the professor was growing older and perhaps the table would not be too heavy between the two of them. It looked like a marble top, but could not have been, for she found it easy enough to manage, though it was heavier than she anticipated. Then she noticed that Van Helsing simply held the lip of the tabletop with his fingertips! He was doing nothing to take the weight of the table himself. She let go and the table dropped with a thud. She jumped back, the vibration reflecting that the table truly was heavier than she had given it credit for.

"What are you playing at, Professor?" she hissed. "I'm not sure I like these little games of yours."

Van Helsing's cool blue eyes held her gaze. "I am sorry, dear Mina. I did not mean to deceive you, but I feared that trying to test you openly would not give me true results. By not knowing which things were tests and which were not, you reacted as you normally would. Not as you thought I would want you to. Not as you would expect yourself to."

"I don't understand any of this!" she cried, stepping away from him. Tears of frustration welled up and slid down her cheeks.

"If I had asked you to lift this marble-topped table and carry it across the room, would you have done it? No. Because you are a lady. What gentleman would ask a lady to do such a thing? And you would have said, 'No, Professor, I cannot do that...', but yet you **did** do it. I was careful to take none of the weight myself. You did it, Mina. You have incredible strength. More than you realize."

"Enough to toss a man across an alley," she whispered, as the import of his words hit home.

"*Ja*, enough to toss a man across an alley indeed." Van Helsing nodded vigorously. "Enough to vanquish Dracula when you had to. And enough to fight the forces of evil that are infecting this city."

Mina stumbled to one of the chairs and sat.

"Now we will have our tea." He left her to her thoughts, departing for the kitchen.

Mina stared at the table. She reached out and touched the cold marble top with trembling fingers. Amazing. She had lifted this table by herself. It had a pedestal base of solid wood, but the top was indeed marble. It was only large enough for a tea tray, but still, it should have taken two grown men to move it easily across the room. Her gaze wandered around the room, taking in wall-to-wall bookcases filled with journals and medical books, philosophies, even novels and books of poetry. The professor's tastes were eclectic, to say the least. His large, battered desk sat by the windows, but the heavy drapes were drawn, leaving the room dimly lit. She thought about opening them, then remembered the vampire who stalked her and changed her mind. The drapes gave at least the illusion of safety. For the moment it was enough.

The professor returned carrying a generous tea tray and followed closely by a tow-headed boy of ten years.

"I have told Freddy that he may join us for tea if that is agreeable with you, Mrs. Harker," Van Helsing said with a twinkle in his eyes.

"Of course," she said with a smile. "Hello, Freddy."

"Oy, Missus," Freddy said, holding out a freshly scrubbed paw to shake her hand firmly. "Pleased to meet yew. Any friend o' the professor is a friend o' Freddy Barnes."

They shared a delightful tea as Freddy entertained them with tales of life on the streets of London. When the professor reminded him that he still had some books to bring downstairs before dinnertime, the boy shot to his feet and dashed for the door.

"I think you have a new admirer, Mina," the professor said with a gentle smile. "Freddy is quite taken with you."

"He's a charming young rascal," she said with a wry smile. "But I don't know that I'd want to trust him very far."

"Nonsense," scoffed the professor. "Once Freddy has accepted you as his friend, he is loyal to the ends of the Earth. If ever you need him, Mina, Freddy will be at your service. On that you may depend."

The smile seeped from her face. "What do I do now, Professor? I don't even know who I am, much less *what* I am anymore. What am I going to do now?"

"You are going to find a new direction for your life, Mina. As so many have done before you. As I had to do once—a long, long time ago. But that is a story for another day. It grows late and Jonathan will be worried. We must not keep you out any later. I want you home safely well before dark."

Mina laughed, though it lacked humor. "Jonathan gave me money for a carriage. He worries about me now, though I'm not sure why."

"He loves you, Mina." Van Helsing's gaze was direct, but his eyes spoke in tones of understanding.

"I don't understand why, after the way I betrayed him." Mina's voice broke, and she swallowed hard to hold back the tears.

"Once again, Mina, you did not betray him. You were deceived by a master liar and devil. You were under his spell, captivated! You must stop blaming yourself like this."

"I chose to be deceived!" she cried. "I wanted to escape. I wasn't strong enough to stand firm while the rest of you fought against this evil. I wanted out!"

"And you fought your way back!" Van Helsing snapped. "For Jonathan. For God. For your own soul's sake. You came back to us."

They stared at one another over the tea tray.

He sighed. "Tomorrow we go together to meet my friend and colleague, Father Michael Gallagher. I will apologize for him right now, Mina. He is … an acquired taste."

"What does that mean exactly?" Mina asked, her eyebrows raised skeptically.

"He can be difficult to deal with, but he is the best man to train you."

"A priest is going to train me? To do what exactly?"

"Yes," Van Helsing said, his tone enigmatic. "He's going to train you to hunt and destroy monsters."

"I've already done that."

"Now you will learn to do it God's way."

CHAPTER 8

Mina and Professor Van Helsing entered the dimly lit church the following morning. The cool interior sent a tremor along her spine. She closed her eyes and breathed deeply, centering her thoughts on the God who had sustained her during her convalescence. Peace enveloped her like the soft feathers of a dove and settled her spirit.

"Wait here," Van Helsing whispered. He walked halfway up the center aisle of the sanctuary, pausing to genuflect, before continuing to the altar to stand beside the priest.

"I thought I told you no," came a strong clear voice from the figure bowing at the altar. A priest's cassock couldn't disguise the broad shoulders as they hunched forward over the railing.

Van Helsing's voice was low enough that Mina could not hear clearly, though she caught phrases— "only man who can train her…" and "…needs your help if she is to survive…"

Mina frowned. *After all, I did destroy Dracula,* she thought. *That was no small feat. What is this priest supposed to teach me anyway?* She felt rebuffed and she resented the feeling.

"… meet her… talk to her…" More fragments drifted her direction.

The man stood and turned. He was ruggedly handsome for a priest, with dark hair and a closely trimmed beard and mustache. His eyes shone fiercely beneath thick brows. Mina almost expected him to sprout wings like some angelic warrior springing into battle. He belonged in armor instead of a priest's robes. He strode down the aisle toward her, his robe swishing with each indignant step. He towered over her for a moment then huffed disgust.

"Go back to your knitting, Mrs. Harker," he said dismissively. "A lady like you doesn't need to learn the kind of things the professor wants me to teach you." He turned to walk away.

"I don't knit, Father Gallagher," Mina said to his back. "But if I did, I'd be sure to dip my needles in silver. Because they'd certainly be of more use to me that way. The things stalking me right now aren't interested in booties or caps." Her words held all the scorn she could give them.

"Stalking you, Mrs. Harker?" He turned slowly, an incredulous smirk twisting his lips. "What would you know of things that stalk in the night?"

"What about 'things' that suck the life blood from humans and leave behind a dried husk? What about evil that preys on young girls and steals their innocence as well as their blood? Shall we talk about Nosferatu, Father Gallagher?"

Father Gallagher's eyes narrowed. He glanced at Van Helsing. "You told her about that? Why would you do that?"

"I learned the hard way," Mina said, drawing the lace collar away from her throat just enough for the scars to be visible. The wounds Dracula had left behind. When his eyes widened, she quickly pulled the collar back in place. "Still think I should be knitting with the ladies?" she asked, her eyes raking him coldly.

His gaze darted around the chapel, then visibly satisfied no one had heard the exchange, he motioned them toward a small door off to the side of the sanctuary. "Come with me." His orders were clipped and his steps quick as he hustled them down a long set of stone stairs to a lower-level cellar. Taking a large key from the ring attached to his belt, he opened a thick lock on a door and ushered them inside, where he lit a lantern and hung it from a hook on the wall.

Then without warning, he lunged at Mina, knocking her into the far wall and pressing his weight against her. Without thinking, Mina's arms came up to block him, pushing back against his chest, but he was like a brick wall — unmovable and solid.

"I'm just a man, Mrs. Harker," he whispered. "What will you do when a real monster comes at you in the night? Scream for help?"

Her fingers reached for the edge of her purse and slipped the silver blade from its sheath. Only when the blade touched his neck did he realize she had armed herself without his being aware. Swiftly he released his weight from her body and grabbed her arms, pinning them against the wall at her sides. The knife fell from her grip with a clatter. It was the alley all over again! Fury filled Mina. Father Gallagher might be a man of God, but he was taunting her, playing her for a fool. With a rush of anger, Mina flung her weight forward and he flew off her and landed on the floor in a heap.

Van Helsing laughed out loud as he leaned over to assist Father Gallagher to his feet.

"I did try to warn you, Michael," he said, shaking a finger at the younger man.

"Yes, you did," Father Gallagher said ruefully. "Guess that'll teach me to doubt your word, Abraham. You would think I'd know better by now."

"Yes, you should," Van Helsing chortled.

Mina frowned at them uncertainly.

"Are you sure you both know what you're doing?" Father Gallagher asked. "Mrs. Harker, this is not a game. These creatures will not stop, will not show mercy, will give no quarter. The cost could be …" He hesitated and glanced at Van Helsing. "It could cost more than you're willing to pay."

"I've already paid, Father Gallagher," she said, her chin raised in a determined set. "I don't think I'm being given much choice at this point."

"Some things cannot be avoided, Michael," Van Helsing said softly. "You know this, *ja*? Mina may not have chosen this path, but now it lies before her. As mine did. As yours did, as well. Should we not arm her, help her? I am an old man. I cannot do it, but you can. I need you to prepare her for the road ahead."

Father Gallagher studied her for several moments, but Mina no longer felt uncomfortable under his scrutiny. "You have strength, but you will have to master your anger. You weren't able to push me off until you gave way to that fury. But anger is a tool of the enemy. Your battle is not against flesh and blood, Mrs. Harker, but against principalities and powers of the dark world, against forces of evil that war with the heavenly realms. You cannot use the tools from the enemy's armory and expect to defeat him."

Mina frowned.

"How well do you know your Bible, Mrs. Harker?" he asked.

"As well as any Englishwoman, I suppose," she said, mystified.

"Well, you are about to learn it a whole lot better than most Englishwomen." He opened a cabinet on the far side of the room and took out a leather-bound Bible. He held it out to her. "It's yours. Take it. Read it. Study it, write in the margins, underline passages, make notes on the back pages. This is your training manual now."

"Write in a Bible?" Mina was shocked.

"Yes, Mrs. Harker. This is your own survival manual. I want you to know it as well as you know your own name. I'll be giving you homework, starting today. Ephesians 6:10-18. I want you to tell me what you think about the armor of God and how you think that might help you in the battles you are to face. Write down a few answers, think them out. Romans 8:28-39. I want your opinions and thoughts, everything that comes to mind. Then take a look at Psalms 139 and 140. Just familiarize yourself with them. We'll be delving into them as we progress."

Father Gallagher had jotted the Scriptures on one of the blank pages in the back of the book as he spoke. He closed it with a snap and handed it to her.

"Excuse me, I thought you were going to teach me to fight vampires," she said.

"You have to learn to walk before you can run, Mrs. Harker," he said, opening the door and ushering them out of the room. He hurried them back up the steps and into the sanctuary. He paused before the altar and crossed himself. Then he nodded to them both before walking briskly away.

"See you in three days, Mrs. Harker," he called softly over his shoulder before he ducked into the priest's side of the confessional booth, where a line of parishioners waited patiently for his attention.

Van Helsing chuckled softly as he took her elbow and escorted her to the door of the chapel. "Like I said, an acquired taste."

CHAPTER 9

Mina walked slowly through Whitechapel on Abraham Van Helsing's arm. Life teemed around them, noisy, dirty, chaotic, but she barely noticed.

"Professor, are you really sure about this?" she asked.

Van Helsing laughed softly. "I know, my dear. Father Gallagher has a wild Irish temper. But he has battled the forces of evil as you have yourself. You can trust him."

"But studying Scriptures?" She indicated the Bible in her left hand. "Maybe I should just see if Arthur can recommend a good swordsman..."

"My dear, Lord Holmwood's friends will not be open to teaching a woman swordplay," Van Helsing cut her off. "British aristocracy is not that open-minded when it comes to feminine capabilities. Besides, Father Gallagher is highly skilled in multiple weapons. And he knows the skill set you'll need to come against these particular evils you'll face. Arthur's friends would not be prepared for their speed or their expertise in evasion. Gallagher is."

"How is it that a priest is fighting vampires in London?" she asked, an incredulous smile creasing her face.

"The Sisters of the Maid have been battling this evil since the days of Joan d'Arc," Van Helsing said, his face suddenly clouding over. "Their order is very old, very sacred. The sisters keep valuable records, and they train each generation, passing along the knowledge they gain. Always there is a priest attached to their order. Michael has been with the Sisters for over thirty years now. He has become hardened by the things he has seen, the things he has done. But you could be in no better hands, Mina, of this I am certain."

Mina frowned. "He doesn't look old enough to have been a priest for thirty years, Professor."

"I didn't say he'd been a priest for thirty years. I said he's been with the Sisters that long. When you've been around him for a while, perhaps he will tell you his story. I don't think you should hear it from me, *liebling*." He patted her hand and smiled down at her.

"Now we shall have some tea, *ja*?"

"So until Friday, I'm supposed to study these Scriptures, write down my thoughts—" Mina's voice cut off as she stared up at Van Helsing. "Then what?"

"Then you will take the next step," he said with a laugh. "And the next step. And the step after that one. It is a process, Mina! See it as an adventure. And with Father Gallagher, I can assure you there will never be a dull moment." He laughed again as they strolled away from Whitechapel.

Tea with the professor was delightful. He treated her to an afternoon tea at a small shop with exquisite strawberry tarts topped with thick whipped cream. The chocolate biscuits melted in Mina's mouth.

"I must order some of these to take home to Jonathan," she exclaimed, rolling her eyes in delight. "I think this must be the most heavenly thing I've ever tasted."

"I have always held the opinion that chocolate can cure most of the world's problems, if only we would take a bit every day." His eyes twinkled merrily. "What a happy countenance that little taste has given you."

Mina laughed. "Let's hope it can do as much for Jonathan. I'm not sure even chocolate will appease him when he finds out about my 'church activities' with Father Gallagher."

Van Helsing frowned. "I am not usually in favor of keeping secrets between husbands and wives, but perhaps…"

"You think I should keep this a secret, don't you?" Mina said when his voice trailed off. Her smile deepened and she pointed her spoon toward him before she dipped it into her strawberry tart. "I'm beginning to think I may have to if I ever want to be allowed outside my house again. Jonathan is far too worried about my welfare." She took a bite, then she frowned. "I hope I'm doing the right thing, Professor."

"You are doing what you must." His gaze lit a fire in her heart.

CHAPTER 10

Betsy met Mina at the door, curtseying as she took her hat. Mina kept the package in her hands, though. It held a half-dozen chocolate biscuits from the tea shop. She wanted to surprise Jonathan with them after dinner tonight. She took a second look at Betsy. Her cheeks were pinker, and she had a happy little smile on her face.

"Back to me dusting!" Betsy announced cheerfully. She actually bounced back into the study. Mina stared after the girl.

Is working in our household really that wonderful?

Shaking her head, she headed to the kitchen to confer with Mrs. Hardman. She found her head housekeeper pounding out dough on the lightly floured tabletop. She watched in admiration, as Mrs. Hardman deftly formed two loaves and set them into pans for the final rising, draping them in towels and setting them on a warm ledge of the old oven.

"Did you have a pleasant afternoon, Mrs. Harker?" asked the elderly lady, wiping her hands on her apron and smiling warmly.

"Yes, I did, thank you," Mina said. "I wish you could teach me how you do that some time," she added with an admiring shake of her head.

"Do what?" Mrs. Hardman asked, looking around. "Knead bread dough? Why, there's no special charm in that, ma'am." Her impish grin belied her words. "You just pretend it's someone you really want to throttle, and you have at it for several minutes. You feel better, everyone gets fed, and you don't go to jail at the end of the day."

Mina burst out in laughter. "Mrs. Hardman! How naughty! I never would have thought!"

"Well, we all have our little secrets, don't we?" she said, with a little smile. "Especially in this family."

"Very true," Mina said, with a conspiratorial wink. "I brought a little something to surprise Mr. Harker." She handed the biscuits to Mrs. Hardman. "After dinner please, with our tea."

She saw the markings on the paper. "Oh, I've heard of this place!

Is that where you went today?"

"Yes, Professor Van Helsing treated me to tea there after we stopped at a church. I'll be doing some charity work there from now on." Mrs. Hardman's eyebrows rose, but she said nothing. Mina continued. "After one bite of these, I knew I had to bring some home to Jonathan."

"I've been meaning to try them myself. Guess it would be worth the effort then." Mrs. Hardman made no further comment, but Mina knew that, even though she wasn't sold on the idea of charity work, she would keep Mina's secret and hold to the story when asked.

"By the way," Mina turned back before leaving the kitchen, "what on earth have you done to Betsy? She's a whole new girl today. I swear she skipped to the study just now to finish dusting!"

Mrs. Hardman chuckled. "I have done not a thing, ma'am, I assure you. She has a beau."

"What?" Mina gave the older woman her full attention as she pulled the pork roast from the larger oven and removed the lid from the cast iron pot. She ladled a bit of sauce over the top of the meat, replaced the lid and slammed the door shut again.

"She met him last Sunday when she went to visit her mother," she said. "Evidently, as she was coming home, three young ruffians tried to seize upon her. This young man was delivering groceries for his father's store. You know, the Tunstall Grocery. We do business with them all the time."

Mina nodded, unwilling to interrupt Mrs. Hardman's narrative.

"Well, young Henry cried out for them to stop, and created such a scene, the police came running and the boys scattered. Betsy was shaken to the core, so Henry took her to his parents' home for a cup of tea and a few minutes of peace. The police came there to talk to her, then Henry brought her home. He's been coming by every day to check on her. Even brought her flowers today."

She nodded to an arrangement of daisies and mums on the corner cabinet away from the heat of the oven. Mina couldn't help the grin that came over her face.

"But she wasn't injured, was she?"

"Oh, no, ma'am," Mrs. Hardman said with a wave of her hand. "I would have informed you immediately if she had been. Just frightened. And it was so late when Mr. Tunstall brought her home, I didn't want to waken you that night. Then... well, you've had a rather frightful week. Betsy didn't want you to worry about it, since she wasn't hurt."

"Very well. But I do want to be informed if you or Betsy is ever accosted by anyone again." Mina frowned. "This time it was mischief. But there are some terrible things going on in London right now, Mrs. Hardman. I don't want to take any chances with either of you. I want to know about any circumstances or encounters that are … unusual. Do you understand?"

"Of course, ma'am. As you wish."

"A beau for Betsy," Mina murmured. "A bit of good news at last."

She left the kitchen smiling.

~~~

"I saw Professor Van Helsing today," Mina said, as she passed the seasoned new potatoes to Jonathan. The tiny pieces swam in buttery bits of savory and onion.

Jonathan frowned. "What did the good professor have to say?"

"We went to church."

Jonathan paused. "Well, that's a refreshing change, I suppose."

"I'm going to be doing some charity work there a few times a week," Mina said, nonchalantly. "I just can't sit around the house all day, Jonathan. I feel like I'm going out of my mind. This is something worthwhile."

He passed her the bread and the butter dish.

"This bread is sublime," Jonathan said, taking a bite of the feathery light slice slathered in butter.

"I know," Mina said with a smile. "I told Mrs. Hardman today that I would love to learn how to make bread like she does."

"Why on earth would you want to do that?" Jonathan frowned. "What do you mean?"

"That's what we have Mrs. Hardman for, Mina. Why would you want to learn how to cook when we have a woman to do our cooking for us? Good God, woman! The things that get into your head."

Mina winced at his blasphemous use of the Lord's name yet again. Maybe she was being too sensitive, but it did bother her.

"Why shouldn't I learn to do a few useful things during my lifetime, Jonathan?" she asked, trying to keep her tone light and off-hand. "You never know when you might need to know a thing or two beyond embroidery and letter writing. Or how to pour a cup of tea." She tried to keep her tone from growing sarcastic, but it was becoming more difficult. They were entering that area of 'what a
~~~

proper British wife could and couldn't do' yet again, and she was not happy about it. Especially in light of her upcoming "adventures," as the professor had called them.

"Oh, speaking of tea, darling," Jonathan said, suddenly switching the subject so quickly, Mina was taken by surprise. "You have an invitation from Mrs. Drummond." He reached inside his jacket and produced a fine linen envelope with her name on the outside. He smiled as he passed it to her.

Mina wiped her fingers on her napkin and took the envelope with a certain amount of trepidation. James Drummond was the top lawyer at Jonathan's law firm, the head of the company. That meant his wife's invitation was no trifling matter.

"Mrs. James Drummond requests the honor of your presence at tea this Friday at three o'clock…" Mina read from the page, but broke off when she registered the day and time. "Jonathan, I can't make it to this tea! I'm supposed to be at the church that day. I just set it up today. I can't back out on my very first day."

"Why not?" He frowned.

"What do you mean, why not!" she sputtered. "Because I gave my word."

"Just tell them that something more important came up and you have to change it. Surely they'll understand. They're lucky you're volunteering your time at all, Mina."

"Jonathan, I can't just break my word every time some lady wants me to have tea."

"**Some** lady? Mina, this is my employer's wife. This is not optional. You have to attend." Jonathan's voice had taken on a harder edge now.

"Am I to have nothing in my life that I can depend on being able to do? Is there anything I will ever be able to say with certainty — yes, I will be available to do that?" Her voice was quiet, but the edge beneath her words held a knife's sharpness.

"This is what a wife is supposed to do." Jonathan's voice was low, but equally unyielding. "You used to understand that concept."

"Maybe I see the world differently now." Her voice remained even, but inside, she felt shaken.

"Mina, you will go to this luncheon." Jonathan's voice remained firm. "You will not embarrass me with the firm."

They finished their meal in silence.

As Betsy began clearing the dishes, Mina rose without a word and went to the kitchen. Mrs. Hardman had just finished putting the chocolate biscuits on a little tray with two teacups and the small pot of after dinner tea.

"A small change of plans, Mrs. Hardman," Mina said, forcing a smile. "I find I have a headache tonight and am going upstairs straight away. I want you and Betsy to enjoy those chocolate biscuits. It's my treat to you both."

"But..."

"No, I insist," Mina said, and with that she left the bewildered housekeeper to mull over this turn of events.

CHAPTER 11

Thursday, Mina climbed the steps of the church with a heavy heart. The building was quiet. She had spent most of the day yesterday studying the verses Father Gallagher had given her, and she had come up with a few notes, but most of them made little sense even to herself.

She encountered Father Gallagher as he rose from his prayers at the altar and turned.

"This is not Friday, Mrs. Harker," he said.

She sighed. "Yes, I'm aware of that. I need to reschedule our meeting, Father."

Father Gallagher pursed his lips and looked up at the ceiling, almost a plea for patience. "Am I wasting my time with you, Mrs. Harker?"

"No. You are not." Her tone was firm. His eyebrows shot up. "This is my husband's doing. A luncheon with his employer's wife. He is demanding that I attend. But I fully intend that it is the first and the last time that I shall allow such an engagement to happen. I can't be the demure little wife he wants me to be. If he wishes to divorce me for that..." She swallowed the lump in her throat. "Then I suppose I shall have to let him do so."

"Are you certain this is what you truly want?" Father Gallagher gaze seemed to pierce her soul.

"Want?" She allowed herself a bitter laugh. "I want this to have all been a terrible nightmare that I presently awaken from. But since that is not going to happen, I am stuck with this reality. It will not change. This is my life. And I must be ready for it, whether Jonathan likes it or not. I am torn, Father. Torn between duty to my husband and duty to God. But my duty to God is more urgent. Is it not?"

"I have always found it to be so." His smile was grim.

"Father?" Her gaze went from fiery to pleading. "Will God forgive me?"

For the first time, she saw compassion in his eyes. "We'll have to pray for His mercy, Mrs. Harker." He made the sign of the cross over her. "I'll see you on Monday."

Mina turned to leave, but Father Gallagher's voice stopped her. "Oh, and Mrs. Harker." She paused in the aisle, turned toward the stern priest who wore only the slightest grim smile on his face. "That gives you the weekend to work on those Scriptures. I'll expect some very good responses." He turned and walked away briskly.

Mina rolled her eyes, her sharpened hearing catching his low laughter ringing against the chilled stones of the old church walls.

~~~

As Mina came up the sidewalk, she noticed a tall young man with sandy hair standing at her door with Betsy. The young man held a bouquet of lilies and Betsy was blushing and smiling like her face would split into pieces with joy. Neither noticed her until she came up the front steps.

"Oh, Mrs. Harker!" Betsy said, dismay written on her face.

"It's all right, Betsy." Mina smiled warmly. "This must be the young man Mrs. Hardman told me about. Please introduce me to your friend."

"Yes, ma'am. This is John Henry Tunstall, ma'am." Betsy's words tripped out so quickly she almost fell over them. "Henry, this is Mrs. Wilhelmina Harker, my employer. We really haven't been talking long, ma'am..."

"Betsy! Mr. Tunstall will think I'm a slave driver." Mina laughed. "You may certainly spare a few minutes of your day. I know I can trust you to not take advantage of that."

"Oh, thank you, ma'am!" Betsy gushed.

"It's lovely to meet you." Henry finally managed to squeeze in a few words. He had a charming smile and a polite manner.

"I understand you saved our Betsy from some street ruffians," Mina said, her tone at once more serious. "I want to thank you most sincerely, Mr. Tunstall. I'm very grateful to you."

"I'm glad to have been of service," Henry said with a nod. "I couldn't let anyone as lovely as Betsy be hurt by thugs." Then he realized how that sounded. "Not that I would have let anyone be hurt when it was in my power to stop..."

"It's quite all right, Mr. Tunstall," Mina said. "I understood your meaning. Very nice to have met you. I'm sure we'll see you again."

He smiled, the relief evident on his face.

They're made for each other, Mina thought, as she entered the house and gave the two a little bit of privacy. *Was I that socially clumsy*
~~~

as a youth? She pondered the question as she removed her hat and gloves. *I suppose I was. Lucy was always the butterfly in the room. The one who drew me out. Or the one who drew attention away from my many mistakes,* Mina thought ruefully. She sighed and headed for the study.

Might as well work on that homework now. She sat down with a small leather notebook of unlined paper and her Bible.

~~~

Friday arrived and Mina's trepidation mounted. She did not want to go to this tea, but there was no way out, short of announcing her own death. And she was fairly certain that Mrs. Drummond would insist on viewing the corpse and obtaining certification that it was indeed Mina's body. Even then, Mina had a horrid image of Mrs. Drummond propping her body up on a settee and asking if she wanted lemon or sugar.

A young footman answered the door of the mansion when Mina arrived at the set time. His short brown hair was perfectly combed and his suit immaculate. A thin face and expressive blue eyes gave Mina no hints of what awaited her, but here, at least, was one kind face in the household. She took comfort in that.

Mina had worn her best afternoon dress, a hand-me-down from Lucy that was a couple of years old, but still had some use to it. It was a lovely light blue voile with dark blue trim, and ecru lace at the neck. Mrs. Drummond was as thin and wrinkled as a raisin, her eyes sharp in a slim face with a patrician nose. Her dress was lavender silk with velvet trim and white lace, cut in the latest style. Every inch of her screamed of wealth and status. Her dark hair showed few traces of gray and was carefully coiffed in an intricate series of rolls and curls.

"Ah, Mrs. Harker," she said. "Thank you, Joshua. That will be all." She dismissed the young footman with a wave of one jeweled hand. "Do come and have a seat, my dear. Allow me to introduce my daughter, Maryanne. Maryanne, this is Mrs. Harker."

Maryanne was a beautiful young woman in her late teens, with thick brown hair drawn back in a similarly intricate hairstyle. Her gown was a brilliant green with blue trim in the finest silk. Maryanne's cold gaze eyed her up and down like a country cousin, and Mina had the immediate desire to bolt for the door.

Jonathan's words echoed in her mind. "You will not embarrass me."
~~~

Mina stepped forward and took a seat as Mrs. Drummond indicated.

"Let's get acquainted, shall we?"

Getting acquainted meant being subjected to hearing about the many social groups Mrs. Drummond led or attended, the art societies, the symphonies, the museums she supported, almost all of them supported and attended heavily by the Royal Family, of course. Queen Victoria's name came up several times, as Mina nodded politely. Though the Queen had herself become a recluse since the death of her husband, the rest of her family remained in the public eye, often more visible than Victoria was happy about, if rumors could be believed.

"I understand you were friends with Lady Westenra," Mrs. Drummond said rather suddenly.

Mina was taken aback by the question. "Why, y-yes, her daughter, Lucy, was my best friend. We grew up together."

"Such a shame," Mrs. Drummond said. "First the daughter dies, then the mother."

"Yes," Mina said softly. "It has been a sad time."

The maid came in bearing a tea tray, followed by three footmen with serving trays. They each set down their offerings on the table in the adjacent room, then vacated as quietly as they had entered.

"Ah, our tea has arrived," Mrs. Drummond said. "Shall we?" She motioned with one languid hand, and they rose. The ladies seated themselves and Mrs. Drummond poured from the ornate teapot. There were a variety of sandwiches and pastries, shrimp in a creamy sauce, and berries swimming in fresh cream. The ladies nibbled and sipped their tea. Only once did Mina exclaim over a raspberry and lemon-filled pastry and wonder how it was made. The look both Drummond ladies gave her told her she could not ask that question in their company again. It was simply "not done by ladies of quality" and she would have to learn to live without the knowledge.

Goodness! No wonder Jonathan thought I was crazy to ask Mrs. Hardman to teach me how to bake bread. If Mrs. Drummond knew that, her head would spin in circles. Mina's thoughts gave her a certain amount of pleasure until Mrs. Drummond turned the conversation back around to her once again.

"And now, my dear, we really must discuss your schedule," Mrs. Drummond said.

"My schedule?" Mina almost choked on her shrimp.

"Yes, your social calendar," Mrs. Drummond explained as if to a child. "There is much to do to bring you up to some sort of acceptable standing. You've remained too long in the shadows. I'm surprised at Lady Westenra. As her daughter's friend, I would have expected her to bring you more into the spotlight, so to speak. It really was quite a dereliction of her duties that she neglected to help you along. But we can turn that around. Can't we, Maryanne?"

"Mrs. Drummond, I really don't think I have the time for..."

"Nonsense, my dear Mrs. Harker!" Mrs. Drummond cut her off as she chose another scone. "You must make time. Jonathan needs all the help he can get. As his wife, you must help him along by being socially active in the community."

"How will my activity in the community help Jonathan be a good lawyer, Mrs. Drummond?" Mina asked, completely perplexed by this logic.

"It's all about perception, Mrs. Harker," she explained. "You must maintain a certain visibility. Thus, he is visible too, you see."

"No, I'm afraid I don't see," Mina said, trying her best to smile. "Besides, I will be very busy. I've just volunteered at a local church, and that will be taking up quite a lot of my time. In fact, I was supposed to start today, but I postponed until Monday so I could accept your kind invitation. I really can't put them off further though. I've already promised to be available to them."

"Oh, church work," Mrs. Drummond waved her hand dismissively. "Leave that to the nuns and priests. That's not for women of our station, Mrs. Harker. You are meant for other duties."

"I'm afraid I do not see it that way, Mrs. Drummond," Mina said, her voice polite but firm.

"Well said, Mrs. Harker," Maryanne spoke up. "All this social nonsense is just that. A dying social mess that could do with a few less tea parties and society gatherings, if you ask me."

"Maryanne!" Mrs. Drummond scolded. "This is not the time for your silly blathering."

"It's not silly blathering, Mother," Maryanne insisted. "Certainly no sillier than all your ridiculous committees and society teas and parties and meetings. What do you accomplish, anyway? Getting rich men to open their wallets and pour more money into your museums, art shows, and symphonies? Why do they need the women to encourage them to do that? They would do it anyway!"

"Maryanne, that is enough!"

"I'm not saying that those are not worthy causes," Mina said, trying to find a peaceful middle ground between mother and daughter. "But don't you feel that we owe a duty to God as well?"

"No, I do not," snapped Mrs. Drummond.

Mina was taken aback.

"I attend church, like every good Christian woman in England, Mrs. Harker. That is more than enough. And it should be enough for you as well. You are a well-bred young woman and it is time you started doing your Christian duty to your husband. There are things we do and things we don't do."

"I see," Mina said. "And you are going to tell me just where those lines are drawn?"

"Yes," Mrs. Drummond said. "It is **my** Christian duty to my husband to help his employee in this situation. Your husband is in need, Mrs. Harker. Whether you realize it or not, he is a liability to this company. His health is not good, yet my husband has kept him at his post in spite of it."

"His health is not good, Mrs. Drummond, because of an assignment your husband sent him on, an assignment that almost cost him his life. An assignment to take contracts to a ..." she stopped herself and amended her comment just in time, "... homicidal maniac who almost killed him. A maniac who imprisoned him and left him in the care of other maniacs who did him great bodily harm. Don't you think your husband owes him a debt for placing him in that position?"

Mina found herself standing now. She took a deep breath and regained control of her emotions.

"Be that as it may, Mrs. Harker." Mrs. Drummond's voice faltered, but she was resolved to try again to regain a portion of the ground she had obviously lost. Maryanne simply stared in awe that anyone could speak to her mother that way.

"Mrs. Drummond, I thank you for a lovely luncheon. It was so nice to meet both of you." Mina's back was straight, her smile firmly in place. "I enjoyed this very much, but I won't be needing your help with my schedule. Jonathan's work is Jonathan's work, and my work is my work. London society will have to keep on rolling along with me. I have other obligations and I will not put them off any longer. Now I really must be going. Jonathan hates it if I'm not there when he gets home." She stared defiantly at Mrs. Drummond, who was now truly speechless. "I'll see myself out. Thank you again for a lovely afternoon."

She turned to sweep from the room, then paused one last time. "You really must ask your cook to pass along her recipe for those delightful raspberry lemon pastries to my husband. I'd love to give it to my cook to try. I might even try my hand at them myself." She grinned widely before departing.

~~~

"Give my husband the recipe? Mina, what in God's name were you thinking?" Jonathan demanded that evening, soon after he had arrived home.

"Did she give you the recipe?" Mina asked.

"**No**! She didn't give me any blasted recipe! Did you really think she would?" His roar shook the lamps in the study.

"How did you find out this quickly? I only left her house two hours ago."

"Mrs. Drummond stormed into the office only slightly less than that. From the shrieks, I had surmised that you had beheaded three or four vampires within her household staff at luncheon. I expected to be hauled before a judge before the end of the day. Imagine my surprise."

Mina tried unsuccessfully to suppress her mirth. "You see? It truly could have been worse."

"It's not funny, Mina. Mr. Drummond is not happy with either of us right now."

"No, Jonathan," she said hotly. "You're right. It's not funny. I was ambushed. That woman wants to run my life. She wants to dictate every moment of my time, and I won't allow it. She knows nothing—**nothing**—about what is truly out there! She knows nothing about what we've seen, what we've fought against over the past year. I will not be relegated to committee meetings and society groups while monsters tear up this city and murder the people I love."

Jonathan's shoulders slumped. "We've been invited to a musicale tomorrow night with the Drummonds. We are going, Mina. And I need you to behave yourself."

"Behave myself? Are you going to put me in chains, Husband?" Her voice was laced with sarcasm, but fear knotted in her stomach. This was a test. A test of her resolve. A test of her love for Jonathan versus her love for God.
~~~

"Just... please don't antagonize Mrs. Drummond," he said wearily.

"Maybe you should think about what happens if she antagonizes me, Jonathan," she retorted.

"Are you going to chop off her head, Mina? Is that it?"

"That's not even fair! I don't kill humans and you know it," she cried. "Although I'm not sure she qualifies," she shouted at his back as he walked out the door.

Jonathan went to bed without supper, and Mina slept fitfully on the couch in the study.

~~~

Breakfast was a subdued affair. Betsy served, eying both of them closely, but saying little beyond a whispered, "Can I get you anything else, ma'am?" and "Will you take some toast, sir?" When both had shaken their heads, she curtseyed and darted to the kitchen hastily.

"Mina, I need to remain employed," Jonathan began softly. "I am not independently wealthy. You know that."

"I do know that, Jonathan," she said, keeping her voice equally controlled. "But I will not allow that woman to lead me around by a leash and collar. I don't care who she is. I refuse to give her that right. I don't know what brought this on so suddenly with the Drummonds, but it must end. You are my husband, and while I love you and I will try to be as supportive as I can be to you, I will not be placed in this position. As my husband, I would expect you to shield me from this unwelcome abuse."

"Abuse? Mina, don't you think that's rather harsh?" Jonathan's eyebrows rose. "Mrs. Drummond simply wants to introduce you to society. She's trying to move you forward among other ladies of social standing in London. I would hardly call that abuse."

"It is unwanted demands upon my time, Jonathan. It is her insistence that nothing else matters unless she deems it worthy. I do not need her approval to determine what makes a pursuit worthwhile."

"Like your charity work?" Jonathan asked. "Is this something Van Helsing is behind?"

Mina frowned. "In fact, the professor did introduce me to the priest at this particular church, but that does not negate the importance of their work. Why do you ask?

Jonathan rubbed a weary hand across his forehead. "Do you
~~~

have a gown for the musicale this evening? We will need to be ready by six o'clock. Mr. Drummond is coming by in his carriage to pick us up. We'll take an early dinner with them, then proceed."

"Where is this grand event taking place?" Mina swallowed her resentment.

"I--I don't remember now. But it is strictly formal. If you don't have anything appropriate, you will have to try to find something this afternoon."

"I have an older ball gown of Lucy's I can wear." Her voice was low and laced with pain.

Jonathan winced, but he nodded. "I'll be in my study. I have some contracts to go over." He pushed away from the table and left the dining room.

Betsy slipped into the room as Mina cradled her head in her hands. "Ma'am, can I get you anything else from the kitchen? You really should eat something."

Mina raised her head and gazed fondly at the anxious servant. She really did fuss over them so, but only because she truly cared about her master and mistress.

"I'm fine, Betsy. You may clear now. All but the tea. I will finish my tea, thank you."

"What about the last of the chocolate biscuits, ma'am?" Betsy asked shyly. "I saved one from last night. I was going to give it to Henry, but maybe you should have it for your breakfast. You really do need to eat something, ma'am."

"Didn't you like them, Betsy?"

"Oh, they were lovely, Mrs. Harker!" Betsy said, her face lighting up. "That's why I saved one special for Henry." She blushed bright pink.

Mina chuckled lightly. "Then you must save it for Henry. He'll be pleased by the gesture, and I'm sure he'll enjoy it more than I will right now."

"But, ma'am, you really do need to eat something," Betsy pleaded.

Mina considered for a moment. "Do you think Mrs. Hardman has any of those delicious orange scones hidden away somewhere?"

Betsy's eyes lit up in delight. "She just made up a batch this morning for afternoon tea."

"Do you think you might filch one without incurring her wrath?" Mina's eyes sparkled with mischief.

"I'll risk it!" Betsy crowed with delight. She ran off to fetch the scone.

So, her romance with Henry Tunstall was going well. And bringing about delightful changes in the girl's demeanor. *Well, good for Betsy*, thought Mina. She also knew that Mrs. Hardman would gladly fill a platter with scones if it would get her to eat! Well, eat she would. These wonderful women were her source of comfort these days. After her scone, maybe Betsy could help her into that ballgown. Hopefully it would still fit, and she would be ready for this dreadful evening with the Drummonds tonight.

"Please, God, help me not to make a mess of it," she murmured. "For Jonathan's sake."

CHAPTER 12

Jonathan's eyes lit up when Mina descended the staircase. Her dark teal satin gown featured an off-the-shoulder bodice with a layer of lace over the shoulders and bosom, but she hid her scars with a wide black ribbon edged with ecru lace and tiny red ribbon roses. The skirt was full, falling gracefully from a dropped waist. She was simply stunning. It was an older style, but she wore it gracefully.

Jonathan wore tails and top hat, obviously obtained quite recently, as Mina knew he did not own anything so fine as these clothes.

"Mina, you are beautiful," he whispered, as she drew near.

"Thank you." She smiled, seeing true appreciation in his warm brown eyes. "You look very handsome as well. New?"

He sighed. "A necessary expense, I'm afraid."

A discreet knock at the door made further conversation impossible. Betsy hurried past Mina to answer the door. Jonathan held Mina's cloak for her, then held out his arm.

"Shall we, Mrs. Harker?"

"We shall, Mr. Harker."

They followed the coachman out into the night. Mina found herself searching the street. That itch on the back of her neck was back. There were eyes upon them; she could feel it. But she could not see the culprit. No matter. She would find him. Sooner or later, she would find him.

~~~

"So, my wife tells me you are doing some charity work," Mr. Drummond said, his voice genial.

Conversation had remained neutral during the appetizer and the soup. Mina knew it was too good to last. He had waited until she had a forkful of roast beef in her mouth. Mina chewed and swallowed carefully while they waited patiently. Jonathan had taken a bite of his potatoes, so he was equally unable to jump into the conversation to divert the direction.

"Yes," Mina finally managed to say. "I've recently become
~~~

involved in a local ministry. I was supposed to have started on Friday, but postponed my plans until Monday."

"What exactly will you be doing, might one inquire?"

"Well, we haven't exactly laid that out, but they have many operations within the city. I'm sure it will vary from day to day. I'm willing to do whatever they need the most, of course. Isn't that the course that the Lord would have taken, Mr. Drummond? To serve where service is most needed?"

"But surely you know what you are volunteering to do, Mrs. Harker," he said, a bit more forcefully. "I mean, perhaps it is something that could be relegated to ... say two hours in the morning a couple of times a week?"

Mina smiled thinly. She smelled a trap, and she was not about to step into it. "Well, until I actually have a chance to get started and see what all they will need, I won't truly know that, Mr. Drummond."

"Mrs. Drummond was saying that she has some wonderful opportunities for you. Perhaps you might find some time to look into those as well." His voice was still genial, but his eyes were a more-than-a-little stern.

If he thinks he's scolding a child, he's in for a surprise, Mina thought grimly.

"Mrs. Drummond had quite a calendar lined up," Mina said brightly. "I just don't think I could live up to that much social interaction. I'm not quite the committee joiner, Mr. Drummond, though I do appreciate the invitation."

"I don't think you quite understand your social obligation, Mrs. Harker—" Mr. Drummond began.

"Mr. Drummond, you really should try this roast beef," Mina said, forking another bite. "It's really very good, but if you allow it to get cold, it's going to grow tough." She inserted the fork into her mouth and savored the juicy meat, chewing slowly.

Mr. Drummond's eyes narrowed.

"I do hope, my dear, that you are not going to ask for the recipe," Mrs. Drummond said softly.

Mina's gaze focused on her with amusement as she swallowed her bite. "Why no, I'm not, Mrs. Drummond. Our own Mrs. Hardman makes a lovely roast beef. But I would still like the one from your own kitchen for those raspberry lemon tarts."

Mr. and Mrs. Drummond studiously applied themselves to their roast beef. Jonathan glared at Mina, but said nothing.

Jonathan mentioned a political situation that might impact one of their cases peripherally, and Mr. Drummond was momentarily diverted. But Mina knew the discussion was far from over. The roast beef already felt like lead in her stomach, and the elaborate cherry and chocolate dessert, which was the last course, did not promise to help matters. The stays in her corset cut into her ribs and she felt faint. She asked for a glass of water, and sipped that rather than the wine beside her plate.

Mrs. Drummond finally asked, "Don't you like the wine, my dear? It's James' favorite vintage."

Of course, that got the attention of the men. Mr. Drummond frowned. *Another black mark against me,* Mina thought. *Drat that woman!*

"No, I just feel a little light-headed," Mina said with a smile. "Not enough water, I'm sure. I'll be fine. The wine is very good." *The wine is terrible. Far too dry. Like drinking the Gobi Desert.*

"Nonsense!" Mr. Drummond said. "Wine is the best thing for a woman feeling faint. Have some more, Mrs. Harker. "

"I'm fine, Mr. Drummond," Mina insisted.

"Mina, are you sure you're all right?" Jonathan's voice sounded concerned, but his frown told her he was more worried about the supposed insult to his superior. "Maybe you should have a sip of wine. Perhaps it will settle your stomach, dearest."

"It's nothing, Jonathan," she said, putting a light smile into her voice. "I'm quite all right. Please do not fuss." She shot Mrs. Drummond a pointed look. She took another sip of her water, as Mr. Drummond snorted in irritation. Mina kept her gaze fixed firmly on the tablecloth and concentrated on slowing her breathing. Gradually, the dizziness subsided. Meanwhile, the men resumed their discussion and Mrs. Drummond smirked behind her wine glass like the cat who had swallowed the canary. Mina's eyes narrowed. *If she thinks this is the way to influence me, she has another think coming. I'm more determined than ever to avoid her company. What an odious, conniving woman.*

Mr. Drummond removed an ornate gold watch from his waistcoat and flicked it open. "Well, we should be going if we are to be seated before the musicale begins," he announced.

Jonathan and Mr. Drummond stood and assisted the ladies with their chairs. As they arose, Mina's gaze swept the room.

That's when she saw him.

The elegantly dressed man with a silk scarf draped over the lapels of his dress jacket raised his wine glass in her direction. Candlelight glinted off the lenses of his dark glasses, but he peered at her over the top rim and his irises caught the light, reflecting eerily. His smile flashed and his incisors lengthened then receded so quickly, no one else seemed to notice the anomaly. Mina's mouth hardened. Was this the reason for her momentary unease? Had he influenced her somehow? And why was he here, of all places? Had they been followed?

"Mina?"

She glared at the vampire who sat with a bevy of women who fawned over him with adoration in their every look and touch. Slaves to his power, no doubt. Then one turned her gaze upon Mina, and she saw the same feral quality in the woman, the same pale skin, sharp incisors, strange eyes. *He's turning them!* She realized it and was suddenly ill again. She stumbled against Jonathan's arm.

"Mina!" Jonathan's voice hissed in her ear. "You must pull yourself together. What is your problem tonight?"

Mina stared at him in disbelief. *Does he really think I'm just trying to be willful? Does he think this is about defying the Drummonds? He fought against Dracula, and he still doesn't have a clue.*

"It's nothing, Jonathan," she said, her voice cold and clipped. "We need to leave immediately."

Careful not to look in the direction of the vampires again, she held her head high and swept from the dining room with as much grace as she could muster. Jonathan held her cloak and she accepted it without a word.

"Is something wrong, Mrs. Harker? You look very pale." Mrs. Drummond frowned, and this time she seemed genuinely concerned. Mina bit back a sharp reply when she saw sincerity on the older woman's deeply lined features.

"I'm fine, thank you," she said. "The fresh air is helping."

"Didn't finish your wine, which would have helped more than the air," groused Mr. Drummond.

"Oh, do stop going on about the wine, James," scolded Mrs. Drummond. As the men stepped forward to call for the carriage to be brought forward, Mrs. Drummond eased closer to Mina and slipped an arm around her waist. "My dear, are you, by any chance, expecting a child?"

"What!" Mina exclaimed, taken aback by the suggestion. Then she chuckled lightly. "Thank you for your concern, Mrs. Drummond, but no, I am not with child at the moment. Truth be told, I think my corset is a bit too tight," she confided in a whisper.

The two women snickered together, a moment of shared torment at the societal expectations in fashion.

"I do believe my favorite time of day is the moment I can rid myself of that prison of whale bone and lacing," Mrs. Drummond whispered. "Although it does seem to help the back pain I've suffered over the years. I'm not sure I would be able to walk upright some days without it on."

"This was one of Lucy's dresses, and I'm afraid it is a couple of years old. I had to lace in pretty tightly to fit into it." Mina found it easier to talk to her in these few moments of honesty. "Before I wear it again, I think I'll have to manage a bit of creative gusseting to let out the side seams. Either that, or learn to manage without breathing quite so much."

The women giggled again, and for a moment, they seemed to share a bit of camaraderie.

Then Mrs. Drummond smiled and asked, "Whoever was that handsome man who smiled at you just before we left our table?"

Mina's blood turned to ice water. She drew herself up, cursing herself for lowering her guard with this odious woman. "I have no idea who you might be referring to, Mrs. Drummond. I knew no one else in the restaurant tonight save our party."

"Oh, come now, my dear," Mrs. Drummond said, smirking widely. "He was looking right at you when he raised his champagne glass in your direction. Quite a handsome gentleman too. Someone your husband is acquainted with, perhaps?"

"There was no one of my acquaintance in the restaurant, Mrs. Drummond. I don't know what you are trying to insinuate, but I do not appreciate it."

The men returned with the carriage, and Mina cut further remarks short. Jonathan noticed that her lips were pursed tightly, and he frowned slightly, but she said nothing as they scrambled into the carriage. They were soon on their way.

The prestigious home of the Lord Westland was lit up brighter than daylight. The halls were crowded with the glittering elite of London society. Jonathan and Mina were introduced right and left until Mina felt herself drowning in a sea of names and titles. Then she saw the trap slamming upon her. This was Mr. Drummond's way of pushing her into society. There was sure to be a spate of invitations following this event for the pretty little wife of Mr. Jonathan Harker. And he would expect her to accept them all! She felt herself suffocating.

A familiar figure appeared amidst the crowd, his dear face slightly pale at the sight of her dress, which was sure to be a reminder of happier days.

"Arthur!" Mina greeted their friend with a relief that almost brought tears to her eyes.

"Mina, how beautiful you look, my dear," he murmured, as he kissed her cheek and shook hands with Jonathan. He turned and kissed Mrs. Drummond's hand and greeted Jonathan's employer.

"It's refreshing to see that Mrs. Harker has at least one friend in London society, Lord Holmwood," Mr. Drummond said, his voice coming out a bit caustically. "We seem to be having difficulty encouraging her to take her place with Mrs. Drummond and the other ladies."

"Well, I've always found Mina to be something of a free spirit, Mr. Drummond. And we mustn't cage a free spirit." Arthur raised his champagne glass in Mina's direction. She felt a swelling of affection for her friend. But when she glanced at the faces around her, she saw that his words had not gone over very well. Even Jonathan looked decidedly out of sorts.

A gong sounded, and the crowds began to move toward the ball room where chairs had been arranged in rows. A small orchestra was set up at the front of the room, and people began filing in and taking their seats, chatting with friends. Arthur excused himself, squeezing Mina's hand reassuringly before returning to his party.

Sitting between Jonathan and Mrs. Drummond, Mina listened to the music floating through the ballroom, but there was no joy in the occasion. She only felt the sinking feeling that her circumstances were spinning out of her control once again.

No! she insisted. *I will not be caught unprepared ever again. I will not. If we are to face monsters in London every time I turn around, I have to be prepared to fight them. If Father Gallagher is willing to train me, then I must go through his process, no matter what. No one will stand in my way. No one will stop me. Not Mrs. Drummond, not Mr. Drummond, not London society, or the Queen herself.*

Not even Jonathan.

Intermission brought Mina a brief respite, as she excused herself from Jonathan and the Drummonds, and sought out Arthur Holmwood. Throughout the first hour, all Mina could think about was the presence of the vampire at the restaurant. Someone else should be told. She would never be able to get away from Jonathan tonight. But perhaps Arthur could get word to Professor Van Helsing. Someone else in their group needed to be aware of the danger they were in. And this was definitely not the time to tell her husband. He would lock her in the attic and never let her out of the house again without an armed guard.

Mina smiled her way past through the crowds until she reached Arthur's side and begged for just a moment of his time. Arthur smiled his excuses to his party and guided Mina to a window seat on the far side of the room.

"Is something amiss, Mina?" He frowned, taking in her pale cheeks.

"I fear we were followed tonight, and I felt someone else in our... group ... should know about it."

"Followed?" Arthur looked about for Jonathan. "Have you told Jonathan?"

"No! Jonathan cannot be told tonight. He... won't take it well."

Arthur's eyes narrowed, and his voice lowered. "Mina, who exactly are we talking about?"

"It was one of ... them," she whispered. "It was the one who accosted me in the alley near Professor Van Helsing's home recently. The one we believe attacked Lady Westenra."

"And he saw you?" Arthur's voice was low and tense. "You're sure?"

Mina nodded. "Quite sure. He had ... women ... with him. At least one of them had... turned."

Arthur's face paled. "My God..."

"There you are, Mrs. Harker." Mr. Drummond's voice cut into their conversation. "Harker! I found her. She's over her with Lord Holmwood. We've been looking everywhere for you. You really shouldn't disappear like that, young lady."

"I hardly disappeared, Mr. Drummond," Mina said, rising and smoothing her skirts to still her shaking hands. "I simply wanted to ask Arthur a question about an old friend of ours, a professor we used to know."

Arthur picked up on the cue immediately. "Yes, I told Mina I would be seeing him again very soon, in fact. We just got caught up in reminiscing about the old fellow's idiosyncrasies. Besides, Mr. Drummond, Mina is hardly apt to disappear in companionship such as this, is she?" He waved a careless hand about the room and chuckled. Mr. Drummond huffed in a disgruntled way as Jonathan and Mrs. Drummond hurried over to join them.

"Mina?" Jonathan looked from her to Mr. Drummond, sensing that something was definitely amiss.

"I simply wanted to ask Arthur a question, Jonathan," Mina said.

"Most young women are content to stay by their husband's sides in social gatherings," Mr. Drummond grumbled.

"Oh, come now, Drummond," Arthur said, trying to be congenial. "You can't cage women like parakeets, can you? Mina and I are old friends. Jonathan knows that. There was no harm in our conversation."

"Of course not, Arthur," Jonathan said. "I just lost track of where Mina had gone off. Just a momentary panic when I didn't see her. So sorry."

Mina frowned and laid a hand on his sleeve. He really did look pale. "Are you all right?"

"Yes, my dear," he said through gritted teeth, "but it would be better if you would refrain from dashing off again, please." He whispered the last, but it was like a slap across her face.

The gong sounded.

"Well, that would be our signal to take our seats," said Mrs. Drummond, just a tad too cheerily. "Come, dear."

"Jonathan…" Arthur tried to say something conciliatory, but Jonathan waved him away.

"It's all right, Arthur," he said. "We can talk another time, please."

Mina looked back at him as Jonathan began to pull her toward the ballroom.

Arthur reassured her with a nod that he would see Van Helsing as soon as he possibly could about the vampire. That was the best she could hope for.

CHAPTER 13

The carriage wheels clattered away over the cobblestones as Betsy took Mina's cloak and Jonathan's top hat and cape, upon their return home from the musicale.

"Did you have a nice evening?" she asked. One look at Jonathan's face sent her scurrying away with the outer garments without waiting for an answer.

Mina mounted the stairs, feeling that her lungs would burst if she didn't release herself from her corset immediately.

"Mina, we need to talk," Jonathan said sternly.

"Well, I'm not in much of a talking mood, Jonathan," she said wearily. "I've been lectured about all I can take for one night. Especially until I can rid myself of this cast iron corset I've had to wear to fit into Lucy's dress. I'm getting out of it now. If you want to talk, you'll just have to follow me upstairs. But I'm getting changed. Then I'm going to bed, and I'm not sleeping on the couch again."

"I don't recall asking you to sleep on the couch last night," he said, following her up the staircase.

"No, you just asked me if I was going to murder your employer's wife, as I recall," she shot back over her shoulder.

"I did not!" He stopped in mid-step on the stairs.

Mina whirled around at the top of the steps. "Yes, Jonathan! You did! I believe your exact words were: Are you going to chop off her head?"

Jonathan paled, then flushed. "Well, as I recall, your parting shot was that you weren't sure she was even human. Are you still wavering on that point now?"

"She might be human, but I'm not so sure he is!" she snapped, stalking to the bedroom.

Jonathan followed her into the bedroom and slammed the door. "Mina, that's enough!"

"Yes, you're right," she said, ripping her way out of the dress and throwing it across the chaise in the corner. "He's a human male all right. Stubborn, opinionated, master of the universe — definitely a human."

"Mina, stop it!"

"What has happened to you, Jonathan?" Mina's voice held real anguish. "You never treated me like an object before. You always valued my opinions; you valued my mind and my goals in life. You never tried to hold me back before. What has happened to you? Why have you changed?"

"You purposely antagonized Mr. Drummond tonight, Mina," he said through gritted teeth. "Why would you do that? You know my job depends on him. They've kept me on in spite of my health."

"As well they should, considering you wouldn't have these health problems, if not for them!"

"But I am having trouble performing my job now, don't you understand that?" He sank to the side of the bed wearily. "They could fire me. It might make a difference if you could just be a little nicer to Mrs. Drummond. Would it really be so terrible going to a few social functions with her?"

"Yes, Jonathan, it would!" Mina threw up both hands in the air. Unable to even take a deep breath, she ripped angrily at the laces until the hated corset followed the dress and the underskirts to the heap with the dress. She slipped her nightgown over her head and breathed her first truly deep breath in several hours. She exhaled and leaned against the windowpane, overlooking the streets of London. "I cannot be that woman, Jonathan. You spent one evening with her. Can you honestly say you want me to be like that? Concerned only with fashions and who is lunching with whom, or who was seen with whom? It's all gossip and clothes and social causes, but heaven forbid they actually *do* anything to truly help the poor or the needy in this city. I thought maybe telling them about doing charity work with a church would get them to back away a bit. No, because the Lord's work is 'beneath' ladies of 'quality,' according to Mrs. Drummond. Is that what you want me to become, Jonathan?"

He was silent.

"Well, I can't do that. I won't. If you want to divorce me for not following your newfound social dictates, then do it." She bit back tears as she said those words, and carefully kept her back turned so he would not see her if they spilled over.

"Is that what you want?" he asked softly. "A divorce?"

"No!" she cried, turning to face him. "It's not what I want! But I will not be made into some caricature of a woman like that one, shallow and empty, scheming, manipulative. I won't do it, Jonathan. Accept me as I am or walk away. But don't expect me to play this game with them."

"Is that your final word?" he asked.

She was silent for a long time. He was so quiet. So resigned. Her heart thumped against her ribs. She had hoped he would take her in his arms. She had hoped he would say, no, of course not, he would never want her to be like that woman. Was he really going to just give up on their marriage? Was she really going to just give up?

"Jonathan, I…" She turned around to try to beseech him to see reason.

Jonathan was gone.

~~~

Mina's dreams were plagued by the vampire in the glasses and the fancy clothes. Why was he following her around London? Or was it coincidence that he had been in the restaurant they had gone to last night? Mina shook her head. She didn't believe in coincidences.

A soft tap at the door made her sit up in bed. When she called out, the door opened, and Betsy peeked in. She smiled and opened the door wider to allow herself entry with a small wooden tray. It held a small teapot, a cup, and a plate of scones.

"Thought you might need a little something to get yerself going, ma'am," she said shyly.

"Has… Mr. Harker had breakfast?" Mina asked carefully.

"Well, he's taking some tea in his study, but he's refusing breakfast," Betsy said, biting her lower lip. "We just… well, we thought maybe you'd prefer… just seemed like you might want to have a nibble up here this morning."

"Thank you, Betsy," Mina said, grasping the girl's hand affectionately. "This is very thoughtful of you, and it is very much appreciated."

Betsy blushed and smiled. Then she left Mina to her tea and scones while she tidied up the room, hanging up the garments from the previous night.

"We definitely need to take out those side seams if I'm ever going to wear that dress again, Betsy," Mina said wryly. "I couldn't take a breath all evening."

Betsy looked inside the dress and smiled. "Nice wide seams, ma'am. I can take it out by a couple of inches easily."

"Don't take it out too much!" Mina laughed. "I don't want it to
~~~

fall off of me either. And there's no rush. I doubt I'll be wearing it again anytime soon. In fact, the Drummonds may never invite us to go anywhere again, so it may be a moot point." Her voice and her face grew somber at that point. *Jonathan might not be taking me anywhere either.* But she didn't say that aloud.

At last, she got up and dressed. In no mood to attend church this morning, she descended the stairs. *Might as well face it now. If he's going to throw me out, I might as well know it, and deal with it. Maybe the Professor can find a place for me temporarily.*

She tapped on the study door, then opened it slowly. "May I come in?"

"Of course." Jonathan stood at the window, but he turned when she entered. He still wore his dress pants and the silk shirt from the night before, though he had removed the coat and vest. A blanket lay rumpled on one end of the sofa. Mina picked it up and carefully folded it.

"You didn't have to sleep here," she said softly.

"I needed to think," he said. "In fact, I did very little sleeping. I'm afraid I'm not in much shape for church this morning."

"I was rather thinking of staying home myself," Mina said with a sliver of a smile.

"Ah, yes, but you'll make up for it this week with all those excursions to the church to do your volunteer work," Jonathan replied, almost bitterly.

"Jonathan, I—"

"No, let me try to get this out, Mina." He sighed. "You are right. I don't know what I was thinking. Drummond started trying to push me into a more political arena, and I let him do it. His first stipulation was that you had to be more 'visible' socially. I should have known it would be a disaster. Oh, that odious woman! You were right, Mina. I don't want you to be like that."

Mina sighed and her body sagged in relief, folding almost in half with her elbows on her knees and her face resting on her hands.

"Mina! Are you all right?" Jonathan knelt in front of her.

She looked up at him, weariness tugging at the muscles in her face. "I truly thought you were going to tell me to go pack my bags." She swallowed the lump in her throat.

"Oh, Mina." Jonathan leaned forward, resting his forehead against hers, as he wrapped his arms around her. "I'm so sorry. I let myself be bullied by the firm. I should have taken a stronger stance with them long ago. You put me to shame, my dear. You are so brave, so strong."

"Me? No, Jonathan!" Mina exclaimed. "You fought off those evil women of Dracula's. You never surrendered. I'm so proud of you. You came back to me. I thought you were ashamed of me for my own weakness against Dracula's enticement. I thought that was why you were trying to change me."

"No, you're the one who finally defeated him, Mina." Jonathan brushed her hair away from the tears on her face. "And you're the one who continues to try to fight off the evil in our streets. I worry so about you. Please, at least promise me you'll be careful. Please promise me that. I couldn't bear to lose you, Mina."

They fell into one another's arms and wept together, relief overcoming the anger they had endured.

Finally, Mina pulled back and wiped her eyes with her handkerchief.

"Jonathan, I must tell you something," she said. "I didn't tell you last night. Well, you weren't in a mood for me to tell you." Her mouth quirked up a little bit.

"What is it?"

"At the restaurant, when we were getting ready to leave," she began.

"When you went so pale," Jonathan said, suddenly realizing that he had missed something important in his efforts to impress his employer.

"Yes." Mina nodded, watching his expression carefully. "He was there. The vampire. He was watching us."

Jonathan rose from his position on the floor and sat on the sofa beside Mina, clearly stunned beyond words.

"He wasn't alone, dearest," she said quietly. "There were women with him. Three of them. At least one of them made a point of … flashing her fangs at me."

"He's turning them," Jonathan whispered in horror. "Dear God…"

"Yes, he's turning them. We have to be careful. Watchful."

Jonathan groaned. "That explains it." He wiped his face with his left hand while still clinging to her with his right arm firmly around her shoulders.

Mina felt cold. "Explains what?"

"Mrs. Drummond." Jonathan shook his head. "Please forgive

me, Mina. You're right about her. She is an odious woman."

"She said something, didn't she?"

"Yes." He swallowed hard. "She said there was a man at the restaurant who seemed to be flirting with you. Were you perhaps hoping to meet someone there? I should never have listened to her, but you disappeared so quickly, and you had been behaving so strangely all evening... I—"

"No, I'm sorry," Mina cut him off. "I should have found a way to tell you. To warn you." She leaned into his embrace. Suddenly chopping off Mrs. Drummond's head didn't seem like such a terrible thing after all, human or not.

Jonathan suddenly sighed and pressed the heel of his hand to his forehead. "Your little talk with Arthur last night..."

"Yes, I had to let someone know who could go warn the Professor at once. I knew you were never going to let me go out last night, and I didn't want to wait until today to try to contact anyone else. Besides, if anything had happened to me last night, no one would have even known that we had been followed to the restaurant. I had to try to take precautions somehow." She gripped his left hand. "Please forgive me for not being more honest with you at once. But with the Drummonds right there—"

"No, you did the right thing," he said, shaking his head absently. "But should we check on Arthur or the Professor today?"

"Yes." Mina smiled. "But first, I really think you should go upstairs and get some rest. You didn't sleep last night and neither did I. What if we both take a little nap? Arthur and the Professor will probably both go to church. Perhaps they will stop in afterwards to see us."

A soft rap on the door, then Mrs. Hardman entered softly. "We're just heading out to church, ma'am. Will you be going yourselves?"

"No, Mr. Harker isn't feeling well, and frankly, neither am I," Mina said. "Must be something we ate last night. We'll stay here and rest today. But you and Betsy go on."

"Are you sure, ma'am?" Mrs. Hardman's face creased with worry. "I can stay home if you need me to."

"No, of course not," Mina said. "You go on. We'll be fine."

~~~

Mina watched over Jonathan while he slept, her eyes finally dry, and her resolve firm. It seemed that the enemy wanted to break up
~~~

her marriage. Well, that would just not do. She and Jonathan were finally on the right path, and she would make sure they stayed there. If Mr. and Mrs. Drummond wanted to make an issue of that, they might find they were biting off far more than they could chew.

True to Mina's prediction, Arthur and Professor Van Helsing showed up soon after church services. Mina told Mrs. Hardman to lay two more places for luncheon, and they retired to the study for a quick consultation while the food was prepared.

"Arthur, I owe you an apology," Jonathan began.

"Whatever for?" Arthur frowned.

"I feel I was … abrupt last evening," Jonathan said. "Mr. Drummond has been bringing pressure to bear, and, well, I'm afraid I have not dealt with it as I should have."

"Political and social pressure?" Arthur asked, nodding.

"Yes. And involving Mina as well. Since the whole Carpathia incident, I am not strong enough to keep up with the long office hours, I'm afraid…"

"Ah, I see." Arthur held up a hand. "I suspected as much from what little I witnessed last night, so I made a few back door inquiries myself, my friend. I hope you will not be offended by that. Say no more. I will offer you this. If Drummond wishes to release you from his employ, let him. I will offer you employment with my estate at the same rate of pay as they are currently giving you, with annual increases thereafter. So, if he wants to give up exceptional legal counsel such as yours, my friend, it's his profound loss."

"Arthur, I don't know what to say," Jonathan stammered.

"Just say you'll put the old man in his place once and for all. Frankly, it was all I could do to not punch him in the face right there in Reginald's ballroom last night."

Mina covered her mouth, unsuccessfully trying to smother an unladylike chortle.

"You're laughing, but Reggie would have been very displeased with me," Arthur said, frowning to hide his own smile. "And Henrietta would have been cross beyond words if I had gotten blood on that marble floor."

Mina gave way to a howl then.

"Mina! It's not funny!" Jonathan scolded softly, but he was smiling too.

"At least Arthur isn't threatening to behead either of them," she snickered.

"Mina!" Arthur feigned shock. "You didn't!"

"Well, actually, Jonathan put the idea into my head," she said with a sideways flicker of her eyes. "I hadn't seriously considered it until after last night. Then I contemplated it very seriously indeed."

"Well, this sounds like a tale worth repeating," Arthur said.

"Perhaps we should get back to the vampire who seems so intent on following you about." Professor Van Helsing's voice wiped away the playfulness.

"In a way, the two subjects are connected," Mina said slowly.

Between the two of them, she and Jonathan related the entire evening to Arthur and the professor.

"Disturbing," murmured Van Helsing. "He is brazen, this one. Far too brazen. Why? Why take his women out in public? Why show them off? Why show them to you? Why take the chance on Jonathan seeing them?"

"Maybe he doesn't know about my connection to Dracula," Jonathan said slowly. "Perhaps he doesn't know that I would react to his 'brides,' as Dracula called them. Maybe he isn't aware of that history."

"Maybe," Van Helsing mused. "But what has he learned about Mina? Why does he want her to know that there are more vampires in the city now? Is it to scare her? She has not shown fear up to now. Does he think numbers will intimidate her? These are questions I want answers to, my friends. We must know these things. Strategy." He seemed about to say more, but cut himself short.

Just then, Betsy knocked on the door and announced that luncheon was ready.

"Come," Van Helsing said with a clap of his hands. "We eat. We gain strength. We live to fight another day."

Arthur clapped Jonathan on the shoulder. "I meant that offer, Jonathan. I would be pleased to have you working for my family. Just give old Drummond the gate and you are immediately hired."

"Thank you, Arthur," Jonathan said, grasping his hand firmly. "I may have to take you up on that sooner than you expect."

"First thing tomorrow morning, if you need to, my friend," Arthur said fervently.

Mina breathed a sigh of relief. *Thank You, Lord.*

CHAPTER 14

"All right, Mrs. Harker," Father Gallagher said briskly, pulling up a chair and motioning her to do likewise. "What did you come up with for Psalm 139?" They were back in the cellar, but this time Mina was alone with the priest. She found herself missing the professor's comforting presence.

She felt taken aback by his direct approach, but she opened her Bible and her notebook, and set them side by side. "Well, God seems to know every detail of my life, every thought, every action, every word I speak."

"Go on."

"This seems to say that I can't get away from Him, no matter what I do, where I go, or how hard I try."

"Very good. Now why is that important?"

Mina stopped and mulled this over, chewing on her lower lip. "I suppose you're telling me that it does no good to try to run away from what God is calling me to do."

Father Gallagher gave a gruff laugh. "A man named Jonah tried to run from the call of God. After spending a very long time in the belly of a large fish, he decided that running from God was not a good idea. I do hope you won't need that much persuasion, Mrs. Harker. The belly of a fish is a smelly place to reside. I assure you, you won't enjoy it."

Mina frowned.

"Ask it," Gallagher demanded.

Mina started.

"The question you have," he insisted. "This is your training. Ask your questions. Always ask. There are no wrong questions. You won't offend God, and you certainly won't come up with anything I haven't heard before."

"If He know every word, every thought, every action…" She bit off her words.

"How can He still love you?" Father Gallagher finished for her.

"How can He stand the sight of me, Father?" she asked, staring at the tabletop.

"Because Jesus paid a terrible price for you, child," Father Gallagher said, his voice challenging her to look him in the eyes. "And don't you ever forget that. You are bought and paid for by the blood of Jesus Christ. He took every sin upon Himself for you." He pointed directly at her. "If you were the only person in the whole world, He would have still gone to the cross to redeem you, Mina Harker. You are that precious to Him. This is your first and most important lesson. Until you absorb this, nothing else will matter. You must know that *you* are loved by God Almighty."

She digested that for a few moments, still staring into those deep brown eyes.

"Now continue with the Psalm," he ordered.

"Before I was born, He knew all about me, even when I was unformed substance. Even before I had arms and legs, hands and feet? Yes, but now I've been bitten. What am I now? What will I become? What if I become evil? That scares me."

"If you were evil, it wouldn't scare you," Father Gallagher said. "You are like unformed substance now, Mrs. Harker. You are being born into a new existence, a new role. Your days have been written in His book, even though you have barely begun to live them. It's new; it's different. But it is still ordered by God Almighty, and He will not forsake you. Not ever."

"What do you mean—if I were evil, it wouldn't scare me?"

"If your heart were evil, you would relish that. You would hate God's Word, and you would delight in what Dracula did to you. You would be ready to go out and replicate that evil. You wouldn't be here, with me, in the basement of a church, learning how to fight against the powers of darkness."

She pondered that for a moment.

"Keep going." He nodded to her notes.

She smiled. "I liked the next couple of verses—17 and 18—about how precious God's thoughts are. The idea of counting His thoughts being like counting sand. Jonathan and I once spent a couple of days at the beach at Hastings. The sand was so vast..." Her voice trailed off as she was momentarily lost in the memory.

Father Gallagher smiled and nodded. When she shook her head to bring herself back to her present moment, she saw his smile and blushed.

"I'm sorry," she said, "it was just such a lovely memory, and that beach was a special place."

"No need to apologize. You need to hold fast to that memory. It will help you when times are difficult. Make a note of that beach in your Bible, Mrs. Harker. Right next to that verse. Use Hastings to tie that Scripture in your mind to the wonder of God's thoughts being as numerous as the sands of that beach."

She paused only a moment before writing "Hastings" beside the verse. Then she took a deep breath and pursed her lips. Verse 19. Father Gallagher laughed. She looked up at him, startled.

"Oh, I see the question coming already!" He chuckled again.

"Yes, I'll ask it. Why can't God just slay the wicked?" she asked.

"We'd be pretty spoiled brats if He did everything for us and just handed it to us, now wouldn't we?" he said. "We need to show our willingness to stand for His truth. If we are not willing to partner with God and fight for what's right, what are our lives worth? Are we just decorations? Ornaments for the doors?"

Mina's thoughts went to Mrs. Drummond and her endless committees and teas and society engagements, and she shuddered. She ignored all of her mother's training and propped her elbows on the table, dropping her face into her hands and pressing her hands to her eyes.

"Out with it," Father Gallagher ordered, frowning.

She looked up at him, and suddenly she felt weary. "It's been a … difficult weekend."

His frown deepened. "Tell me."

So, she did, leaving nothing out. He listened intently. When she had finished, he sighed, then stood and paced the room a couple of times.

"Jonathan is now prepared to stand up to this Drummond on your behalf?"

"Yes," she nodded. "He saw the manipulation for himself. It was … grotesque."

Gallagher waved his hand dismissively. "The Drummonds are not your problem. That's a distraction. I'm not quite sure where the instigation is coming from though. There is something else going on here. We just don't see it yet. How did the vampire know where you would be? And who is he? Why is he so focused on you? I need to talk to Van Helsing about this."

"Yes, he wants to talk to you as well," she said. "He may be waiting for us to finish our session. Do you want to cut this short?"

He hesitated. "No," he decided. "No, this is too important. Continue, Mrs. Harker."

She sighed. "This is a hard one for me. 'Thine enemies take Thy name in vain.' Jonathan does this, but he is not an evil man!"

"It bothers you?"

"Yes!"

"You must tell him."

"But he'll take it as criticism. Things have been so difficult between us. We're just starting to do better. I'm..." She paused.

"You're afraid of rocking the boat," Father Gallagher stated. "But you are going to have to build your marriage on a solid foundation. If you are holding back because you are afraid of bruising his feelings, those little wounds will fester into gangrene and damage your relationship. Tell him that if it wounds your heart, you feel it must be all the more hurtful to a loving and generous God Who has given him so much. Tell him tenderly. Tell him lovingly. But tell him."

"But if I love him, shouldn't I be able to look past his faults?"

"Compromise is deadly, Mrs. Harker. This sin is so small, does it really matter? We ask ourselves that, but before long, the whole world is rotten. I believe Jonathan will hear your words, but there will be others who will not. This is a lesson you need to learn now. If you can't approach Jonathan, how will you deal with others who will be less reachable? Look at verse 22. Did you write anything down?"

Mina nodded. "Those who will not heed the truth will become your enemies whether you want them to or not."

"Exactly. And the last few verses?"

"I wrote out my own prayer," she said with a little smile. He nodded encouragingly. "Search me and know my thoughts. See if I'm becoming anxious or harboring worries. Lead me in the way I should go."

"This also supposes that you will follow where He leads." Father Gallagher grinned. "Very good, Mrs. Harker. With everything that happened to you this weekend, I'm surprised you managed this much."

"Oh, I finished all of them, Father," she said.

His eyebrows shot up. "Proceed. Let's move on to Psalm 140. This one is very important."

Mina flipped a page and began with the first few verses. "Evil is out there. It's a plea for God to rescue us from evil men."

"Yes, the threat is continual. This is a war that will never be over. Van Helsing said you were all taken aback to find that there were more vampires still out there. The fact is there will always be more. In one way or another, there will always be evil to vanquish." He nodded. "Later I'll introduce you to Sister Joan Phillippe. She's been at this for a very long time. Maybe it's time you heard her story. She's not terribly different from yourself."

At the wave of his hand, she continued. "Traps and snares. How do I avoid them, Father? Is that part of this training?"

"Yes and no. Yes—you will learn new skills. You'll learn to see the snares coming, you'll learn to smell trouble. But you'll also learn to lean on the leading of the Holy Spirit to such an extent that He will be able to whisper to you and you'll respond. There are some traps you won't be able to avoid, but God can still rescue you from the ones that you can't sidestep. He can still give you victory when all looks lost."

Mina pondered those words for a few minutes. "The next part—a prayer of supplication? I'm not sure I'm getting the full importance of these three verses."

"All right, let's break this down," Father Gallagher said. "Write this down, Mrs. Harker, because this is important. Can you write quickly?"

"I can take shorthand if I need to, Father," she said with a smile.

His eyebrows went up another notch, and he nodded toward her notebook. "Thou art my God—that's your statement of faith. Second—Believe you are heard. Third—Believe He gives you strength. Fourth—Believe He protects you in battle. Fifth—Don't let the villains win! Sixth—Don't let them have reason to be raised up or exalted. Those are six very important points within those three verses. Remember them. Your life will depend on those six points, Mrs. Harker. I mean that quite literally."

She stared into his eyes again, gauging the truth, weighing his words. He meant every bit of it. The sentences she had just written. He had spoken in a firm, even tone, so she had written everything long hand. Each statement marched across the page like soldiers in black and white, the lead of her pencil standing in sharp contrast to the stark paper.

"Next?"

She sighed. "Their own words condemn them, so when people seek to burn others, they end up burning down their own houses instead?"

"All too often, people burn their own positions to ashes when they try to come against God's people. Maybe it looks like they are winning at first, but in the end, they bring themselves down by their own deceitfulness."

"Deep pits they cannot rise from," Mina mused.

"They become buried under their own sins," Father Gallagher said. "Rather like our vampire foes. They keep going and going until their sins destroy them. They are eventually found out. They continue in their violence until they become the hunted ones."

"Lastly, the Lord maintains the cause of the afflicted and justice for the poor. The righteous give thanks and the upright dwell in His presence." Mina smiled. "That felt like a ray of hope to me."

"Very good, Mrs. Harker. You've done well," Father Gallagher said. "And trust me when I say, I don't believe I've ever said that to a student on their first day before. Now very quickly, because we've taken so much time on these two passages, I want to cover Romans 8 and answer the questions I know you have written down."

Mina gave him a wry grin. "Maybe a couple."

"Of course."

She sighed and flipped another page in her notebook. "All things work together for good. I'm sorry, Father, but I just don't see that."

"Really."

"I see nothing good in Lucy's death. I see nothing at all good in Jonathan's imprisonment at the hands of those foul creatures of Dracula's. And while there may benefits to my new abilities, I'm still not sure I'm very happy about being a weapon either."

"Do you do needlepoint, Mrs. Harker?"

"Excuse me?"

"Are you skilled at needlepoint? Most women are taught at an early age. Were you taught needlepoint?"

"Yes, but—"

"Can you tell the design by looking at the back of the fabric?"

She paused. "No."

"What does it look like?"

"It's usually a tangle of threads and knots."

"Exactly. We may never see the full picture this side of Heaven, Mrs. Harker. But God sees the entire tapestry. He knows what the right side of the picture is supposed to be. We don't. Trust Him. All things will work together for good, whether we see it or not."

Mina wrote the word 'tapestry' beside verse 28 in her Bible. Then she moved on in her notes. "Who will bring a charge against us? It is God who justifies us." She paused. "This may be a loaded question, Father, but if one of these cases ever had to come before a court, where would it stack up, legally speaking?"

Father Gallagher laughed. "Well, I've never seen a vampire try to sue a slayer, largely because to appear in a court of law, they would have to be sworn in on a Bible. Laying hands on the Word of God would be painful to the point of burning off a layer of skin. On a younger vampire, it might send them up in flames entirely. I've never tried that, but it might be an interesting exercise. Besides, what would be his defense? 'Your Honor, this woman stopped me from drinking the blood of a child three nights ago. I resent that. She tried to stab me with a silver dagger to make me stop. I wish to sue her for that.' I doubt the judge would see things his way. If the vampire is dead, there is never any remnant left over to show his or her existence. Even if others witness the event, there must be corroborating evidence of a wrongdoing to convict."

Father Gallagher watched her struggle with this concept. "Look at the next part of this section, Mrs. Harker. Nothing separates us from the love of God. It says nothing about vampires. If tribulation, distress, and famine won't do it, a vampire isn't much of a threat either."

She smiled a bit uncertainly, then dove into the next note in her book. "We were considered sheep for the slaughter. Frankly, Father, that's not much comfort." Her left eyebrow cocked up at an angle.

"Paul is quoting the Old Testament in that verse, Mrs. Harker." He waved it away. "He is contrasting that with the very next verse, which was his real message to the Roman church. We overwhelmingly conquer through Him Who loved us. We conquer through *Him*. And look at the last two verses. Nothing can separate you from the love of God. You must believe that with all your heart and soul. That is your most important lesson today, Mrs. Harker. This confirms the other verses we've been over. Mark them down. These are the cornerstones of your training today. Nothing can separate you from your God. Cling to that fact. Believe it with all your heart and soul. Let it sink in."

He gave her a few minutes to write a few notes in her book. When she sighed and flipped the page, he smiled.

"We've come a long way today."

She nodded. "This one brought back a few hard memories."

"I thought it might." His wry smile had her chewing her lower lip again.

"Be strong in the Lord and the strength of His might." Mina sighed and closed her eyes wearily, suddenly seeing a windy pass in Carpathia, the snow and sleet whipping around her as Van Helsing circled her with a crucifix held before him. "The Professor used to speak these words over and over as I struggled against the power of Dracula."

"Yes, I made sure he memorized it early. You will need to as well."

"I don't think I will ever forget it." A dry sob caught in Mina's throat. She cleared her throat.

"All right, let's just go over these verses one at a time," said Father Gallagher. "I can see you wrote down a few phrases—probably adequately describing each one, so I'm just going to do this part for you. You can take some notes if something strikes you.

"Verse 11—Stand firm. You need the full armor of God. Every resource that God can give you. Never think that any part of it is unnecessary. You need it all or you'll have a vulnerable area in your life that the enemy can take advantage of.

"Verse 12—this battle is not against flesh and blood. You know that better than most, but it's not just against vampires either. You have your eyes fixed on one particular foe, Mrs. Harker, and it's not necessarily the one that will be after you. The enemy coming after you is a spiritual force of wickedness, principalities and powers, rulers of darkness, beings far beyond this world that we can see and touch. Win that battle first, then you can take down anything in this world without breaking a fingernail.

"Verse 13 — Resist evil. And again, *stand firm*. You'll hear me say that often, Mrs. Harker, so you might as well write it down in big letters and underline it a few times. Stand firm. Resist evil. You've done that. You could have just followed Dracula, but you resisted and came back to humanity. Now God can use you, can heal you. That's resisting evil. Yes, you did it once, but you will find yourself doing it over and over for the rest of your life.

"Verse 14—Stand firm. There it is again. Stand firm. Gird your loins with truth. You are protecting the soft areas of your body with truth, rock hard, solid truth. Nothing can penetrate truth, nothing gets past it, nothing sneaks around it. What is truth? God is truth and His truth sets mankind free. His Son sets us free. The breastplate of righteousness. That covers the heart, the lungs, the organs that keep us living and breathing. Our righteousness? Never! Whose righteousness?"

"The righteousness of Jesus Christ." Mina spoke for the first time in several minutes.

"Exactly! His righteousness covers our hearts, protects us, cradles us, shelters us. Verse 15 — feet shod with the Gospel of peace. Why do we armor our feet?"

Mina frowned. "To protect them from rough roads, from thorns or sharp objects, things that might wound us?"

"Your road will be difficult, Mrs. Harker." Father Gallagher's gaze shot through her. "But your ultimate purpose is not just to slay vampires. It's to save humanity, not only *from* vampires, but *for* Christ. The Gospel is not always easy to spread. And it is not always accepted. If you do not keep your focus, you will end up wounded and unable to keep traveling."

She nodded, making a few notes in her book as he continued.

"Verse 16 — the shield of faith. We've talked about building your faith. If you don't keep your faith strong, your shield will break. What does a shield do in battle, Mrs. Harker? Do you know?"

Mina floundered. "A warrior hides behind it?"

Father Gallagher laughed. "Well, I guess it looks like that, doesn't it? No, a shield is mobile. A warrior can shift it to intercept whatever is coming his way. But it also protects the face. You don't want to be blinded by an arrow or a sword. A shield blocks the blows of the enemy. Keep your faith strong. Remember the words we've gone over today. Build yourself up until you know beyond the shadow of a doubt that *your* God is always and forever by your side.

"Verse 17 — the helmet of salvation protects your head. Know in your mind that you are saved from your sins. Know it with all your intellect. Know it, understand it, accept it, and be unshakable in that knowledge. And lastly, but most importantly, take up the Sword of the Spirit, which is the Word of God. You will be memorizing a lot of Scripture. You may find this tedious, Mrs. Harker, but it is absolutely necessary. When all else fails you, the Word of God will never let you down."

"How am I to win a battle with a Scripture verse, Father?" she asked.

"You'll be amazed," Father Gallagher said, his eyes taking on a faraway look for only a moment. "We'll get to that another day. Lastly, with all prayer and supplication, be ever on the alert. You cannot ever let your guard down. You discovered that just this weekend. You must be alert every single day. You must always expect an attack, because you will never know when the enemy will pop up."

He stood suddenly. "I think we've covered enough for today. Besides, I need to find Abraham and have a long talk with him."

"Father Gallagher, when will I learn to fight?"

"First, you'll do pull-ups, running, some jumping. I'll have an obstacle course set up down here before your next session." He looked pointedly at her skirts. "You might want to dress accordingly, Mrs. Harker. Or at least bring a change of clothing."

He grabbed her notebook and scribbled a couple of Scriptures in it. "Are you able to return tomorrow?"

"Yes," she stammered as he handed her the notebook and ushered her up the stairs toward the sanctuary. Abraham Van Helsing was waiting patiently on the back pew. "But, Father, is this really necessary?"

"You must walk before you run, Mrs. Harker." His voice drifted back to her as he strode toward the professor. An older priest came out of the confessional and frowned at her sharply. He stared at Father Gallagher and Van Helsing, and Mina felt a shudder pass through her. Why did he appear so angry?

CHAPTER 15

A small nun tugged on Mina's sleeve and smiled at her. She was dressed in the white muslin of a novitiate, a thin waif of a girl. The wooden cross on her chest looked heavy enough to topple her, but she moved with the light grace of a little bird.

"You are Mrs. Harker?" she asked softly.

"I am."

"Sister Joan Phillippe requested an audience with you if you can spare a moment," she said, the smile never wavering. "She sent me to wait until Father Gallagher was finished with his counseling for today."

Mina looked at the two men, their heads close together in heated conversation. She longed to join the debate, since she knew it concerned herself and Jonathan. But she also knew her presence would not be welcome. She smiled reluctantly at the little nun and motioned to her to lead the way.

"Of course, Sister. I've heard about Sister Joan Phillippe. I'd be delighted to meet her."

After following the little nun down the hallway to a passage deeper into the recesses of the back portion of the church building, which also housed a hospital for the poor, Mina finally spoke again. "I didn't catch your name, Sister."

"Oh, I'm sorry," she said, giggling. "I'm not used to being noticed by outsiders. I am Sister Anne Marie. I am Sister Joan Phillippe's assistant. Really more of a servant, though it is a great honor to serve her. She is an amazing woman of God. I am blessed to be here." Her voice was so earnest. Mina wondered what made this Sister Joan Phillippe such an amazing woman.

They passed through the hospital, but not quickly enough for Mina. The smells assaulted her and she felt physically ill. Men and women moaned from their cots, the two wards shielded by mere sheets, as white-robed nuns moved efficiently from bed to bed, smoothing a cover, offering a cup of water, washing a feverish brow, changing a bandage on a festering wound. Mina wondered how they managed these duties day after day, yet they carried themselves with a serenity she envied. She fished a handkerchief from her handbag and dabbed her nose delicately, hoping it was not obvious that she was trying to mask the smell of the ward.

They stopped before a thick wooden door and Sister Anne Marie tapped lightly before entering. Whatever Mina expected, Sister Joan Phillipe took her breath away. It was difficult to tell her age, for her face was unlined, her features even and pleasing in an austere way. Dressed in the black of her order from head to toe, she exhibited none of Sister Anne Marie's friendly warmth. But she radiated ... strength, power, purpose. Here was a woman who knew who she was and what she needed to do with her life.

What did that knowledge cost her? Mina wondered.

"This is Mrs. Harker, Sister Joan Phillippe," Sister Anne Marie said quietly.

"Thank you, Sister. You may go prepare tea now. I'm sure Mrs. Harker could use a bracing cup after spending the morning with Father Gallagher." A trace of a smile barely twitched on Sister Joan Phillippe's lips.

"Of course." Sister Anne Marie smiled and left the room.

"Please take a seat, Mrs. Harker." Sister Joan Phillippe motioned toward two easy chairs by the fireplace in the corner. "Knowing Father Gallagher, you have not been in comfortable quarters this morning. Sit and relax for a few moments."

"Thank you, Sister." Mina took the proffered seat with a sigh. "I never realized that studying Scriptures could be such exhausting work."

"It is when you study with Father Gallagher," Sister Joan Phillippe confided.

Mina laughed, then covered her mouth to smother her mirth.

Sister Joan Phillippe's eyes took on a serious note. "I have two reasons for inviting you here today, Mrs. Harker. The first is that I understand we might need to provide you with — what would they call it? — a cover story. A reason for coming here to 'study' with Father Gallagher daily. So what shall we do with you? Would you be able to nurse?"

"I'm afraid I had a hard time walking through the ward just now," Mina admitted, shame-faced, as she weakly waved her handkerchief before stuffing it back in her purse. "I'm amazed at the nuns who can manage those duties, and I'm full of admiration for all of you."

"Shall I tell you a secret, Mrs. Harker?" Sister Joan Phillippe's eyes shone with compassion. "Many of our sisters go about their duties for a few hours, then slip out back to the alley and quietly throw up in a basin before returning to tend to the sick again. They are no different than you are. But they are dedicated to helping the suffering, treating each person as though that person might be Jesus Himself. For did He not say that if you have done it to the least of these, you have done it unto Me?"

Tears burned in Mina's eyes. The good Sister's faith shone in the room like a warm fire, and Mina drew near.

"Very well, perhaps not nursing then," Sister Joan Phillippe said.

"I did learn short-hand and typing skills," Mina offered.

"Typing?" Sister Joan Phillippe queried.

"It's a machine that pounds out a letter at a time, but makes everything neater. For documents, notes, letters. Perhaps for keeping records on the patients here. Establishing birth and death records, what was done for them in the way of cures..." Her voice trailed off lamely.

Sister Joan Phillippe considered her for several minutes thoughtfully. "Such a machine would be loud though, would it not?"

Mina grimaced. "Yes, it does clack a bit with the strike of the keys."

"How is your hand?"

"My hand?"

"Your writing. Mine is little better than chicken scratches, I fear, especially as I've gotten older." Sister Joan Phillippe held out our hands, and Mina was surprised to see joints swollen with arthritis that belied the youthful look of her face and carriage.

"My handwriting is clear, Sister," Mina said. She looked down and thought about the notebook in her hands. "I just scribbled these notes, not intending anyone to see them, certainly not thinking to use them as a means of securing work —"

Sister Joan Phillippe held out her hand and opened the notebook. Her eyebrows rose. She nodded. "Very well. You shall be my scribe for the moment. I will have you write up our notes from the clinic. That may mean you have to come into the wards occasionally. But I'll try to keep that to a minimum. I'm afraid I was going to ask that of you anyway. But that's another subject."

Sister Anne Marie tapped on the door again and entered when Sister Joan Phillippe called "Come."

Their tea was very simple. Sister Anne Marie had brought them rolls and a pat of butter, a small pot of black tea and a pot of honey.

"One of our parishioners has a son with beehives just outside of London. He brings us several jars every month for our apothecary," Sister Joan Phillippe explained. "There are many good uses for honey besides sweetening our tea. It will also cleanse a wound and treat an infection."

"I did not know that," Mina said with a smile. Maybe working in the hospital wouldn't be so bad if she could expand her knowledge. If only she could control her rebellious stomach.

They chatted for a few more moments about the church, the area, the neighborhood, and Mina wondered why Sister Joan Phillippe was keeping to such mundane topics when she clearly had something else on her mind. Then the tap came on the door again.

Sister Anne Marie returned, cleared away the tea tray, and turned to leave.

"That will be all for now, Sister. I want some time alone with Mrs. Harker," Sister Joan Phillippe said, face once again austere. Sister Anne Marie nodded once and slipped from the room.

Sister Joan Phillippe sighed.

"Now we're going to talk about that second thing you brought me here to discuss, aren't we, Sister Joan Phillippe?" Mina tried to smile, but her mouth wouldn't cooperate.

"Yes, Mrs. Harker."

Suddenly Mina felt her stays were too tight. What had Father Gallagher said of Sister Joan Phillippe? *She's not too terribly different from yourself.* What had he meant by that?

"I understand we have a few things in common, child," she said. "I felt it best to get this out in the open right away. You see, you are the first woman that Father Gallagher has ever trained. The first to come here for training. And there will be certain … resistance to this from others. But you will have my assistance, and I think you should know why. If all else should fail, I will train you myself. You will not leave us unprepared for what you must face."

Mina stared at the serene nun before her. "You… will train me? To—"

"To destroy vampires, my child."

Mina digested that, and Sister Joan Phillippe waited for a

moment. When she saw Mina take a deep breath and nod, she continued.

"I'm sure you think of me as a middle-aged nun who has spent her life among clerics, sheltered from evil. But I assure you, evil can find you, no matter where you go, no matter where you hide. I was a young nun, eager to serve God, with a heart for the mission field. I was to be sent to Ireland with four other sisters and a priest to establish a ministry. Along the way, we collected three more monks who were to travel with us, then part company to form their own abbey. We had such hopes. Then one of our sisters became ill. She grew weaker and weaker. The one disadvantage of our habits is that they can hide what should be seen, what would have told us of the terrible curse that we had allowed into our midst."

Mina felt sick. She knew what was coming.

"When she died, I was the one to wash her body and I saw the marks upon her neck. As I ran my finger over the marks and pondered what they meant, I felt hands grab me from behind and I felt fangs sink into my neck. I prayed for help, then I grabbed the only thing I had in my possession. I grabbed my silver crucifix and rammed it over my shoulder into his eye socket, as I screamed and screamed."

Mina's hands instinctively went to the identical scars at her own throat, and she felt tears sting her eyes. She had been surrounded by people who fought with her, fought for her. What must it have been like to have tried to fight off this monster alone?

"When I turned, I saw that it was the priest, his face contorted into a mask of rage. Blood poured from my neck, but the wound from his eye pulsed with a thick black substance that stank like sulfur. One of the monks came running and rammed a wooden stake through the priest's heart, and he dissolved into ash. The monk fell to his knees and genuflected, then he begged my forgiveness. He said he had begun to suspect a vampire among us, when Sister Mary Grace became so ill, but he didn't know who it was. He knew of them, had heard the legends from his people, but had never seen one before. He had been sharpening that stake in case he needed it."

"So I am not the only one," Mina said.

"To survive? No, child, you are not alone in that. But you partook of a vampire's blood, then repented, as I understand it," Sister Joan Phillippe said. "That is something I have not heard of before."

Mina's eyes lit up a bit and her smile widened. "Ah, I see. This is something like a probation, isn't it? Are you to watch me, Sister, to make sure I'm not going to turn out bad after all?"

"My dear Mrs. Harker, if there was any chance of that, I would certainly not be allowing you back here with our patients, who would not be in any condition to fight off a vampiric being." Sister Joan Phillippe's tone held no reproof, and only the tiniest hint of amusement.

Mina was thoroughly chagrined. "I apologize, Sister. How thoughtless of me."

"You have every right to be a little bit skeptical of our motives, Mrs. Harker." Her lips really did quirk into a smile this time. "Father Gallagher is a difficult man to become accustomed to. In time, you'll come to trust him, as we do. But I understand your misgivings right now. No, my purpose today is to assure you that if all else fails, I will complete your training. And yes, I am well equipped to do so." She sighed. "After that attack, we rested for several days before continuing our journey. I plied that monk with questions until I thought he might pitch me into the sea. I learned everything he could teach me. One of the other brothers had, at one time, been a soldier. He had left that life behind, but I begged him. In light of what had happened to me, he relented and taught me enough that I was able to defend myself. Only against the undead, mind you. Against a human, I would accept death, if God so willed it. I promised I would never take a human life. I have kept that vow." She crossed herself and kissed the crucifix around her neck. "But never again would the undead feed on a man, woman, or child, as long as God gave breath to my body. I have kept that vow as well, as best I could."

Mina absorbed that information and silence wrapped them like a soft cloak as the sun drifted down through the bars in the window.

"Now, I want to take you into one section of the wards," Sister Joan Phillippe said, rising. "This will be the only section where I will require you to come with me daily. We will work together, you and I, in this particular ward." Mina felt the blood drain from her face. "Don't look so worried. You'll soon understand my reasons, and I think you'll agree to come along willingly."

Mina rose and followed her. They proceeded down the hallway past the wards she had seen on the way in. Tucked in the back was a long room lined with cots. Twelve patients occupied the room at the moment, and two were being bundled out wrapped in binding clothes for the undertaker. Sister Joan Phillippe crossed herself as they passed. A nun passed her a paper with names on it. Jane Claymore, age thirty-four, and Joseph Hanson, age seventeen.

"Your first duty, Mrs. Harker," whispered Sister Joan Phillippe. "Two death certificates for these poor souls."

"Cause of death?" Mina asked softly.

"Exsanguination, Mrs. Harker," said a familiar voice.

Mina whirled to face… "Professor Van Helsing!"

"Yes, Mina. They were bled dry."

"Then all of these people—"

"Yes, my child," Sister Joan Phillippe said softly. "This is where we care for the victims of vampire attacks. We do what we can. We try to rebuild their blood. The professor has been helping us for many months now. We give them transfusions, we try to feed them, give them his tonic, but when their masters call them, they wander out. Sometimes we find them in time. Sometimes we don't. Sometimes it feels like we are fighting a losing battle, but we will never give up. Not as long as we can draw breath."

Suddenly Mina saw in her an ancient warrior, the raw determination of a prophetess from the pages of the Bible. No, that was fanciful. But she was definitely a woman Mina could see with a sword in her hand, if the need arose.

"I'll help, Sister Joan Phillippe," Mina said quietly. "Just tell me what to do."

She felt Van Helsing's hand land heavily on her shoulder as he patted her, then he walked heavily down the long hallway.

"Let's go back to my office," Sister Joan Phillippe said. She paused for a moment, calling to the nuns attending patients nearby. "Sister Annabeth, Sister Julienne, this is Mrs. Harker. She will be joining us in the clinic. Feel free to discuss the patients' conditions with her. She will understand their needs and how we must treat them." The nuns exchanged a glance, then nodded. "She's training with Father Gallagher," Sister Joan Phillippe added, to which both nuns smiled broadly and with much more enthusiasm.

Sister Joan Phillippe guided Mina back down the corridor and closed the heavy door behind them with a heavy thud. She sighed and motioned toward the seats by the fireplace, which Mina accepted gratefully. When they had settled back into the chairs in the corner, Sister Joan Phillippe offered Mina a cup of water, and she drank eagerly.

"I can't say I quite expected that," she said ruefully.

"I understand, child," Sister said kindly. "I told Father Gallagher some of this story would be best coming directly from me. And I suggested that some of your time would best be served down here with us. If questioned by others, you would be quite truthful in saying that you were helping the nuns treat the sick in the hospital, and that you were assisting me with the records. Though, of course, that was an extra blessing I did not expect."

"So, once you were attacked, you knew this was what you were supposed to do with your life, Sister?" Mina felt mystified. Perhaps, if Lucy had lived, they could have done this together.

"Oh, goodness no! In fact, I almost left the religious orders." Sister Joan Phillippe sat back in her chair as memory took her back. "My superiors thought I was brain damaged. That I had imagined the entire incident. Even the corroboration of the monks and the other nuns did nothing to further my cause. I was put in solitary confinement as a punishment for lying. I was berated for perpetrating tall tales. The others eventually recanted rather than face the continual punishment from the bishops who were sent to examine our case. I was deemed unfit and sent home. In a fit of rebellion, I ran away to France.

"Weak from hunger, destitute, wracked with doubt, fearful for my very sanity, I came to a nunnery." Her smile grew soft. "The Sisters of the Maid took me in, fed me, clothed me. They asked no questions. They let me pray; they let me wander in the gardens. Then one day, I wandered into the infirmary. They were caring for a young girl, no more than twelve or thirteen. She'd been bitten. I saw the marks plainly. I fell into a panic. Mother Superior came at once and took me to her office. She calmed me down, gave me herb tea, allowed me to rave. When I tried to tug at my collar to show her, she patted my hands and said, 'We know...' Just that. 'We know.'

"They explained that their order had long fought against this form of evil, going back to the days shortly after the death of Joan d'Arc. You know, many of her opponents were vampires. Yes, indeed. On both continents. The nuns kept records of those wicked days. Their order came about from a strong desire to never see people victimized by these demons again. And so, they destroy them whenever they find them. They protect the defenseless. I stayed for many decades."

"Decades?"

Sister Joan Phillippe smiled sadly. "I've heard you have many gifts, Mrs. Harker. I only have one. I have been given a very long life. I don't know how long it will last, but I will continue to use it as long as I can. And I will help you in any way I can."

She might be a nun, but it still seemed impolite to ask the woman her age! Mina's curiosity burned within her, but she couldn't bring herself to utter the question.

"You said we might face opposition, Sister Joan Phillippe," Mina said with a frown. "Might I ask where this opposition will be coming from?"

The Sister exhaled deeply. "Our senior pastor here is Father Matthew. I'm afraid he does not approve of Father Gallagher's brusque manner. Your presence here has been 'noted' and not in a good way."

Mina nodded. "Short man, white hair, face set in a scowl that looks like it's permanent?"

Sister Joan Phillippe nodded. "He has been most determined to get rid of Father Gallagher for months now, and you may provide the best reason yet. If the Father is giving you private instruction in the basement, Father Matthew will come to the worst conclusions, I assure you."

"He's welcome to come down and spar with me," Mina said, with a mischievous twinkle in her eyes. "He could see for himself just what is going on in the basement."

"That would not be wise either." The Sister's countenance held no levity. "You must be careful not to take Father Matthew lightly, Mrs. Harker. His voice carries more weight than you or even Father Gallagher realize, and the repercussions could be significant. We need to be able to keep this ministry open. And we need the protection of the Catholic Church to operate safely within the city of London. Otherwise, we are subject to more oversight and government interference than you can imagine. We need to keep Father Matthew pacified, if at all possible. I have a hard enough time reining in Father Gallagher. I'm asking you to please not make my situation any more difficult."

"Of course, Sister," Mina said, thoroughly chagrined by her own lighthearted banter in the face of the serious situation these nuns faced on a daily basis. "You'll have my full cooperation."

"Thank you, Mrs. Harker. Now let me show you where I keep the certificates, the paper supplies, and things you will need."

They spent some time on the mundane office needs of Mina's upcoming duties. She filled out the two death certificates, mourning the deaths of these people she had never met, who had barely lived before their lives were cut short.

As Sister Joan Phillippe bid her goodbye at the door, Mina turned one last time.

"May I ask one question, Sister?"

"Of course." The Sister's face was austere, but her eyes twinkled.

"Did Father Gallagher train you like he's training me?" she asked.

"No, Mrs. Harker, he did not," Sister Joan Phillippe said, closing the door. "I trained him."

CHAPTER 16

Mina had much to think about as she headed home. Sister Joan Phillippe's story whirled in her mind as she absorbed the details over and over. But the last was the most startling. She trained Father Gallagher? That made her a woman of some lethal substance, despite her serene appearance.

"A tuppence for your thoughts, *liebling?*"

The familiar voice brought a smile to Mina's lips. "Even after all this time, you still find ways to surprise me, Professor."

Van Helsing laughed as he tucked her hand in the crook of his arm. "What pleasure that gives an old man, Miss Mina, that I can still find ways to amaze a brilliant young woman like yourself. Yes, I was waiting for you to finish. I am a curious old man, I wanted to know how your first day went. So I waited and watched. Now I will walk you home and we can talk."

"How long have you been treating patients at that clinic without telling any of us?"

His face lost all levity. He looked up at the grey skies above the London rooftops. "Too long. These poor wretches provide an absolute playground for the beasts that infest our world. They come here to the poorest of the poor, and they know that most of these poor people will never even be missed. They have no loved ones to cry out for their lives, and even if someone does try to alert the authorities, who will pay attention? She ran away to escape her lot in life, they'll say. Or he ran away to seek his fortunes in some other city on the European continent. Why would they remain in Whitechapel if they found a way to get away from this misery?"

"But Lady Westenra…"

"She was targeted for your benefit, Mina," the Professor said softly, gripping her hand tightly, but refusing to look directly at her as he spoke. "Make no mistake about that."

Mina studied his profile for a moment, then looked away, steeling herself against the sting building in the corners of her eyes. *I will not cry on the street. They will not make me cry.*

"Your resolve grows, my child," Van Helsing said, still refusing to look directly at her. "It's good. You will need it."

~~~

Jonathan sat at his desk when she returned home. Her heart sank. To be home so early. Could that mean anything but dismissal from the firm?

"Jonathan?" Her voice quavered.

"No, dearest," he said, smiling with that weary expression he seemed to wear most often these days. "I have not lost my position."

Mina leaned against the door and exhaled. "Is that good or bad?"

He laughed. "I suppose it's good news for the moment. Even with Arthur's generous offer, it's never a good thing to be sacked from one of London's prestigious law firms."

"How did it go? Were you … Did you have to threaten to leave? Does he know about Arthur's offer?"

"Actually, he called me into his office, and I thought I was going to be told to leave the premises right then. He was … well, provoked would be putting it mildly, I believe."

"He was provoked? Why?" Mina stepped forward and sat in the chair opposite Jonathan's desk.

"It seems Arthur called on him early this morning."

"What?" She leaned forward in her chair.

Jonathan chuckled. "He told Mr. Drummond that he was looking for a private solicitor and was hoping he could talk Drummond into parting with me. He knew of my health problems, and felt that he could provide a position that would be less taxing for me physically, and less socially grueling for you. You could pursue your charity work, which was so dear to your heart, and Mr. Drummond could find a more malleable couple for his firm to groom."

Mina's eyes widened with each word, then she broke into laughter. "He did *not*! You're teasing me, Jonathan! Arthur would not do such a thing."

"Oh, I am assured that he did. He added quite a few frills and furbelows to it as well. Although I got some of the story from Mr. Drummond's clerk later in the day. Arthur made it clear that you were a dear family friend, and that socially manipulating you was not going to tolerated. And that if you were unhappy, Arthur could most assuredly make certain that Drummond could be made equally
~~~

uncomfortable in many ways, both in his social life and his business circles." Mina felt her face grow pale. "Though Drummond did not divulge that part to me directly. His clerk told me that part with great relish. He was once engaged. Mrs. Drummond tried to take the girl under her wing to such an extent, the poor thing called off the wedding and refused to see him again. He can't afford to give up his position, but he has never quite forgiven Mrs. Drummond, either. I think it gave him a certain amount of pleasure to see the Drummonds brought down a few notches for the way they've tried to manipulate us lately."

"But why didn't Drummond just let you go? Why make you stay?"

"For one thing, I'm a very good lawyer," Jonathan said, his smile becoming wider as her face warmed so much, she knew she blushed bright red.

"Oh, Jonathan, I didn't mean…"

"It's all right, Mina." He laughed. "I think it would wound his pride if I left his firm. I am a good lawyer, and while my health did suffer at the hands of a client he sent me to, I've still done my job. And I've handled a good many affairs for him, even when I've had to work from my office here at home. Besides, most of London knows my health problems arose from a job I did for his company. To leave would be a black mark against his firm's good name. He can't say I haven't done my job, because it is well-known that I have performed my duties. Besides, if I am taken on by Lord Arthur Holmwood as his personal attorney, there is no greater affirmation I could have. Drummond's reputation would be called even further into question. Clients would pull out like rats deserting a sinking ship. Arthur put him over a barrel, and he knew it. He wanted to make sure I knew he knew it and he didn't like it one bit. So basically, we're stuck with one another. If I leave his firm, I'll destroy his company."

"But he can't force you to stay, Jonathan…" She frowned as she tried to pull all the pieces together. "Wouldn't life be easier if you just left and took Arthur up on his offer?"

"You are now married to a full partner in Drummond's law firm, Mrs. Harker," Jonathan said quietly.

"What?"

"We signed the papers this afternoon." Jonathan nodded. "I'll work the cases I want to work. I'll work from home as often as I wish. The pressure is off."

"Of you, yes." Mina stood and gripped the back of her chair. "Jonathan, Mrs. Drummond is going to expect more than ever from me if you're a full partner." Her face was stricken.

"No, Mina, she won't." Jonathan stood and came around the desk. "I just told you what Arthur said to him. And I reiterated it before I signed the papers. No society teas, no committee meetings. They are to leave you alone. You are my wife. You are not their puppet, and you have no strings for them to pull. I promise you, Mina. They will not back you into any corners again."

Mina wrapped her arms around his waist. "Oh, my husband! I am so happy for you. Truly I am. Partner! You earned it a thousand times over with all you suffered for those people and their contracts."

"Let's celebrate," he whispered into her hair.

"Yes, let's."

"Dinner out, just the two of us."

"Of course! I'll tell Mrs. Hardman."

"And then I want to hear about your day," he said as she headed for the door.

She hesitated at the door and smiled back at him. Well, he'd get an edited version of her day, at least. Just how much could she safely tell him about the church in Whitechapel with its priests and nuns who fought vampires and knew secrets that spanned decades, if not centuries?

CHAPTER 17

The next morning, Mina chose her clothing with care. She would begin her physical training with Father Gallagher today, and she would need to be ready for it. But she couldn't just walk through the streets of London in trousers either. She was still a lady—and now she was the wife of a solicitor, a full-fledged partner in the firm. Her behavior must be above reproach.

After a lovely dinner with Jonathan and an even better night of lovemaking, she slipped away from her snoring husband and took her brown skirt to her dressing room for a few alterations. She blessed her mother for teaching her to sew at an early age, and she managed her own cunning changes to her wardrobe easily, still getting in a few hours of sleep before awakening with Jonathan for breakfast as usual.

Then dressing herself for a change, she walked to the church and slipped in quietly. Father Gallagher was waiting for her and urged her through the door to the basement more quickly than usual.

"I'm afraid my superior is curious about my activity in the basement these days," Father Gallagher said softly. "We're going to have to be a bit surreptitious in our comings and goings."

"So I've been warned," Mina murmured.

"Ah yes, Sister Joan Phillippe." Father Gallagher nodded. "I trust your afternoon was … enlightening?"

"That's certainly the word for it." Mina's tone was tinged with amusement.

"And did she tell you how we met as well?"

"No, she did not. I think she left that for you to tell. She only divulged her own tale. And she laid out duties for me to perform to make my presence here more socially acceptable, if questioned."

"Oh, so nursing those bitten by the damned is socially acceptable now?" His voice was bitter.

"No, but nursing in a hospital for the poor and destitute is. There are a good many things I'm unable to tell the general public these days, Father, as I'm sure you yourself can attest to."

"Touché, Mrs. Harker," he said with a raised eyebrow.

He opened the door to the basement area, which had been set up strangely to Mina's eyes. After closing the door behind her, he eyed her clothing.

"I believe I told you this would entail physical training, Mrs. Harker. You're going to have a hard time in skirts."

"Give me just a moment, Father Gallagher," she said with a smile. She raised her skirt by just a couple of inches — enough to show the hem of trousers and boots beneath her skirt. "I couldn't very well traipse through London in men's clothes, now, could I?"

"Will you have a moment on the street, Mrs. Harker?" Father Gallagher took three steps away from her and whirled around with a sword in his hand, leveled at her chin.

But even as he had turned, Mina had snapped off the skirt by means of a fastener on the waist and whipped it around his sword, as she spun to the right and ripped a gun from her waistband to hold level with his head.

Father Gallagher's eyebrow rose another notch. He slid her skirt from his sword and handed it back to her. "Handy." His nod was approving. She lowered her gun and smiled as she reached for her skirt. "But you will need to be faster next time. And you lowered your gun too soon. Never lower your guard, Mrs. Harker."

He took her through several moves, showing her how to improve her defenses, proving where her weaknesses were. Then he ran her through a make-shift obstacle course of metal drums she had to crawl through and ropes she had to climb, even rings suspended from the ceiling that she had to use to cross from one side of the room to the other by launching herself hand by hand from one ring to the next. By the time she had completed the course twice, she was exhausted, and ringlets of dark hair clung to her face and neck, thick with sweat. Sister Anne Marie came down to fetch her at lunchtime and Mina was more than ready to go. She fastened her skirt in place before leaving the basement, lest Father Matthew should see her dressed so inappropriately.

Sister Joan Phillippe greeted her warmly, then took in her disheveled appearance with a sigh. "Sister Anne Marie —"

"Water and soap?"

"Yes, please, then you may bring in lunch." She smiled as the younger nun left the room. "Lunch will taste much better after you have cleaned up a bit. I'd forgotten just how challenging Father

Gallagher's training can become."

"So this is normal?" Mina asked wryly.

Sister Joan Phillippe paused and looked her over with a critical eye. "No, I'd say he's giving you the advanced course. You must be bringing a good deal to the table at the onset, Mrs. Harker." Her smile was warm. The door opened and Sister Anne Marie was back with a bowl and pitcher, and two large towels over her arm.

"We'll give you a moment of privacy," Sister Joan Phillippe said.

Mina washed her face and neck with the hot water and used the bar of soap liberally. It felt good to get the sweat off her skin again. She opened her bodice and sponged as much of her body as she could, toweling off and redressing rapidly. Then she coiled and re-pinned her hair. The heavy door opened behind her.

"Thank you so much, Sister Joan Phillippe, I do —" She stopped abruptly.

It was not Sister Joan Phillippe standing in the doorway. It was a short, white-haired man in a priestly robe. His scowl deepened.

"And just who are you?" he demanded.

"I am Mrs. Wilhelmina Harker," she said, summoning a frown. "Do you always enter a woman's room without knocking?"

"How dare you, young lady!"

"No, how dare you, sir! It's quite rude to enter a lady's quarters without requesting entry, even if that lady is a nun. You did not even knock!" Mina knew she should not be challenging this man. She knew full well who he was, but he did not know that she knew. And he had almost walked in on her semi-dressed!

"This is the office of Sister Joan Phillippe. What are you doing in here?"

"Father Matthew!" Sister Joan Phillippe's voice was so welcome, Mina almost wilted in relief. "What is going on here?"

"Who is this woman? And why is she alone in your office?" he demanded.

"Mrs. Harker has kindly offered her services to us as a volunteer," Sister Joan Phillippe stated. "She had a ... rather nasty encounter on her way to the church today and needed a moment to recover. We left her with water to wash away the sweat from her exertion and gave her some privacy. That is hardly an act that warrants your cross examination, Father. Why on earth would you wish to berate her for taking us up on a kindness?"

"If she was accosted in the street, she should have called the police," he said, his eyes narrowed in suspicion.

"I did not say she was accosted, Father." Sister's voice was cool. "I said she had a nasty encounter. She ran from that encounter and needed only to relieve herself of the perspiration. Examining her clothing is an indignity I don't think you should be putting her through. Her husband is an attorney. You wouldn't want to cause offense. She has come to us out of the goodness of her heart."

"I rather doubt that," Father Matthew huffed.

"I beg your pardon?" Mina voice carried enough frost to ice the North Pole.

"I've seen you here before, young lady," he said, pointing a finger in her direction. "And in the company of Father Gallagher and that Van Helsing character. There's a bad seed if ever there was one."

"Well, Sister Joan Phillippe," Mina said coldly, her eyes still drilling holes into the self-righteous little priest. "I didn't realize I might need to bring in a list of references when I offered to help you in your clinic. Perhaps I should have my close friend Arthur come in with me and provide some validation. After all you wouldn't want a bad seed in your clinic. Surely you would take his word for my good name, Father. You do know Sir Arthur Holmwood, don't you? I would send for Lady Westenra, who was like a second mother to me, but she died recently, so I fear she won't be much help. Alas, but perhaps, Arthur can speak for her as well. He knows how close we were, seeing as how I practically grew up with her daughter, Lucy."

Mina's gut twisted with every word, and she hated this priest for putting her in this position. She hated using her friends' names like this, hated using their reputations, hated dragging Arthur into yet another situation of her own creation. But she knew that it wasn't just her own neck on the line. Sister Joan Phillippe had said as much only yesterday. They needed the protection of this church to keep their work against the vampiric forces in London open and operating. This terrible little man would shut down the Sisters of the Maid and Father Gallagher all in one terrible blow if she did not do something drastic.

"I don't believe you for one minute," he huffed.

Mina raised one eyebrow coldly. "Very well. I'm afraid I won't be able to stay today, Sister. I'll go see Arthur immediately. But when I come back tomorrow—and I will come back tomorrow, Father—Arthur will be with me. Correct me if I'm wrong, but didn't he just donate money for the hospital recently? Yet, I was here yesterday, and I saw a pretty pitiful operation back there."

Bullseye.

Father Matthew reddened. "Those funds are still processing through channels. We are eager for them to be released so we can upgrade our facilities. Of course we are most grateful for Lord Holmwood's generosity. He is one of our kindest patrons."

"Well, I would have assumed so when he recommended that I spend time here with the Sisters, but by your behavior today, Father, I was beginning to have my doubts. I would hate to have to tell Arthur that I was poorly received after his encouragement to volunteer my time here." Her eyes pinned him to the wall as surely as a bug to a child's cork board.

"Lord Holmwood told you, a lady, to come to Whitechapel to volunteer your time?" His suspicions were aroused again. "Now why would he do that?"

"I'm not your average lady, Father," Mina said with a feral smile. "Arthur knows that well. I've never really fit the mold. God bless Arthur, he understands that. But if you don't believe me, please do feel free to contact him yourself. Mrs. Wilhelmina Harker." She enunciated each syllable. "Now do I work with the Sisters today, or do I leave?"

"By all means, Mrs. Harker," Father Matthew motioned with one hand, "far be it from me to stop an angel of mercy from helping the poor and downtrodden." He strode from the room, murmuring to Sister Joan Phillippe, "I'll speak to you about this later."

Sister Anne Marie took the water pitcher and towels away, her hands still shaking from the intensity of the encounter. Sister Joan Phillippe closed the door carefully and sat at her desk with a sigh.

"Were you bluffing?"

Mina sat in the hard wooden chair opposite Sister Joan Phillippe. "To a certain extent, yes." She saw the Sister wilt. "But I do know Arthur Holmwood quite well — that part is true. And Lady Westenra was very much like a second mother to me, that was true as well. So, if Father Matthew goes to him, he will back up my story, including the part about me never fitting the mold. Sister, Arthur Holmwood fought Dracula with me. He is very much in this battle too. If Father Matthew is going there looking for an ally, he will not find one."

Sister Joan Phillippe smiled, then she shook her head. "Well, you are full of surprises, Mrs. Harker. That was quite a performance. But why? Especially after what I said yesterday about Father Matthew?"

Mina frowned. "I have a question, Sister. Why did Father Matthew just walk into this room without knocking? Why would he barge in here—into a woman's chambers—without a courtesy knock? What is he up to? He almost caught me with my blouse open. Two minutes sooner and he'd have gotten more than he bargained for. Was that what he hoped for? Did he know I was in here? Was he hoping to catch me? If so, why? If not me, what did he hope to catch you doing? Something about that man is not right. I know you are worried about his influence. Well, now I've given him cause to worry about my influence. I can put one little word into the ear of his biggest financial contributor and an entire house of money falls down around him. Lord Holmwood is not just one man. He's one man among a sea of other lords of the realm, men of substance. Father Matthew is not going to endanger his standing with someone like Arthur, especially over someone as lowly as a woman who volunteers in the hospital. I'm not worth it to him."

"But what if he goes straight to Lord Holmwood right now?" Sister Joan Phillippe said.

Mina grinned. "Professor Van Helsing was standing in the hallway when I delivered my spiel, Sister. He heard the whole thing. He'll get to Arthur long before the good Father will."

Sister Joan Phillippe laughed. Really laughed. Mina was startled by the sound, but it made her smile. "I really thought you had lost your mind, Mrs. Harker. I have never seen anyone who can think as fast on their feet as you can. I think I will enjoy working with you more than I have enjoyed anyone in the past sixty years."

Sixty years? Mina hid her expression. "Then I think you must call me Mina, Sister."

"We cannot dispense with all the formalities, alas," the Sister sighed, "but you may call me Sister Joan."

The two women smiled across the desk, then laughed again. That was the way Sister Anne Marie found them as she brought in their lunch. They were still laughing.

~~~

Father Matthew did indeed visit Arthur Holmwood, who extolled Mina's virtues beyond even Mina's wildest dreams. Father Matthew remained suspicious, but with Arthur backing her, there was little he could say without losing his greatest financial backer. Money did become available for the clinic, but it was nothing close to what Arthur had contributed. When Mina broached the subject
~~~

with him, he admitted with a sigh that he suspected as much. Some of it went to Rome, as with all monetary bequests, some of it went to administrative costs and to the upkeep of the church as a whole, and some of it went to other projects in the city.

"It's never simple to donate to one cause, Mina," Arthur said. "I hate it too. I would rather be able to stipulate that I want this amount to go to this cause, but the oversight that would be required to handle that kind of management is just not possible in this day and age. I suppose there is going to be a certain amount of duplicity in any business, even if that business belongs to God."

"I must be terribly naïve," Mina murmured, leaning her forehead against the windowpane overlooking Arthur's exquisite gardens. She had accepted an invitation to tea so they could discuss the problem of Father Matthew. "I expected at least the church to run their affairs honorably."

"In a way, they do," Arthur said. "The money they send to Rome is a form of tithe they give to their superiors. And they don't hoard all the money for their own 'pet projects,' but they try to share with the other charities around the city. You aren't naïve, Mina; you just don't realize how many truly destitute people there are out there." He took another sip of Earl Grey.

"My family was poor too, Arthur," she said, turning to face him. "I didn't come from money. I wouldn't have even had contact with you or the professor, if not for meeting Lucy at school. I was Lucy's whim, her crazy quest to have one friend who didn't fit the mold of every other society debutante in London."

"But you were a different type of poor, Mina. There's poor and then there's the kind of poor that you're seeing in Whitechapel. Those poor devils have no hope, Mina. Not one shred of anything that might lead them to think that they might even survive the day. You were never that kind of poor." His eyes followed her as she rose to pour them each a fresh cup of tea from the silver service.

"And speaking of Whitechapel," he continued, lighting his pipe and grinning up at her impishly. "Does Jonathan know you're going to Whitechapel every day to church? I can't imagine he's on board with this."

"No, he does not." She crossed her arms and grimaced at him. "You're not going to turn me in to the lawyer now, are you?"

Arthur approached her and placed his hands on her shoulders. "Just be careful, Mina. Jonathan will have my head on a platter if he finds out I helped you get away with this right under his nose and did nothing to stop you. You're putting me in a terrible position, you know."

She hung her head. "I know, and I'm sorry. Truly I am. But Father Matthew is up to something and you're the only person I could think of to hold him off. If I can't get this training from Father Gallagher, I won't be able to protect Jonathan, much less myself or anyone else. They've already come after Lady Westenra. Whoever that vampire is, he's going to try to hit Jonathan, I just know it. I have to be ready, Arthur."

Arthur pulled her into a hug. "I know, Mina. I know. I'll do all I can. You know I will."

~~~

The weeks slipped by. Father Gallagher doled out Scriptures and made the obstacle course more challenging. He challenged her fighting skills more too, trying to catch her off-balance. Mina was making it more and more difficult for him, as she anticipated his traps and avoided them more frequently now. She became more adept at entering a room, then spinning to the other side of the room in the blink of an eye, so that if he did pull a blade or a sword where he expected her to be, she was no longer there. She even somersaulted into the room more than once, and her heel clipped him on the chin, leaving him with a bruise that turned a lovely shade of purple just in time for mid-week mass.

They no longer sat down to study Scriptures, but rattled them off as they darted around the room, dodging swords and daggers, and rolling beneath each other's fists.

After one particularly stressful session, Sister Joan noticed Mina wincing every time she rose from her chair to move to the tall filing cabinet in the corner. They were tackling the end of the year records, so she had been back and forth several times for folders, and she held her lower back with her left hand when she bent to the lower drawers.

"Aha, I recognize that maneuver," Sister Joan said with a smile. "I believe it was the Father-flipped-me-to-the-floor move. Correct?"

"No, that was last week, Sister Joan." Mina grimaced. "This is the Father-dodged-my-kick-and-sent-me-flying-into-a-stone-wall-then-I-bounced-backwards-against-his-desk-when-I-spun-too-fast-to-avoid-his-sword."

"Ooooh. Yes, that would have been my second guess." Sister
~~~

Joan reached into her bottom desk drawer. "I've noticed you moving a little more awkwardly of late. I saved you some of my special liniment. We just made up a new batch. I had a feeling you would be needing it."

Mina uncorked the bottle and the scent of eucalyptus and wintergreen stung her eyes. "Oh my! Guaranteed to kill or cure, Sister Joan?"

"Oh, it will definitely cure, but the smell does take some getting used to." Sister Joan smiled. "Hot bath, hot as you can stand, then rub that in every muscle that hurts."

"I'd need a gallon of it," Mina groaned.

"Well, the muscles that hurt the worst then." She laughed. "I promise you'll feel better in the morning."

~~~

Mina asked Betsy to prepare her a hot bath when she returned home that night. The girl nodded but looked more pale than usual.

"Betsy, are you feeling all right?" Mina asked.

"Oh, yes, ma'am," Betsy said with a wan smile. "Just a little tired."

"I hate to ask it, but I really need the bath water hot tonight. It might mean an extra trip or two."

"Oh, that's all right, ma'am. I'll do it for you." Betsy smiled, but her normal spark seemed to be missing.

Mina collected her robe and undergarments along with the bottle of liniment. Betsy had filled the tub and then brought up a pitcher of cool water and one of hot water. "Just in case you need to cool down or heat it back up," she said, before slipping out of the bathroom.

Mina slid into the water and groaned with relief. Sister Joan was right. The heat was just the ticket. Steam billowed up around her. She even submerged herself and washed her hair, an indulgence she hated doing in winter. But the heat felt so wonderful. And tonight even her scalp hurt. About twenty minutes later, Betsy knocked timidly on the door. Mina bid her enter.

"Master Harker is home and wondered if you'd be coming down to dinner." Then her eyes widened when she saw the bruises on Mina's shoulders.

"Oh, Betsy, I've just washed my hair," Mina said. "Could you please add a log or two to the fire up here and have a tray brought up tonight? I'm really tired."
~~~

"Ma'am, do you need some help?"

"No, Betsy, I'm fine," Mina said, pouring warmth into her voice as she stood and wrapped towels around her body and her hair. "Really I am. I'm just a little sore. I tripped and fell on the stone steps today. It looks far worse than it is, truly!"

Betsy nodded. "Yes, ma'am…" she murmured as she backed out of the room.

Mina sighed and stepped out of the tub to finish drying off. She was trying to apply the liniment to her shoulders and her upper arms when Jonathan entered the bathroom.

"Mina? Betsy said you took a fall today and aren't feeling… *Mina*!" Jonathan stared at her in shock.

"It's really not as bad as it looks, Jonathan," she said, trying to smile.

"This was not a fall, Mina." His voice was hoarse. "Who hurt you? Who has done this?"

"Jonathan, it's not what you think."

"Mina, I demand to know who has attacked you."

"Jonathan, no one has attacked me."

"Mina, those are finger marks on your arms." Jonathan pointed as he spoke, and his voice shook. "I demand to know who hurt you. I'm your husband, Mina, and I will not allow this to continue."

Mina sighed. "All right, I'll tell you everything. Can you help me put this awful stuff on my back, please? Then I'll get dressed and we'll sit down quietly, and I'll tell you everything. I promise. But I'm telling you now, Jonathan. No one has attacked me. I'm fine."

She poured some of the liniment into the palm of his hand and turned her back to him. She heard a gasp when she moved the towel, but he gently worked the lotion into her back muscles, and she refrained from moaning as the potion worked its magic on her.

"You have bruises across your shoulder blades too," Jonathan said softly. "Do you want more across your upper back?"

She turned and saw pain in his eyes. She nodded slowly, pouring more liniment into his hand, then she capped the bottle and set it down. She gathered her hair with one hand, where it had fallen from the towel, and held it up out of the way while he gently worked the lotion into her shoulders and her neck. Then he held her robe for her and helped her wrap a towel around her hair once again.

"Thank you, Jonathan," she whispered.

He nodded.

They sat in the twin chairs before the fire while Betsy bustled in with a tray. Mrs. Hardman had made a hearty stew, one of her signature dishes for cold winter nights, filled with thick chunks of beef, potatoes, carrots, and green beans. A beautiful loaf of homemade bread, thickly sliced, was wrapped in a cloth and nestled in a basket with a dish of whipped butter beside it on the tray. Mrs. Hardman followed Betsy with a large pot of tea and their cups, saucers, and sugar on a second tray. After wishing them a good evening, she hustled Betsy out of the room.

They ate for a few minutes in silence, and Jonathan rose to pour the tea, insisting that Mina remain seated and resting before the fire.

"Jonathan, I—"

"Eat first, Mina." Jonathan's voice was strained, but tender. "Whatever has happened, you need your strength. You tell me you have not been attacked. I believe you. So I will wait for you to eat, then you can tell me what's going on. I can't guarantee I will take it well. But I will try, my love. I owe you that much."

"What do you mean?"

"Every time I've accused you of some wrongdoing, I've been horribly wrong. So I'm going to believe in you, Mina. You've told me several times, quite calmly, that you were not attacked. I'm going to trust you—as I should have trusted you before and didn't. So for now, please eat something and try to regain some strength."

Mina reached out to grip his hand. "My love, I am not in distress. Truly I am not. I'm fine. I have some bumps and bruises, but I am perfectly all right. Please do not think I need my strength. I'm not ailing. I'm just tired."

His eyes searched hers. Then he nodded, and they ate in silence for a few moments. Mina reached to butter one last slice of bread and savored each bite.

"If Mrs. Hardman ever left us, she could open a bakery and make a fortune!" She smiled at Jonathan, but his eyes were still troubled. She sighed. She swallowed the last bite and washed it down with her tea.

"Several weeks ago, Professor Van Helsing took me to a church to introduce me to a priest, Father Gallagher. He specializes in fighting … vampires. He agreed to train me. That's what the bruises are from. I'm learning how to deal with how they fight, the way they attack, and more importantly, Father Gallagher is teaching me the right frame of mind in dealing with battling evil."

She proceeded to tell him everything—the obstacle courses, the Bible sessions, the mock battles. She told him about the clinic and Van Helsing's involvement, and about Sister Joan Phillippe. She even told him about the resistance from Father Matthew. She was tempted to leave out Arthur's involvement, but then she looked at his dear face, and she couldn't do it. No more secrets. So she told him how she had been forced to include Arthur in the scheme against Father Matthew in order to keep their band of warriors from being shut down.

"And in all this scheming, you didn't think to come to your husband for help?" he asked, pain etched in his face.

"Jonathan, I didn't want you to worry." Mina felt tears well up in her eyes. "I'm sorry. I should have told you, but you had been so opposed to everything I had tried to do. I just didn't want another fight. I didn't want to you to be upset with me—or for me."

He sighed. "I guess I deserved that. If I had been more supportive from the beginning, you wouldn't have felt the need to be secretive about this. So where is this church?"

Here it comes, she thought. But she was in for a penny, in for a pound now.

"Whitechapel."

"What?" Jonathan's face went deathly white. "Mina, are you out of your mind?"

"Jonathan, you've never seen poverty like those poor people down there. They need help. No one protects them. Father Gallagher and Sister Joan are all that stand between those poor people and the kind of evil that you and Arthur and Van Helsing and I all stood against. Are you really asking me to walk away?"

"Yes! Please, Mina!" Jonathan dropped his face into his hands. "I can't lose you. I can't lose you like Arthur lost Lucy. Like we lost Quincy. Even like we lost that poor devil, Renfield. How many more will we lose? Must I lose you too? I can't do it."

"Do you not realize that I feel that way too, Jonathan?" Mina tried to grab one of his arms, but his grief was too deep and he would not look up at her. "I have more strength than you can realize right now. For all the bruises you've seen on my body, I can almost guarantee you that Father Gallagher looks far worse than I do. I've tossed that man all over the basement of that church! However much I regret my encounter with Dracula, and believe me, I wish every day that I could go back and change things that I did, I came out of it with more strength, more power than I ever dreamed a human being could possess. I can use it to protect you, my love. I have to protect you, Jonathan. Otherwise, it was all for nothing. This is my chance to bring something good out of the awful mess I made of that whole encounter. I have to finish this. I can't fail this time. I can't."

Jonathan looked up at her, his face a mask of agony. "I should be protecting you, Mina."

"But you are," she said, holding his face in her hands. "By letting me do this. By supporting me as I finish the race I have to run."

"Even if it means I have to sleep with a woman slathered in that smelly lotion?" He wrinkled his nose, even as his eyes watered. He bent his forehead to touch hers gently.

She burst into laughter through the tears that streamed down her cheeks. "Oh, yes! The smelly lotion is definitely part of the bargain."

"No more secrets," he murmured.

"No more secrets."

CHAPTER 18

1872

A crash brought Mina from Jonathan's study. Betsy stood in the hallway hanging onto the doorframe while tea streamed across the carpet and the old teapot lay shattered along with her favorite teacup.

"I'm so sorry," Betsy cried, her face pale as tears streamed down her cheeks. Her knees buckled just as Mrs. Hardman reached the doorway behind her. Between the two of them, they guided her to a chair and sat her down.

"It's only china, Betsy," Mina said. "It can be replaced. Don't worry about that. But it's not the first time you've dropped something lately. Do you need to see a doctor? Are you ill?"

"No, ma'am!" she insisted. "I'm fine. I don't need no doctor."

"All right, Betsy, all right." Mina patted her shoulder, but she shared a look with Mrs. Hardman over the girl's head. Something was amiss, and they were both concerned.

"Why don't you go lie down for a bit before supper time?" Mrs. Hardman suggested.

"No! I have to clean up. I've made a terrible mess. I've —" Betsy struggled in their arms, but it only showed just how weak the girl really was. As she wriggled to free herself, the neck of her dress shifted, and Mina glimpsed a small mark.

Was that a scab? A bite mark? She shivered and felt the blood drain from her own face. She took a closer look at Betsy. Pale skin, dark circles under her eyes, bloodless lips, blueish tints around the nail beds of her fingers. *Dear God! Just like Lucy. No...*

"I insist, Betsy," Mina said, tossing a bit of authority into her voice. "I can help Mrs. Hardman clear up the crockery. You need to go rest. Just for a couple of hours. Then you'll be right as rain. After all, this is Thursday night. Doesn't Henry come over on Thursdays?"

"W-we aren't seeing one another anymore," Betsy mumbled.

"Really?" Mina's heart sank. "That's too bad. I liked that young man very much."

"Yes," Betsy murmured. "So did I…"

"Well, you go rest like a good girl." She gave Mrs. Hardman a pointed glance and the older woman ushered Betsy down the corridor to her room.

Mina had already gathered most of the larger pieces of china onto the platter by the time Mrs. Hardman returned. "I can get that, Mrs. Harker. There's another pot on the shelf that will do until I can order another tea pot. I'll fix your tea in a moment."

"No, that's all right, Mrs. Hardman," Mina said. "I'm going to have to go out for the afternoon. When did Betsy stop seeing Henry Tunstall? And why?"

"Well…"

"This isn't gossip, Mrs. Hardman," Mina said sharply. "I'm truly worried for her well-being."

Mrs. Hardman nodded. "About a week ago, she met some young man. I think his name is Lucas. She told Henry she couldn't see him anymore. Just like that. Poor Henry. He's totally baffled by it. I think he meant to ask her to marry him, then this happened. It just blindsided the poor boy."

"And we don't know anything about Lucas?" Mina asked.

"No, ma'am, not a thing."

Mina nodded. "I'll be back later. Try to keep her from leaving the house if you can."

"Leaving the house?"

"Yes, I don't want her going out for any reason, and I don't want anyone gaining admittance to this house in my absence unless it is someone we know well. For any reason, Mrs. Hardman. Anyone who turns up will have to come back when I am at home. Is that clear?"

"Perfectly."

~~~

The doorbell jingled lightly as Mina entered Tunstall's store. An older man with graying hair and a full mustache and muttonchop sideburns approached her with a smile.

"May I be of some service?"

"Yes, I am in need of a new teapot," she said brightly. "I'm afraid we had a bit of a mishap today."

"Why certainly." His tone was jovial, but not overly familiar. "To serve how many?"

"I believe this one held about six cups," she said with a smile.
~~~

"I've finished deliveries, Father—" A young man entered from the back door, then realized she stood in the corner. "Oh, I beg your pardon—Mrs. Harker!"

"Good afternoon, Henry," Mina smiled. "How lovely to see you again."

Henry paled. Belatedly, he pulled his cap from his head and twisted it between his hands.

His father turned to look from Mina to Henry and back to Mina again. "So you are Mrs. Harker? Tell me, ma'am. Are you wasting my time here? Or did you come to see my son?"

Mina met his acerbic expression with an understanding flicker. "While I would like a moment with your son, I truly do need a new teapot. It seems my maid dropped my tea set this afternoon and broke my pot and my favorite cup. So this visit covers a dual purpose, if you wouldn't mind."

Mr. Tunstall sighed. "Henry, why don't you help Mrs. Harker with her purchases? You can talk while she browses our selection. Just..." He paused. "Please don't get his hopes up for nothing, ma'am."

Mr. Tunstall lumbered to the back of the store again, taking Henry's delivery box with him.

"I'm sorry, Mrs. Harker—"

"No, Henry, I quite understand," she said, stopping his protests with a wave of her hand. "I'm sure he's upset on your behalf over Betsy's behavior. I had no idea until today that anything had gone amiss."

"You said your maid dropped the tea service. Did you mean Betsy--?"

Mina nodded. "She's not well, Henry, and I'm very worried."

"She's sick?"

"I believe she's very sick, and I believe it may have to do with this young man she's met. Do you know anything about him? His name? Where they met?"

Henry shook his head miserably. "I only know she ran into him in the park near her mother's house about two weeks ago. Father got a last-minute order for some groceries for the church in Whitechapel. They insisted they had to have them right away, the message said. So I was late getting there to walk Betsy back to your house that night. She met him then."

"Groceries for the Catholic church in Whitechapel?" Mina

questioned, frowning. Sister Joan ordered on a regular basis, and there was never a need for last minute groceries. Their pantries were always well stocked.

"Well, that's what made it all so strange," Henry continued. "When I got there, Father Matthew got very angry with me. He said they had not ordered any groceries, certainly nothing above and beyond what they normally ordered. He accused me of trying to pad the account. I would never do that, Mrs. Harker. I swear it."

"I believe you, Henry." Mina was quick to reassure the lad.

"He called Sister Joan Phillippe to come, and she insisted it must have been a mistake as well. I had to take the order back to the store and explain to my father. He was angry, thinking I had gone to the wrong church. By that time, well, it was terribly late. I went the next day to explain to Betsy why I didn't show up, but she told me never to come back. She acted so strange. Almost like she was afraid of something, but just kept saying I should never come back. And then she said that Lucas wouldn't like it."

Mina chewed her lower lip for a moment. "Henry, I've been working at that church in Whitechapel for quite some time now. I'll speak with Sister Joan Phillippe tomorrow. I can't do much about Father Matthew. He's something of a curmudgeon, but I will speak to Father Gallagher. I believe you were manipulated to keep you from meeting up with Betsy that night. They kept you away from her by sending you on that wild goose chase."

"Why, Mrs. Harker?"

"I don't know yet, but I promise you I will find out." Mina's eyes became hard as stones as she contemplated the possibilities. Then she shook her head and smiled at Henry. "But I don't want you to worry about it, because you did nothing—absolutely nothing—wrong. Now let's find a teapot."

She chose a cheery cream-colored pot with a rosy mum and daisies painted on it. It was perfect for her afternoon teas by herself. Then she chose a new, bigger pot for company. It would easily serve at least ten cups of tea. Tucked away in the corner, she found the identical Victorian Rose teacup she'd always loved. Henry wrapped each piece carefully and promised to deliver them to Mrs. Hardman personally. She signed the account slip, and reassured Henry once again that none of the recent events were his fault. She hoped that Betsy would soon be well again and return to her senses.

But deep in her heart, she feared for her maid.

"No!" she resolved as she headed for Van Helsing's home. "You aren't going to win this one."

It was getting late when she knocked on the professor's door. She knocked several times and was almost ready to give up when he finally flung the door open, disheveled and out of breath.

"Mina! What are you doing here at this time of the evening?" He pulled her into the house, scanning the street as he did so. "You know how dangerous the streets are right now."

"Of course, but it was necessary," she said grimly. "It's starting again."

"What do you mean?"

"Someone is targeting my maid, Betsy."

"Tell me."

She related the whole story as he listened intently.

"You are sure?"

"I only caught a glimpse of what looked like a bite mark," Mina said, and bit her lip for a moment. Then her words came out in a rush. "But everything else fits. The pale skin, the blue tint to her fingernails, the bloodless lips. Then there was the breakup with this young man who she was so enamored with, Henry Tunstall. He's a good man, a hard worker, a young man with good prospects, and she meets some young man in a park, and suddenly she dumps Henry? It makes no sense unless this young man is a vampire."

Van Helsing paced in his study. "There is an old saying, Mina. When you are a hammer, everything looks like a nail."

Mina frowned. "I'm sorry, Professor, I don't understand. Are you saying you don't think this is a vampire?"

"I'm simply saying, yes, it might be. Or it might be that this young man took his lady for granted and she is teaching him a lesson. Or that she felt slighted and found someone else. Maybe it's good; maybe it's bad, but it's for her to decide. You don't know yet that it's a case of a vampire. You have seen too much evil, Mina. Now you see it everywhere you turn. Maybe it is, maybe it isn't. But we must have more than a broken tea set and a fainting maid before we accuse someone of being a vampire."

"I don't believe this!" Mina stood, astonished and more than a little bit betrayed.

"You may be right, Mina," Van Helsing said, still nodding his head. "But we must have proof. And we have to find this young man. So we watch your Betsy and we wait. For now, we can do nothing else. *Ja?* I take you home now, yes?"

"Is this your way of getting an invitation to dinner?" Mina pursed her lips to keep from grinning.

Van Helsing shrugged. "That works too. Come." Then he held up one hand. "No. You wait here. I'll go hail a cab. You wait inside."

Mina frowned. She had noticed that the more agitated he became, the more clipped his English and the more pronounced his accent became. She wondered if he was taking this more seriously than he wanted her to know.

She slipped closer to the window and peered around the curtains. Barely visible in the dimming light, she spotted the glint of gaslight off a man's eyeglasses and the shadow of his top hat. Her assailant was back. Her blood boiled. Well, she wasn't so unprepared this time. She started for the door, rage pushing her to burst into the street—

You can't defeat the enemy by using his own tools. You're letting your rage control you. She remembered Father Gallagher's words that very first day. Putting on the armor of God. Armor… She'd raced out of the house in such a hurry to see Henry Tunstall, she'd neglected to arm herself with so much as a kitchen knife! She had almost run out of Van Helsing's house to tackle that vampire with nothing but her bare fists and her fury.

Brilliant, Mina, just brilliant. Father Gallagher will be so proud. She leaned against the doorframe as shame washed over her. She heard the clop of a horse's hooves on the cobblestone streets just before the professor returned to the house to retrieve her.

"What is it?" he asked, seeing her stricken expression.

She wavered between admitting her hubris and remaining silent, but a predator was still waiting for them to walk outside. She told him.

"He's out there waiting for us right now. I saw him from the window."

Van Helsing's eyes twinkled in the dwindling light. He pulled a gun from his pocket. "Silver bullets." From his left sleeve, he pulled a silver-bladed dagger, and from his left inner breast pocket, he produced a silver crucifix. When he pushed a button in the center, the bottom shot down to reveal another sharp-edged dagger. "And you?"

"I dashed out of the house to meet with Henry Tunstall with absolutely nothing," she said dismally. "Some warrior I turned out to be. And I was ready to hurl myself out there and take him on with my bare hands. How's that for a warrior? Father Gallagher may throw me out of his school for advanced vampire slayers."

"I doubt that," Van Helsing said. "His greatest worry has been your temper. But just now, you kept your head. You didn't run out the door, even though you were tempted. You stopped. You thought first. That's good. Yes. So for now, maybe you take my dagger. Just in case, our friend out there is not so prudent as you. *Ja?*"

~~~

Betsy looked better as she served dinner for the three of them. Even Mina had to admit that she could very well be mistaken.

As she brought in the tea tray with the new tea pot Henry had delivered that afternoon, Professor Van Helsing leaned back casually and spoke directly to Betsy for the first time.

"So, Miss Betsy, I am told you fainted this afternoon," he said in his easy way.

Betsy looked at Mina, her expression that of a trapped rabbit. "N-no, professor. Just had a little bit of a dizzy spell, that's all. I'm fine. Just fine."

"Are you sure? I would be happy to give just a very quick examination. No charge, of course, because you are in this household whom I consider as my own family." His deep blue eyes held hers in only the kindest of gazes.

Jonathan looked up. "You were unwell today, Betsy? Please do allow the Professor to see to you. If there are any medical expenses, we will gladly pay them. You serve us so well, Mina and I will more than willingly take care of you, should you need anything at all."

"No, sir, please think nothing of it. I'm fine. Truly I am. Just a little tired. Mrs. Harker insisted I rest, and I'm perfectly fine now. You are more than kind, sir. I'm grateful."

"Betsy, please let us help you," Mina said.

"I'm fine, ma'am. Really I am." Betsy hurried from the room with a quick curtsey.

The trio was silent for a few moments.

"We can't force her to be examined," Jonathan said softly. "If she says she feels fine…"

"Jonathan, I'm worried for her," Mina snapped. "What if it's a vampire? What if she's been bitten?" She whispered the last part.

"I can see no visible signs yet," Van Helsing said. "If she has, it is early yet. Perhaps we can yet stop the progression. But perhaps it
~~~

is just a love affair gone awry."

Mina sighed. She served tea and they talked of other subjects until the professor took his leave.

~~~

Mina lay beside Jonathan, listening to his breathing as it became deep and even. She slipped quietly from his side and into her dressing room. Fumbling for her clothes, she dressed quickly and quietly in dark pants and a shirt with a jacket that fit her well, but had multiple pockets for blades, stakes, and even a gun with silver bullets. She also carried a vial of holy water and a silver cross, though not one as intricate as Van Helsing's. She would have to inquire as to where he had obtained it.

She watched from the window in the study downstairs until she saw Betsy slip from the house. Following from alley to alley, she kept her distance from the girl, while keeping her ever within her sight. Mina stopped when Betsy reached the edge of the park. To cross the street would be to expose her presence. If it was a human male, it would be embarrassing for Betsy, and Mina could well lose her maid. She didn't want Betsy moving away, perhaps into an unsavory position, because she had acted too quickly. But if it was a vampire, he might kill Betsy rather than risk exposure. No, this night was about discovery.

She scanned the area, then noticed butter-colored hair, wavy and glittering in the moonlight. A slender form rose as Betsy ran across the park and flew into his waiting arms. A lover then. They seemed to speak earnestly for a few moments, though Mina could hear nothing from this distance. They kissed passionately, and she felt embarrassed to be spying on her maid like this. Van Helsing was right. This was none of her business if Betsy wanted to dump Henry Tunstall, it might be a bad decision and in poor taste, but —

Just as she was about to return home, she saw Betsy lean back in the man's arms, her eyes closed and her neck exposed. The man's mouth opened wide and fangs extended, long and gleaming, then he sank them into Betsy's flesh and she wilted into his arms. He drank for only a moment, then released her, leaving her gasping for air and clinging to the lapels of his dark jacket. Mina's gaze burned with intensity. She came out here to find out. Well, now she knew. And now she would end it.

Suddenly arms grabbed her and yanked her back into the alley. She whirled, prepared to fight — until she recognized the Professor.
~~~

He held a finger to his lips. Mina turned to watch Betsy and her vampire again. They must have made noise, because he studied their surroundings carefully, his handsome features tense, deep-set eyes scanning the darkness for signs of threats. His fangs retracted, and his tongue darted out to lick the blood from his thin lips. He whispered to Betsy, caressing her hair away from her face and wrapping a silk scarf around her neck gently. She fingered it, smiling adoringly up into his gaze. He kissed her again, then they sat on a park bench with her head leaning on his shoulder.

"We came to watch and learn," Van Helsing whispered. "Now we know."

"I have to stop him," Mina hissed. "I can end him right here, right now, and save that girl's life."

"No, I don't think you can," the professor said. "But I must check on something first, and I must know…"

"Know what?" she whispered. "He's definitely a vampire. Why are we waiting?"

"First rule of engagement, Mina, is know your enemy. I am not so sure we are looking at some youngling here. But I must be sure. He will not kill her tonight. She will live another day. Unless you attack him. Then he could kill her for spite."

Mina frowned. "What do you suspect, Professor?"

He paused. "No, not until I am sure. Wait for her here, then walk her home. But be careful about ultimatums, *mein liebling*. The young, they do not like to be told what to do."

Van Helsing backed into the shadows and disappeared. Moments passed and Mina saw a smaller shadow take his place.

"Freddy?" she hissed.

The shadow jumped guiltily.

"Oy, Missus."

"What are you doing out here?"

"The Professor says as 'ow I'm to watch until you head for 'ome. If that one out there makes any nasty moves, I'm to fetch Father Gallagher at a run."

"And just how are you supposed to get all the way to Whitechapel and back before I get my head whacked off?" Mina tried to keep the annoyance out of her voice.

"Father Gallagher ain't in Whitechapel, Missus," Freddy scoffed. "'e's only a couple o' blocks away. 'e's been watchin' that other bloke what's been watchin' you and the professor lately. Only tonight, 'e's keepin' an eye on this here fella."

Mina shook her head, trying to make sense of the convoluted mess Freddy had just relayed.

"Yeah, I know." Freddy snickered softly. "Everybody's watchin' everybody, and nobody's gettin' any sleep. Bloody mess is what I say."

"You're more right about that part than you know, my friend," Mina whispered grimly.

"She's comin'!" Freddy said. "I've gotta' tell Father Gallagher."

Mina watched as the vampire held Betsy close and talked to her, then pointed in Mina's direction. Betsy held onto his arm, not wanting to leave him, but he insisted and kissed her tenderly one last time before smiling in Mina's direction and waving arrogantly.

Betsy stumbled in Mina's direction like a lost child, making her way across the square. Mina stepped forward and caught her before she fell.

"Why did you follow me, Mrs. Harker?" Betsy mumbled. "Why are you here? I wanted to stay with him, but he said I had to go home with you."

"Who is he, Betsy? This friend of yours?" Mina asked softly, guiding the girl as she tripped and stumbled on the uneven cobble stones.

"Lucas. His name is Lucas, and he loves me." She looked plaintively at Mina. "Don't make him go away, Missus, please don't make him go away. I love him. I can't live without him. Don't you understand?"

"I understand better than you'll ever know, Betsy," Mina said bitterly. "But for now, let's just get you back to bed."

Father Gallagher materialized from the alley to her right. "Fancy meeting you out here tonight, Mrs. Harker. Out for a stroll?"

"Just walking my maid home after a rendezvous with her new boyfriend, Father Gallagher," Mina said, her sarcasm equal to his own.

"Stop for a moment," he said, pulling a small vial from his pocket. Murmuring a prayer in Latin, he anointed Betsy with oil on her forehead. He paused for a moment, then moved the silk scarf aside enough to place some of the oil over the marks on her neck as well. She cried out as though it caused her pain. Mina pulled the scarf back over the scars and between the two of them, they hauled the girl back down the street toward Mina's home. Father Gallagher helped her to the back door, then disappeared into the night with Freddy close behind him. Mina maneuvered the girl back to bed and sat with her until the sun had risen.

When she entered the bedroom, Jonathan had risen and was dressing. He noted her attire and frowned.

"Mina, where have you been?"

"I followed Betsy tonight," she said.

"You—you what? Mina, that's a terrible invasion of her privacy!"

"She met with a vampire, Jonathan, and I watched him feed off of her." Her words were far more abrupt than she had intended, and he reacted as though she had slapped him. He sat on the edge of the bed with a suddenness that alarmed her.

"I'm so sorry, Jonathan," she said. "I should not have been so abrupt. I simply had to know if this man was only a man or if he was a monster. Van Helsing was there as well. I would have tried to destroy him then and there, but the professor stopped me."

"Why?" whispered Jonathan.

"I don't know," Mina confessed. "But I think there is more going on here than meets the eye. Father Gallagher was there as well. He helped me get Betsy home. For whatever the reason, the vampire— this Lucas—actually let her go. He seemed to know I was there waiting for her."

"He knew? How did he know? Mina, did he see you?" Jonathan's face was a mask of panic.

"I don't know, Jonathan. I just—I just don't know," she said, running a weary hand over her face. "Van Helsing says he needs to check on something. I didn't even know either of them were going to be out there tonight. I just needed to know whether it was a human or a vampire that Betsy was seeing. I almost hoped it was just some boy that swept her off her feet."

"Did you just make it home? The sun is up. You were out all night with vampires running around the city?"

"No, Jonathan, no." She sat on the bed and put an arm around him. "No, my dearest, I've been home for a couple of hours. I sat with Betsy to make sure she didn't try to leave again. I was afraid to leave her alone."

Jonathan sighed and leaned his head toward hers. "You were right. We should have pressed the issue last night."

"No, it wouldn't have done any good," she said. "Jonathan, you were right. We can't take away Betsy's free will. We walk a thin line here. We have no right to dictate what she can and cannot do. She's not a slave and she's not our child. We have no legal rights to make her do as we say. Yet we still have a moral obligation to try to save her from destroying her own life by surrendering to this blood-sucking monster. I don't know how we're going to keep her safe if she insists on throwing her own life away."

"Is this what it was like with Lucy?" Jonathan asked. He had been a prisoner in Dracula's castle while the Count had brought his reign of terror to London.

"Yes," whispered Mina. "It was exactly like this. And I can't lose Betsy like I lost Lucy. I just can't. No matter how diligently we watched Lucy, she still managed to slip out to meet with Dracula. No matter what countermeasures we took, he was always a step ahead of us. But this pup is not in the Count's league and I'm going to make him pay for what's he's done to Betsy."

Mina felt fierce determination rise up in her spirit. She and Jonathan sat on the edge of the bed and held each other for another half hour, unwilling to give up the few moments of comfort they had found with each other.

CHAPTER 19

Jonathan tried to get her to lie down for a few hours, but Mina couldn't rest. She spent most of the morning with Betsy. The girl rested fitfully, often moaning as she slept, and frequently crying out in her sleep. But it wasn't Lucas's name she called, and that gave Mina a surge of hope.

Betsy called for Henry. Perhaps her love for Henry Tunstall wasn't dead after all. Maybe there was hope that the boy would be able to pull her back from the abyss.

But Mina wondered if he would even be willing after all that Betsy had done to push him away. And what about Henry? Did she have any right to pull him into a war with the supernatural that could place his life in jeopardy? She chewed on her thumbnail until it bled. Wrapping a handkerchief around it, she tried to calm herself enough to direct her thoughts to prayer.

Mid-morning, Mrs. Hardman brought her tea and scones on a tray.

"You wouldn't eat breakfast, and I know you've had no sleep. You can't keep this up without some form of sustenance." Her words conveyed a scolding, but her voice held the worry and the caring heart that Mina cherished in the older woman.

"Thank you, Mrs. Hardman. This is indeed welcome." Both women kept their voices soft and low, hoping not to awaken the pale form in the narrow bed.

"Do you need anything else?" Mrs. Hardman whispered.

"Yes, please," Mina asked. "My Bible and my notebook are in the study. I don't want to leave her just yet. Could you bring them? I can at least do my homework for Father Gallagher while I'm here."

"Certainly," Mrs. Hardman said, patting her shoulder as she slipped from the room.

Mina poured her tea and sipped, allowing the warmth to seep into her. Mrs. Hardman had chosen a hearty Ceylon tea with cinnamon and cardamon. The spices provided as much invigorating aromatherapy as the warmth of the tea did, and suddenly Mina felt ravenous for the cranberry and orange zest scones. She had inhaled one of the generous pastries entirely before Mrs. Hardman returned with her books and a quill and ink. When she held out her hands for the supplies though, Mrs. Hardman kept them out of her reach.

"I want you to promise that you'll finish eating and have at least two more cups of tea before you even begin to work on these assignments of yours," she demanded, a hint of a thin smile tugging at the corner of her lips. "I know it's God's Word, but He knows you need to eat once in a while too."

Mina smothered a laugh. "I promise, Mrs. Hardman. And your scones are delicious as always."

"I'm glad I've found something I can tempt you with." Mrs. Hardman relinquished the materials into Mina's hands and waited with a cocked eyebrow until she set them aside on the small table by Betsy's bedside. Once she had taken up another scone and her teacup, Mrs. Hardman nodded and left the room, satisfied that her orders were being obeyed.

Mina shook her head in amusement. Mrs. Hardman was a true gem. Whatever would they do without her? Even when she presumed to get a bit bossy, she did it from a place of loving care. How many people had a servant who actually loved them enough to worry about their health and well-being? Who thought beyond the proper behavior and the walls between domestics and their employers? Mrs. Hardman was one in a million.

And now they would have to introduce her to a whole new level of reality. If she was going to help them protect Betsy, they would have to tell her the entire truth about the dangers that lay just beyond their doorsteps.

Mina sighed. Suddenly she wasn't sure she wanted to eat any more. But another sip of tea revived her and after one more bite of the delectable scone, she dug in and finished all three on the plate. After her third cup of tea, she felt refreshed enough to set the tea tray on Betsy's tall chest of drawers by the door. She refilled her teacup with the last cupful from the tea pot and returned to the chair by Betsy's bed. Setting the cup on the little table, she pulled the books onto her lap and looked over the verses Father Gallagher had given her after their last session. Her notebook was filling up fast with all the verses he had been giving her to study and dissect.

She looked up II Kings 6 and read the story of Elisha and his servant just before the battle. The servant was fearful when he looked out and saw all the enemies surrounding them. Then the prophet prayed for the servant's eyes to be opened. When the servant looked again, he saw the hills full of horses and chariots of fire. The armies of God had come to join in the battle. "There are more of us than there are of them," spoke the prophet Elisha.

"Well, we're going to need a few of those armies for this battle too, Lord," Mina mumbled as she jotted in her notebook. "Still got a few of those battalions handy?"

She flipped over to II Samuel 22:35 and read, "He trains my hands for battle, so that my arms can bend a bow of bronze."

"I get that You are training my hands for battle, but what does a bronze bow have to do with this?" She jotted the question down for Father Gallagher. Was it a heavier bow? Harder to draw?

She flipped to Psalm 18:39-40 and read, "For Thou has girded me with strength for battle; Thou hast subdued under me those who rose up against me. Thou hast also made my enemies turn their backs to me, and I destroyed those who hated me." Well, that was encouraging, but she couldn't imagine Lucas turning his back to her or being subdued any time soon! Or her mysterious stalker either. Father Gallagher was laying it on thick with the battle Scriptures.

She turned to the last notation for today. Psalm 37:8 said, "Cease from anger and forsake wrath. Do not fret, it leads only to evil doing." That one stopped Mina cold. Cease from anger? She looked at the restless form tucked between Mrs. Hardman's clean white sheets. Mina felt nothing but anger right now. She didn't want to forsake wrath. She wanted to drop a ton of her own brand of wrath right on the blond curls of that arrogant monster and crush him to a pile of dust. Her fingers tightened so hard the quill in her hand snapped and the feather hung limply to one side.

Mina stared at the mangled quill in her hands and a shiver raced up her spine. Was she about to be snapped in half by her own anger? She suddenly felt that she couldn't get to Father Gallagher fast enough for answers to her questions. But she couldn't leave Betsy either. Suddenly she felt weariness catch up to her.

"It's too much, God," she whispered. "I'm not strong enough for this battle. I'm so afraid I'm going to fail You again, and more people are going to die. I can't go through this again. I can't."

A soft knock at the door announced Mrs. Hardman's arrival before she entered the room, a quizzical look on her face.

"You — and Betsy — have a visitor," she said, her voice reflecting a bit of mystery. Mina nodded, and Mrs. Hardman stepped aside to allow a slight figure in white to enter behind her.

"Sister Anne Marie!" Mina gasped.

"Father Gallagher said you might need assistance today," she said brightly. "So I am here to serve. I can sit with your maid, protect her, pray over her, and keep her safe. But you are supposed to get some rest. I'm told you had an … eventful night." She smiled.

"What an excellent idea," Mrs. Hardman said. "Rest—something you are in sore need of, if I do say so myself."

Sister Anne Marie ducked her head to hide the smile that bloomed across her face. Mina rolled her eyes. Between the two of them, she knew when to give in.

"You're sure you can manage if she tries to get up?" Mina asked with a smile.

"I'm used to it with the patients on the ward, Mrs. Harker," she said with a nod. "I'll call out if I need assistance, but I assure you, I can manage one young girl. Besides, I came armed." She opened the bag that Mina had not even noticed she was carrying. The pungent aroma of garlic filled the room, and Betsy flinched on her bed, moaning a bit more loudly. Mina took one end of the garland of garlic and helped Sister Anne Marie drape it carefully around the metal headboard of Betsy's bed. They secured it carefully so the girl wouldn't dislodge it if she flailed about.

"What on earth—?" Mrs. Hardman exclaimed, her face scrunching up from the strength of the aroma.

"I'm going to explain everything in just a few moments," Mina said quickly. She turned to the little nun once again. "You have protection? You're armed?"

Sister Anne Marie produced a crucifix, a bottle of holy water, and a silver dagger from the little bag. Then she pulled out a heavy wooden stake and brandished it as well. Mina nodded her approval. "Call out and I'll be here in an instant." She turned to gather her Bible and notebook, then she paused and smiled at the nun. "And I thank you very much for coming today."

Sister Anne Marie knelt beside the bed and took out her rosary as Mina led Mrs. Hardman out of the room.

"We need to have a chat, Mrs. Hardman. I have a few things to explain to you." She stopped and gave her housekeeper a soul-searching stare. "Things you'll need to understand in the days to come."

"Well, first you need to rest, then we can talk." Mrs. Hardman might be curious, and she might be flustered by the strange little nun in Betsy's room with her unusual armaments. But she was even more concerned about the welfare of her mistress.

"No, I'm afraid this can't wait. I promise I'll go rest, but first we need to have this talk. I'm afraid it's long overdue."

It took over an hour to explain their history, hers, Jonathan's, Van Helsing's, Arthur's—and Dracula. But when she had finished, and Jonathan had corroborated the story over a light luncheon, Mina did finally succumb to a couple of hours of much-needed sleep.

When she woke, Jonathan was sitting in the chair by the fireplace in their bedroom, reading a book.

"You look much better," he said with a smile.

"How's Mrs. Hardman?" Mina worried about the effect their story might have on the no-nonsense housekeeper.

Jonathan laughed lightly. "I caught her sharpening the silver steak knives and placing them strategically around the kitchen for easy accessibility. Then when she took a tea tray to the nun, I overheard her asking where she obtained her wooden stakes. I think Mrs. Hardman will be fine."

Mina's jaw dropped, then burst into giggles. "You're joking, aren't you?"

"No, I am not," he said, holding up a hand as though to swear himself into a court hearing. "I believe our Mrs. Hardman is gearing up for battle. God help any vampire foolish enough to try to get past that little Scotswoman. He's in for one fierce encounter."

"Think she's related to William Wallace?" Mina giggled. "Maybe we should get her a battleax or a broadsword."

"And some of that blue face paint they used to say he wore into battle," Jonathan added, snapping his fingers as he joined her on the bed. They both collapsed in giggles.

"Oh, the mental image of Mrs. Hardman in blue war paint with a broadsword in her hands is one I will not soon shake from my mind," Mina gasped.

"Well, we'd better dress for dinner or she'll be wearing war paint and pointing those silver knives in our direction." Jonathan reached over and pulled Mina out of bed. He sighed. "I suppose you'll be staying in Betsy's room tonight to keep watch?"

Mina stared back longingly at the bed they had just vacated. "Yes, I will have to watch her, or she'll be answering his call the minute we let our guard down."

Jonathan leaned forward to kiss her on the forehead. "Thought so. Well, Betsy must be protected. And you have the church tomorrow, isn't that right?"

Mina nodded.

"I hate to say it, but I do have those tickets to the ballet tomorrow night."

"Tomorrow?" Mina asked biting her lip.

"Yes, in Arthur's box, not the Drummonds'. Just so you know. Do you want me to let him know we have to cancel?"

Mina hesitated a moment. "Let's see how Betsy fares tomorrow. In spite of all the madness going on around us, Jonathan, we still have to carve out a little bit of time for our marriage too. It can't all be about vampires and monsters."

He gave her a gentle kiss, then they set about preparing for dinner as the sun sank toward the horizon.

CHAPTER 20

Mina relieved Sister Anne Marie after she and Jonathan finished supper. They insisted that she have supper with Mrs. Hardman before returning to Whitechapel, and Jonathan refused to allow her to travel alone. He hired a carriage and escorted her personally to the door of the church. When he returned, he joined Mina briefly in the hallway outside Betsy's room.

"My God, Mina! That's where you've been going to 'volunteer' your services? That neighborhood is frightful." He ran a trembling hand through his graying hair. Then he grimaced. "If I thought it would do any good, I would forbid you to go there unescorted again."

Mina stood on tiptoe and kissed him lightly on the cheek. "But you won't do that, because you are a kind and loving husband who trusts his wife implicitly. And you know I am quite capable of defending myself, particularly in broad daylight."

"And you wouldn't listen to me even if I did," he said with a wry frown.

"Don't pout, Jonathan," Mina said, tugging playfully at the lapels of his topcoat. "You know this is something I must do. We've discussed it—"

"Endlessly," he interrupted.

"Yes, endlessly," she acceded. "And you know we can't just back away from this. They've attacked someone in our very own household now. It's personal. In fact, it was personal the moment they killed Lady Westenra." Her face darkened.

"That was not your fault." His voice was firm, but sadness had already filled Mina's heart with a bleakness that no amount of affirmation would ever be able to erase.

"He followed me straight to her home," she said, her voice barely audible. "I led him to a vulnerable, grieving old woman, and he…"

Jonathan wrapped his arms around her and held her close, feeling the grief stiffen her body with resolve.

"Just promise me one more time that you will be careful traveling through Whitechapel, Mina."

"Believe me, Jonathan, I'll make sure they have more to fear from me than I do from them."

~~~

The night passed uneventfully, and by morning, Betsy sat up and consumed some tea and biscuits. Her face was still pale, and dark crescents underlined both eyes. She was embarrassed to find Mina sitting beside her, having obviously been there all night.

"You shouldn't have put yourself out, Mrs. Harker," she protested. "I don't know what came over me, but you didn't need to sit here watching over me like this. What a bother I've been."

"Nonsense, Betsy," Mina said, trying to erase her worry for the girl and put as much warmth into her smile as she could. "You are part of our family. We were all so worried about you."

"What is that awful smell?" Betsy looked up and saw the string of garlic attached to her bed frame. "Why-ever is that hangin' above me? Saints above! What's that thing doing in my room?" She shrank from the garlic, fanning the air frantically with her hand.

"Just humor me for now and leave it where it hangs," Mina said, trying to draw Betsy's attention away from the offending garland. "Betsy, I need to be gone for a while today."

"But you don't go to the church until tomorrow, ma'am."

"You slept through the day yesterday, my dear. This is my day to go to Whitechapel," Mina said gently.

"I-I've lost a full day? But how? How did that happen, Missus?" Betsy grew frantic. "Have I been ill?"

"Yes, in a way, you have." Mina debated how far to push the issue. "Do you remember going out to meet your new friend night before last? In the middle of the night?"

"Oh, no, ma'am, I would never…" Her voice trailed away as she saw sympathy in Mina's gaze.

"You met a man named Lucas in the park." Mina paused to allow her to absorb that information. Obviously, Betsy didn't remember the encounter. But her hand rose subconsciously to the scarf still tied around her neck. "Yes, Betsy, he left a mark on your neck."

Betsy shook her head frantically. With trembling fingers, she tugged at the knot in the scarf and flung it away as she stumbled from her bed and staggered toward the small washstand in the
~~~

corner. An oval mirror hung over the stand and Betsy examined her pale neck. Her fingers shook as she touched the swollen, red holes where fangs had pierced her. She closed her eyes and swayed. Mina caught her firmly and guided her back to the bed.

"It's all right, Betsy. You're safe here. We're going to do everything we can to keep him away from you, but you must help too. You must resist going to him again. Can you do that?"

"What have I done?" Betsy mumbled. "What have I done? Oh, dear God, I'm ruined."

"No, Betsy, we can help you,"

"No, Missus, you don't understand… he'll come back for me. And Henry! I've sent him away. He'll never see me again. I've lost Henry." A sob rose up in Betsy's voice.

"I've seen Henry myself," Mina said softly. "I don't think it will take much to get him back here at your side, Betsy. You made a mistake. I don't think Henry will hold it against you. But for now, we must get you better. You need to rest and recover, and we'll need to keep you safe from that man."

"Oh, what have I done?" Betsy sobbed.

Mina sighed. She would never get answers from Betsy if she couldn't get the girl to calm down.

Mrs. Hardman knocked softly on the door. At Mina's bidding, she entered and took in the scene with a motherly sigh. "Here now, what's all this fuss? You were looking so much better when I came in with your tea. Now look at you! Let's stop this fussing now and calm down. It's not as bad as all that."

"But I've lost Henry, and I'm marked by the devil, and I'm ruined…"

"Well, I saw Henry Tunstall just yesterday when he delivered groceries, and he was very concerned about you. I almost had to throw myself across the doorway to keep him out of your bedroom! The very idea…" Mrs. Hardman smiled at Betsy.

Bless you, Mrs. Hardman! You know just what to say to a hysterical girl. Mina marveled at the housekeeper. *The woman is amazing.*

"Professor Van Helsing is here. He wishes to see you in the study, then I think he'll want to see Betsy."

"Oh, no! I can't see the Professor! He'll think I'm just a fallen woman. He'll drive me out into the street. He'll—"

"He'll do nothing of the sort," Mina interrupted firmly. "He's here to help you. Betsy, he was there in the park, as I was. Father

Gallagher was there too."

"A priest?" Betsy almost shrieked. "I'm to be excommunicated?" She stumbled away from Mina and face-planted into the wall, shrinking into the corner in a heap.

"Betsy, stop!" Mina commanded. She took a deep breath. Grasping Betsy by the shoulders, she guided her back to the bed. "Father Gallagher helped me get you home. He wouldn't have helped me if you were some lost cause. And Professor Van Helsing has helped many people with similar problems to yours. You need to trust us, Betsy. We're going to help you. You know that Mr. Harker and I would never allow anyone to harm you. You are part of our household, and as such, you are under our protection." She stopped again and forced herself to be more gentle. The child was clearly scared out of her wits. Of course, she had no idea what she was really up against, no idea of the battles they had fought together against this very evil, no concept of the prices they had all paid.

"Betsy, there are many people in London who have been attacked and deceived by men and even women like that Lucas, and the professor has been treating them at the church I work at in Whitechapel. There is a clinic there. We've seen many wounds such as those you bear. You are not going to be excommunicated or driven out into the streets. Please trust me. We are going to help you. Do you understand me? We are going to help."

Betsy cowered on the bed, as Mrs. Hardman held her trembling body and tried to calm her back down. "Go, Mrs. Harker," the older woman said softly. "We'll be fine until you and the professor finish. I'll stay here."

Mina gave her one last questioning glance, to which Mrs. Hardman gave her a firm nod and a sad smile. Maybe a little mothering would go farther than firm 'bucking up.' At least, that was Mina's fervent hope.

She headed for the study to confer with the professor. They kept it short. Van Helsing wanted a detailed report on how the day had gone previously, when the girl had awakened, what she had been like, and how she was reacting now.

"So she does not seem to remember her encounter with Lucas? Did she give you a last name?"

Mina sighed. "I was attempting to ask some questions when she became hysterical."

"Yes, I remember the same tactic used by Miss Lucy," Van

Helsing mused, eying her sharply. "It was a ploy to keep us off balance so we would lower our guard and allow her to run to Dracula."

Mina met his gaze for only one startled moment before she turned and bolted for the door.

When they reached Betsy's room, they heard the crash of china and entered to see Mrs. Hardman grappling with Betsy, as the maid fought like a wildcat to free herself. Mina flung Betsy away from Mrs. Hardman just as the girl lunged to rake her fingernails at the housekeeper's face. Betsy hit the wall with more force than Mina intended and slid to the floor. Van Helsing hurried to see to his unconscious patient, while Mina clasped Mrs. Hardman by the arm.

"Are you all right?"

"Yes," she said, trying to catch her breath and smooth back her disheveled hair with shaking fingers. She adjusted the pins to catch up the strands that had been yanked from her prim bun. "I didn't quite expect to be engaged in a brawl this morning." She turned to the tea set, which lay in pieces on the floor.

"You might ask Henry if they have another teapot in stock," Mina said wearily. "Perhaps I should just buy three or four of them and be done with it."

"One will be sufficient," Mrs. Hardman said, as she bent to pick up the pieces. "From now on she'll get a cheap piece of crockery for her cup, perhaps even an old bowl. When she can behave again, we'll see about allowing her to have a teapot."

"I shouldn't have left you alone with her, Mrs. Hardman. I'm so sorry." Mina bent to help the older woman.

"Nonsense! She caught me off guard. Clinging to me, begging me to help her, pleading with me not to let her be turned out. Then she shoved me aside and bolted for the door. When I tried to pull her back into the room, she said that Lucas was calling her and she had to go. When I tried to calm her, she flew at me like a hellion."

"I'll make sure I have someone else with you at all times, Mrs. Hardman, I promise," said Mina. "She had me fooled too. But I should have known better. I apologize."

"Piffle!" exclaimed Mrs. Hardman, standing up with the broken china once again on the battered little tray. "Next time, I'll be ready for her." She threw Betsy a withering look and marched toward the door to dispose of the trash.

Van Helsing had picked the girl up and placed her gently on the bed. "Come, Mina," he said. "Look."

He pulled back Betsy's upper lips and Mina gasped. Fangs broke through the gums.

They were not yet long enough to do damage, but it was a beginning—a sign of the evil to come. Betsy moaned and sweat broke out on her forehead. Her hair began to stick to her face in strings. The dark circles under her eyes grew more pronounced. This was not good.

Van Helsing examined her neck. "See here." He pointed to the abrasions on her neck. Mina frowned.

"I'm not sure what I'm seeing, Professor," she admitted.

"There are overlapping bruises here and here. This is turning yellow, while this one is darker, indicating a more recent injury, and this is swollen and red—inflamed."

"You mean—?"

"Yes, her encounter two nights ago with Lucas was not their first rendezvous. Our little friend has been bitten several times already."

"But I had told you I already suspected she'd been bitten," Mina said.

"Yes, but this indicates habitual feeding. She's further along than I realized. She's beginning to turn."

CHAPTER 21

Van Helsing insisted that Mina go to the church for her routine appointment time with Father Gallagher and Sister Joan Phillippe.

"But I am needed here!" she said. "I can't possibly leave Mrs. Hardman alone with Betsy."

"She will not be alone," he insisted. "I will be here. And here I will stay for as long as I am needed. Her condition is much more serious than I anticipated, Mina. I had thought that their meeting was perhaps only his second encounter, his second sampling of her blood. But I was wrong. He has taken her several times, and it is possible that she has tasted his blood as well. I must run some tests on her blood in order to tell. And she will need constant care. More care than you alone can give her. You will need help."

"All the more reason I need to be here," she protested again

"Listen to me, Mina." The professor's piercing blue eyes locked onto her face. "This Lucas is pressing closer. You need the training that Father Gallagher can give you. You need his counsel. We are both concerned that you will allow your anger to make your decisions for you. That will not do."

Mina remembered the verse in her book. "Cease from anger and forsake wrath..."

"Besides, I will need help, and you will be my messenger, *ja*?" He scribbled on a piece of paper, folded it and wrote a name on the outside. "You will see Freddy on the way to Whitechapel. He will be watching for you."

"What if I don't run into Freddy today?"

"You will. He has orders to watch out for you."

Mina rolled her eyes. "You too? Are you in league with Jonathan to keep me safe? I have been making this walk for the past several months now."

"Yes, and now the maid within your very household has been attacked. We cannot take any chances. Freddy is not there to risk his life, but if you were to run into trouble, he would sound the alarm. That is not so terrible, is it?"

Mina bit her lower lip. It was a wise move, though she was loathe to admit that. She took the note from the professor.

"Arthur Holmwood? Why are you sending for Arthur?"

"Betsy will need blood. I need volunteers. I am asking Arthur to rally some men he can trust. Jonathan is not strong enough, though I know he will hate it that I won't allow him to help."

"I'll help," she said impulsively.

Van Helsing's gaze was filled with a sudden compassion. "*Mein liebling*, you cannot give her your blood. We have no idea what that might do to her."

His words were like a blow to her stomach. Mina's knees gave way and she sank onto the chair where she had spent so many hours beside Betsy's bed. "I could make matters worse." Her voice was a whisper.

"Yes. We don't know enough, therefore, we cannot risk it. Mina, your job is much more important right now. I can find any number of people who can help give this child back some blood. Only you can finish your training with the good Father. Only you can do these things that need to be accomplished at the church. Only you. So much rests on your shoulders, my child. We need you to do your part, and we will do ours."

Mina swallowed the tears that threatened to overwhelm her. All she could think was *tainted blood*.

"I give you my word, I will not leave her side. I will stay here. I will guard her. And I will guard Jonathan too. As will Arthur. I have asked him for men to guard your household. You know he will assist us."

"Yes, Arthur will never let us down," Mina said dully. "Dear Arthur." She paused by the doorway. "I do know of one other person who would most likely give blood."

"Oh?"

"Before this Lucas came along, Betsy was seeing a very nice young man named Henry Tunstall. His father runs a grocery and dry goods store. A very prosperous business. It wouldn't take much to persuade Henry to help. I believe he is still quite fond of Betsy."

Professor Van Helsing stared at her for a moment longer. "You can send this young man a message?"

Mina managed a wry smile. "Actually, we'll need a new tea pot. Mrs. Hardman could perhaps mention that Betsy needs help when he comes to deliver it. My guess is that he'll be most obliging. But if he isn't willing, I won't be putting him on the spot by asking him point blank to give such a vital part of himself to the girl who threw him over for a monster."

Van Helsing's gaze held the barest hint of a smile. "Well played, Mina. It will be up to the young man to decide if he will help or not. *Ja?* Very good."

She conferred with Mrs. Hardman and left her to contact Tunstall's store through her usual messenger. It was better to make the transaction appear as normal as possible. Then it would be up to Henry whether he wanted to help Betsy. As it should be.

Her walk to Whitechapel was uneventful except for the appearance of Freddy, who she caught peeking around a corner a few blocks from the church. She motioned him forward and gave him the message and instructions for delivering it. She even hailed a carriage and paid to have him delivered directly to Arthur without delay. She didn't want to risk Freddy being intercepted and the message going astray.

When she finally made it to the church, Father Matthew glared at her from the door of the confessional as he led an elderly woman to the front of the church to pray in private. He hesitated, and she feared he was going to question her presence. However, the long line waiting for him forced him back to his side of the wooden booth, though she could see it vexed him terribly.

Father Gallagher motioned to her from the basement door, and she scurried toward him with as much dignity as she could muster while moving quickly and quietly in a sanctuary that echoed every tiny sound.

"You're late," he said through gritted teeth.

"With good reason," she whispered. "It's been a very eventful morning."

They both waited until they were down the stairs and safely tucked in their workout room. Then Father Gallagher turned to her.

"What has happened?"

As thoroughly as possible, Mina told him everything that had happened.

Father Gallagher sighed and rubbed the back of his neck with both hands. "Van Helsing is right, of course. You need to be here, finishing what you've begun. Time is running out."

"What do you mean?"

"I mean that whoever this Lucas is, he is pushing for a

showdown. Eventually, he is going to come at you directly. God help us if you are not prepared, Mrs. Harker."

"I'm ready now," she said, fury igniting the blaze in her heart.

"That—" Father Gallagher pointed right at her face. "That tells me right there that you are most definitely *not* ready."

"You cannot expect me to take these attacks as anything less than personal!"

"And that's exactly what's going to get you killed."

A chill ran up her spine.

"Mrs. Harker, did you read the verses I gave you? I understand life has been hectic…"

"Yes, I did. I read them while I sat with Betsy last night."

"Good. Let's go over them." Father Gallagher pulled up a chair, and after a moment of hesitation, Mina sat down at the table opposite him. They usually sparred while they went over verses. This felt odd and off-balance to her.

"You're talking about the one in Psalm 37, aren't you?" she asked.

"Yes, I am. What were your impressions?"

Mina bit her lip and frowned. "I'm not quite sure I understand. We're talking about monsters here. Terrible beings that prey on the innocent, who destroy people's lives, who kill without mercy—" Father Gallagher nodded with each point she made. "If you agree with me, then why should that not make us angry? Doesn't it make God angry?"

"In the first place, you're not God." Mina made a face at him, but he continued. "In the second place, anger and wrath are considered sins. God does not want you living in a sinful state. What was the second part of the verse?"

Mina looked at her notebook, though the words were seared into her memory. "Do not fret, it leads only to evil doing."

"If we are worrying and fretting, what are you not doing?" he prodded.

She frowned and mulled it over. "I suppose you mean you aren't trusting God to take care of things?"

"Exactly. If you worry and fret, you let anger take over your life, because you figure God is not going to deal with the problem, so you are going to have to step in and do His job for Him. God does not need you to do His job, Mrs. Harker. He needs you to do yours."

"Do mine." She repeated the phrase. "Then what exactly *is* my job, Father? I must be missing something. I thought I was here to learn to destroy evil."

"You are here to learn to live in response to the Father." He let her digest that for a moment before he continued. "No matter what the enemy is doing to distract you, you have one job—to respond to the Father when He calls you to act. The enemy wants you to **react**. He wants you jumping to his calls. But God wants you to act on His Word. He wants you to be in tune with where He wants you to be and what He wants you to do. When you can respond to the Holy Spirit with that kind of intensity, you won't need anger to fuel your strength. Your strength will come from God. And no enemy can overcome that kind of power."

Mina sat back in her chair. Her mind spun. Somehow that one little verse put something new into perspective for her and the pieces began to click into place like pieces in a jigsaw puzzle.

"This verse in Psalm 18," Mina said slowly. "I'm not sure I understand it. No one is subdued under me, Father. If anything, they are attacking more fiercely than ever. Is this supposed to be prophetic?"

Father Gallagher smiled grimly. "I gave you that verse for a very specific reason, Mrs. Harker. I want you to memorize that verse. Brand it into your brain and hold it close. 'For Thou hast girded me with strength for battle; Thou hast subdued under me those who rose up against me.' Psalm 18:39. I believe this is why God allowed you to be partially turned."

Mina froze, her eyes widened.

"Yes, I believe this is God's purpose for your life, Mina." It was the first time he had ever used her first name, but he leaned forward, his deep brown eyes burning with his fervor. "God has armed you with strength for the battle that you will face—quite possibly many battles to come, and because of the abilities you now possess, your adversaries will eventually be subdued and you will win the war over them. Not because of your greatness, but because of the greatness of God flowing through you. Through the One who will direct your every step."

Comprehension dawned in Mina's heart. The pieces fell into place, fitting together, all the clues from the many Scriptures he'd given her. He let her absorb the information. This was the culmination of the many months of preparation.

"May I ask you a question, Father?" she asked quietly.

"Of course."

"How did you come to live this type of life? What made you a warrior who kills vampires and trains others to battle like this?"

Father Gallagher chuckled. "I'm surprised it took you so long to ask. Especially after you met Sister Joan Phillippe and heard her story."

Mina's lips tipped to one side in a half-smile. "I kept hoping you would tell me on your own."

"My father died at the hands of robbers. He took our produce to the market when I was about six years old. We had done well that year. Mother said he was prone to stopping at a tavern or two along the way to celebrate when a harvest had been particularly large. Evidently, he had not been very careful with his money pouch. Neighbors later told my mother that Father had even bought a round of drinks in one establishment and that a couple of shady-looking men had been watching him closely. When he left, a little unsteady on his feet, they followed and soon knocked him from his wagon, and killed him. They also relieved him of the remainder of his money and several of the items he had bought, including a locket for my mother and a bracelet for my sister. He had shown them to one of his friends in the tavern. When the men were later found, they still had those items. It was the evidence that damned them in the eyes of the local judge. They were hanged in the village square. Little good that did my family. Though the villagers took care of us to an extent, we were much poorer without my father, who had been a hard-working farmer. He wasn't a wise man, but he was a kind one. Or so I'm told. I have very few memories of him now.

"Anyway, I lived with my mother and my older sister until I was ten years old. That was when I met my first vampire. I don't remember how he talked his way into our house, but I remember he was very persuasive, and acted as though he had an offer of a position in his household for my mother. The next thing I knew he had pounced upon Mother, bit her, then dropped her to the floor, still bleeding and dazed. Then he grabbed my sister as she tried to run for help. He drained her in moments. She was only twelve, and quite small for her age. It didn't take much and she was gone.

"At first I was terrified. I cowered in the corner by the fireplace, afraid to move. But when I saw him toss aside my sister like a rag doll, something in me snapped. Rage took over. I grabbed the poker from the fireplace and flew at him."

Father Gallagher paused for a moment. His face paled as he remembered the horror for his ten-year-old self.

"He laughed at me and with one swipe of his arm, he backhanded me against the wall. My head spun and I almost passed out from the pain. I couldn't even move at first. He made fun of me and said, 'I was going to turn her — your mother — and give her back to you. But for your insolence, I'll give you this instead.' Then he picked her up off the floor with one hand. She was a tiny woman. When he bit her again, his mouth went halfway around her neck. Then he... just ripped her throat out. Blood gushed everywhere while he laughed over my screams. Then he threw her body into the flames of the fireplace. I tried to tug her body out of the fire, but her clothes caught quickly and just the act of trying to yank her body away from the hearth scattered the logs. The cottage became an inferno.

"Neighbors heard my screams and saw the smoke. They ran to help. Some of them managed to drag me from the building just before the roof fell in. My hands and arms were burned badly."

Father Gallagher pulled up his sleeves and Mina gasped at the brutal scars that remained on his forearms. He pulled the sleeves back down again and stared at the table. "One of the men knew I needed more help than they could give me, so they took me to the convent a mile down the road. The Sisters of the Maid took me in, treated my burns, cared for me. When I finally healed enough, they helped me learn to use my hands and arms again. I did manual labor for them, and in return, they provided me with an education, both religious and practical. The worst of it was the nightmares, reliving that horrible moment when he told me that he would have given me back my mother if not for my 'insolence.' I was wracked with guilt. One Sister held me through the worst of the nights when I woke up screaming. She told me over and over again that the vampire had no intention of giving me back my mother. If he had given her back at all, he would have given me a vampiric being who would have attacked me and drained me dry because she would have had no choice. The hunger would have been too great. And he would have enjoyed that too, because he was an evil being.

"Why couldn't I fight it off? I asked her over and over. Why couldn't I save my mother and my sister? And she told me. You cannot fight evil with evil. If you are angry and you allow rage to control you, you are fighting evil with one of its own weapons. That will never work. The only way to fight evil is to tap into the power of God Himself and let Him do the fighting for us and through us.

"I pleaded with her to teach me how to fight. She wanted to teach me to read and write instead, but I kept at her. Teach me to fight. Finally she did. But only after I learned everything else she could possibly teach me first. I memorized Scriptures day and night for years, learned mathematics and languages. Finally, when I was seventeen, she agreed to begin my training as a warrior. By then the convent had been attacked three separate times, and I'd seen these incredible women defeat monsters so vile, I could not believe my eyes when mere women took them down. But this was one incredible woman."

"Sister Joan Phillippe!" Mina said, the connection falling into place.

"Yes," Father Gallagher said. "She finally showed me her scars. Scared me to death. I thought she was one of them. But no, she is not. God healed her. And blessed her with incredible longevity. She was not a young woman when I met her, and that was over thirty years ago." He chuckled. "But don't tell her I told you that part."

Mina grinned. "My lips are sealed."

"So you see, Mrs. Harker, I've struggled with anger too. I know that trap. And I know how difficult it is to break free of the rage. But you cannot defeat an enemy like a vampire by trying to fight it with one of evil's tools."

"I wanted to ask you about this passage in II Kings 6."

"Ah, yes!" Father Gallagher nodded and smiled. "When you are filled with fear, you won't see anything clearly. All you will see is the horror of the circumstances around you. You'll shake and your bones will feel like mush, because surely nothing can stop such a terrible force such as is coming against you.

"But when Elisha prayed for his servant's eyes to be opened, what happened? The servant looked around with the eyes of faith instead of fear. And he saw the hills filled with the horses and chariots of fire—the armies of the Most High God. Those armies are there for you too, Mrs. Harker. But you will only have eyes to see them, to call on them, to recognize them, when you can release all the sins that hold you back."

"Like fear and rage," Mina added.

"Exactly like fear and rage," Father Gallagher said.

"One last question, Father," she said. "Is there a special

significance in the bronze bow?"

Father Gallagher smiled. "Ah, the bronze bow. Mrs. Harker, you would indeed have to be very strong to bend a bow of bronze. It would require far more muscle than it takes to use a wooden bow, for instance. But look at the context of that passage. David had just defeated Saul and was singing a song of praise to God. He knew that he could not have accomplished that on his own. It was only by God's power—God's strength moving through him—that he was able to win that victory. If you are going to be victorious over these creatures, it will not be by your own strength alone." He watched her absorb that for a moment.

"Now let's get in a little bit of practice before you are needed in the infirmary. Then I think I will need to devote some time to trying to help your little maid. Sounds like she needs a priest."

"Just be careful not to mention the word excommunication. She was in a terrible fright that that was her fate."

"Or that was what she wanted you to think, so you would believe she was penitent and would not expect her to run back to Lucas," Father Gallagher said, his voice heavy. "Deception is the first trick they seem to learn."

A little nun slipped into the room, her face clearly frightened.

"Forgive me for intruding, Father Gallagher," she whispered, peering cautiously over her shoulder.

"What is it, Sister Gertrude?" he asked.

"Sister Joan Phillippe sent me. Mrs. Harker is urgently needed in the infirmary." She peered over her shoulder again. "And I am to warn you that Father Matthew is looking high and low for you... and he is ... well..."

"Breathing fire?" Father Gallagher asked sardonically.

Sister Gertrude blushed. "Please come quickly, Mrs. Harker! There is a back way to the clinic."

"Go," Father Gallagher commanded with a sigh. "I'll deal with the dragon."

CHAPTER 22

"I did warn you," Sister Joan sighed, coming around her desk to greet Mina. "We need to get to the ward right away and it will need to look like we've been busy little bees for hours. Grab this." She shoved a clipboard into her hands. "Quickly as you can, transcribe some of those notes into your shorthand and destroy the originals, or put them into your notebook or your coat. Sister Gertrude took the notes earlier today. I told Father Matthew you were running a quick errand when he dropped in a bit ago. When he sees Father Gallagher alone, he will come here looking for you. I want it to appear that you were only away from me momentarily and now you have returned."

"You lied for us, Sister Joan?" Mina's eyes widened in shock.

"Of course not! You were just not running the errand I told Father Matthew you were on. A simple mistake. I am human, after all. I had to send Sister Anne Marie to the pharmacy in your place. Which is where you were, if asked. She is hiding in the kitchen up to her elbows in dishwater at the moment and praying that she escapes notice. We will not mention her name, if you please."

"I never knew the church contained so much intrigue," Mina murmured under her breath as she scribbled out the notes in hurried shorthand, then folded the originals and tucked them down into her corset. Sister Joan's eyebrow rose a notch and she fought to control the twitch in her lips.

Mina shrugged. "Even Father Matthew won't bodily search a lady."

"While I wouldn't put it past him to be tempted if he suspects what you just did, I hope you're right about that. Come along."

"He'll regret it deeply if he does try," Mina growled as she followed Sister Joan down the hallway at a brisk pace. "He won't be half as challenging as Father Gallagher to take down, but I'm fairly confident that he'll bounce nicely."

"Dignity, Mrs. Harker, dignity," Sister Joan murmured.

They had only made it through two new patient charts when Father Matthew burst into the room.

"Am I supposed to believe that you've been here all afternoon?" he sneered.

Mina gave her most innocent "who-me?" look and cast her gaze from one person to another as if mystified by this line of questioning. "Why, yes, Father, I have been here this afternoon. Well, no, that's not entirely true either, not all afternoon."

"Aha! I knew it!"

"I ran to the pharmacy for Sister Joan a bit ago. But other than that, yes, I've been taking notes on all of our patients. We have several new people, and some of the older ones had a difficult night last night."

"You and Father Gallagher are up to something, Mrs. Harker, and I will not stand for it. This is my church, and I won't tolerate any shenanigans in my church!"

Mina's eyes grew stormy. "You are coming very close to impugning my character, Father, and I don't appreciate it. Father Gallagher is my priest and my counselor, but he has never been improper in his behavior whatsoever. I cannot say the same for you."

"What?" The old man's face turned red.

"This is twice now that you have verbally attacked me, Father Matthew. I came here as a volunteer because I believe in the good work that these Sisters are doing in this clinic, and I intend to continue coming here. But I am growing weary of—"

Sister Joan's alarmed expression caught her attention. *Not helping, Mina!*

She closed her eyes for a moment and took a deep breath. When she opened her eyes, she smiled into the eyes of the fiery little priest.

"Father Matthew, please forgive me. I am so sorry. I was up all night with an ailing servant, and I'm afraid I just let my imagination carry me away. Surely you didn't mean what I thought you were insinuating. Please forgive me for leaping where I shouldn't have. I know you could not have meant that you thought I was having some sort of liaison with another priest. That would be ridiculous! Why, the only communications I have with Father Gallagher concern this clinic and my soul." She paused to gaze at him with clear eyes and a serene smile. "Again, I apologize for my outburst. I must be overly tired to have mistaken your meaning for anything more than that, Father Matthew."

"From now on, Mrs. Harker, perhaps you would be better served by confining yourself to this clinic only. As for your soul, you may come to me if you need someone to hear your confession." He saw the flicker of anger spark in her eyes and his lips curled in victory.

But Mina felt the Holy Spirit flow in her heart, felt a soothing calm enter her emotions and settle her. She relaxed into a smile that was far more sincere than his and nodded. "Of course, Father Matthew. If that is your wish. Maybe we should get to know one another better."

He frowned, his eyes narrowing, then he whirled away, his cassock whipping about his ankles as he strode down the stone hallway.

She turned back to Sister Joan apologetically. "I'm so sorry—"

"No, Mina, you did quite well. However did you regain control like that? I thought for a moment you really were going to try to bounce Father Matthew off the walls like a child's toy." Sister Joan fanned herself with her hand, sagging slightly in relief.

"It had to be God," Mina said softly, her mouth curving in wonder. "Father Gallagher has been talking about the Holy Spirit's leading, and today something just fell in place for me as we went over some of my Scriptures. I was ready to rip into Father Matthew when I felt this calm inside. I knew I was supposed to let him think he had won." She grimaced ruefully. "I do believe that's the hardest thing I've ever had to do. I'd rather slay vampires than give in to belligerent priests, especially when they're wrong." She shook her head.

"Harder for you, my dear, but better for us at the moment," Sister Joan said. "Come, let's finish our rounds. I may need some help with this last one."

She was a child of fifteen, and Mina noticed her bite marks were quite similar to Betsy's. She moaned as she tossed and turned on the thin mattress. As Mina was turning to walk away, she heard the child moan a single name. "Lucas."

She spun back to the bed and knelt close, smoothing the little girl's dirty blonde curls away from her face.

"Lucas, please come back to me. Don't leave me. Lucas, I'll come with you this time. I promise…"

"No, child!" Mina cried frantically. "Fight it. Don't go to him. Lucas will only harm you. Stay here. Stay with us. We can keep you safe. Stay here in the church walls. Don't leave the church walls. Do you hear me, child? Don't leave the church walls."

The little girl opened her eyes and stared at Mina, frozen. Then slowly her eyes drifted shut.

Sister Joan moved quickly to her side and felt for a pulse. She sighed with relief. "She sleeps. If we can just keep her from slipping outside."

"Do we know who she is?" Mina whispered.

"No, not yet. Just another nameless waif from the streets. Their favorite prey. No one will miss them. No one will mourn their passing."

"Except all of heaven."

The deep masculine voice startled both women. Father Gallagher slipped around the corner.

"Are you all right?" Sister Joan asked, motherly concern evident in her voice and her gaze.

"Yes, we've been expecting this for some time." His smile was grim. "Father Matthew wants to be rid of me, but will have to find an excuse to send me elsewhere. If I give him no further reason for censure for a while—"

"I don't want you to get in further trouble," Mina said, "but what about the rest of my training?"

"You're ready," Father Gallagher said. "At least as ready as I can make you. I have never had a pupil advance as quickly as you have. The rest will come as you study, as you watch, fight, and pray. We will be on hand to fight with you, and to pray with you, too. But formal lessons have ended, Mrs. Harker. If you have questions, bring them to Sister Joan. She can answer them as well as I could anyway, and she will get you into far less trouble with Father Matthew."

"Father Gallagher." Mina paused. "Thank you."

"You said that like you were saying goodbye, Mrs. Harker." He laughed. "I'll be dropping by your house later this afternoon. The professor sent me a message. Seems that my presence may be needed. Something about a blood donation?" He smirked. "But if asked, your husband requested spiritual guidance."

Mina covered her mouth with her hand to keep from allowing her laughter to echo off the stone walls.

"By the way, I was praying in the hallway back there. You did a remarkable job with the old dragon yourself, Mrs. Harker." Father Gallagher's gaze held admiration, the first she'd seen. "You controlled your temper. You remembered the needs of others over your own pride. And you listened to that still, small Voice. You just passed your final exam. Well done."

"That was some sort of test you devised?" she asked, her eyebrows raised.

"Oh, no." He raised both hands in surrender. "Not my test. This wasn't my doing at all. I'm in trouble here. Remember?" He pointed upward. "His test. And you passed." He grinned. "Now if you'll excuse me, I have an obstacle course to disassemble." His footsteps echoed against the stones.

"You'd better transcribe those notes quickly so you can hurry home, my dear," Sister Joan said. "I'll have Sister Gertrude fetch us some tea."

~~~

Mina arrived home to find Arthur and three other burly men sitting in Mrs. Hardman's kitchen, sipping tea and holding clean rags to their arms to staunch the bleeding. Mrs. Hardman took the kettle from the stove and prepared another teapot of strong Earl Grey tea.

Mina nodded at the gentlemen, who only briefly met her gaze then stared into their teacups again. Arthur was withdrawn to the point of surliness. Mina patted his arm gently, then left him to his own thoughts. *Too much like Lucy*, she thought, as Mrs. Hardman pulled her into the hallway.

"They've all given blood, and Henry is in there now. He came with the new teapot. When Mr. Greenwald came out, Henry wanted to know what was going on. Arthur tried to explain that they were helping Betsy by giving blood to help her recover from 'something that attacked her,' so he insisted on helping too. He's in there now. He doesn't totally understand, but the look on his face when he saw Betsy in this condition—" Mrs. Hardman didn't have to finish her sentence. Mina knew.

She entered and watched as the professor shut off the needle on Henry's end and removed it from his arm. He dropped the apparatus into a basin to be sterilized once again by Mrs. Hardman, then moved over to Betsy's side.

"Is that it? Will she get better now?" Henry asked.

"We shall see," Van Helsing said, his voice non-committal. "We will hope, we will pray, and maybe by morning, we see a change in Miss Betsy."

"By morning? But if she has had so much blood given to her, why do we not see changes now? She's so pale. Sir, why is she so pale? What did this to her?"
~~~

"Hello, Henry," Mina said softly, entering the room and smiling at him.

Henry leapt to his feet. "Oh, Mrs. Harker, I hope you do not think I am overstepping myself here, but I—"

"Of course not, Henry. Please sit down." Mina's hand caught him as he staggered a bit. "You should not try to get up so quickly after giving blood to someone. That's a good way to faint, even for a man." She put a smile in her voice, as she eased him back into the chair. "Henry, the professor is helping us take care of Betsy, and I assure you that she could be in no better hands. We'll spare no expense to make sure she has all she needs."

"Mrs. Harker, I just don't understand. What happened to her? That man she was seeing—did he do something to her? Is that why she is so ill?"

Mina looked to the professor. How much should they tell this young man? How much could they tell him before he declared them all insane?

"Yes, Henry, he did do something to Betsy. But that's really all I can tell you right now. For the moment, we are focused on making Betsy better. Then we'll focus on stopping this 'Lucas' and bringing him to justice." Van Helsing had stepped in to speak the words, to help the young man deal with the problem before them.

Henry pounded his knee with his fist. "I knew it! I'll find him! He'll never touch Betsy again, I swear it."

"He has done this to others, Henry. You can go off in a fit of rage and make things worse. Or you can stay here with us and try to help the woman you say you love. Which choice will you make?" The professor's words marched across the room and let the air out of Henry's tirade.

"What can I do?"

"She may try to leave, Henry," Mina said softly. "Of all of us, you have the greatest chance of stopping her. Love is our most valuable weapon, but it won't be easy. She may say… hurtful things to you. You are going to dheave to determine in your mind and soul that you are going to do what Betsy needs most. You are going to ignore what she says and keep her from leaving this house. Even if she tells you to go away. Can you do that?"

His face crumpled for a moment, then as he wrestled with his own feelings for the woman beside him and the injuries she had already dealt him, Mina saw the birth of a true man. Henry's face resolved into lines of determination. "Yes, Mrs. Harker. I'll do whatever it takes."

"Good! Good!" Van Helsing said. "Now you will go get some of Mrs. Hardman's tea, and you will rest. All is well for the moment. Tonight we will be put to the test." He placed the remaining needle from Betsy's arm into the basin and handed it to Henry. "You will please give that to Mrs. Hardman and ask her to sterilize my equipment again."

Henry took the basin, looking a bit greener than before and stumbled from the room.

"He has guts, that one," Van Helsing said, nodding as Mina took his place beside Betsy's bed and held the girl's limp hand.

"But he's right," Mina said, a lump forming in her throat. "She looks no better. Are we too late?"

"Do not give up! It's too soon to tell." Van Helsing sighed. "We watch. We pray." He patted her shoulder softly. "We wait."

Mrs. Hardman stepped into the room. "Mr. Harker is in the kitchen."

"Time for a conference?" Mina said, looking to Van Helsing. "But we can't leave her alone."

Mrs. Hardman smiled. "Sister Anne Marie is here with that nice Mr. Greenwald to watch Betsy for you. Oh, and Father Gallagher is here as well."

Mina and the professor switched places with their relief guards gratefully and slipped into the narrow hallway.

"Well, ready or not, Henry Tunstall is probably going to get more than he bargained for." Mina's forehead puckered with worry for the young man.

"Oh, no, Mrs. Harker," the housekeeper said. "Henry left a few minutes ago. He said he had to go back and tell his father that he wouldn't be available for the store until Betsy was better. But he promised he would be back before nightfall. I made him promise that he would be back within a half hour, or he would wait for morning. I told him we could manage without him for one night if we had to, but he was not to venture out after dark. He gave me a curious look at that, but I made him promise me."

Mina felt her stomach go into free fall. If Henry tried to travel London streets after dark and Lucas intercepted him... *Lord, please set angels around that young man*, she prayed.

Jonathan embraced her lightly when she entered the room, and she tried to smile for his benefit.

"Have you met Father Gallagher, Jonathan?"

"Yes, we introduced ourselves," Jonathan said, his smile tight.

"You have an extraordinary wife, Mr. Harker," Father Gallagher said. "You should be quite proud of her."

Jonathan looked down into Mina's eyes and his smile deepened. "I am, Father; even when I don't understand everything she's doing, I'm very proud of her for standing up for what she believes is right."

"Well, I take it this squashes plans for the ballet tonight," Arthur said with a sardonic smile. He took another sip of tea. "What is our plan of action?"

"Ballet?" Father Gallagher frowned.

"Yes, we had planned to go to the Alhambra with Arthur tonight," Jonathan explained. "It was supposed to be a bit of a night out for Mina and me with our friend. But Betsy's well-being is far more important."

"Always another vampire to kill, right, Van Helsing?" Arthur's tone held more bitterness than any of them expected. They stared for an awkward moment. Arthur passed an exhausted hand over his brow. "I apologize. I--I'm not myself this evening."

"Too many memories, my friend," Van Helsing said as he rested a kindly hand on Arthur's shoulder. "The pattern—it hits too close to home. *Ja?* Of course. Perhaps you should go to your ballet after all."

They stared at him, and Jonathan protested at once, with Arthur chiming in close behind him.

"But we can't!"

"You'll need every man here to protect that girl!"

"Betsy is vulnerable tonight."

"Remember when he came for Lucy…" The name hung in the air. Arthur froze, surprised that his voice had uttered her name.

"Lord Holmwood, we are only men. This entire situation must be God's battle. When you leave God out of the equation, you have lost the war before the battle begins." Father Gallagher's voice settled in the walls of the kitchen, and Mina felt a calm drape over her spirit where only chaotic turmoil had existed a moment before. "But when God is in control, one small child can hold off an army. We'll have the manpower we need. It will be enough."

He looked up at Mina. "Something more is going on here. What are you feeling deep in your spirit, Mrs. Harker? What are you supposed to do?"

Suddenly she was never more certain of anything in her life. "We have to go to that ballet tonight."

CHAPTER 23

As their initial shock died down, a knock at the kitchen door startled them all, and brought a few of Arthur's friends to their feet with pistols drawn and ready. Mrs. Hardman opened the door and Henry Tunstall paled to find himself faced with so many weapons.

"It's good to see that my Betsy has so many able bodyguards," he said with a nod, as they settled back down.

"Henry! You promised me you wouldn't come after the sun set," Mrs. Hardman scolded.

"Well, it hadn't set when I left the house," he said with a weak smile. "And I must admit I did walk a bit faster those last few blocks. Your ... er... watchfulness must be catching." He nodded to the gunmen. "I felt like I was being followed. Like an itch you just can't reach, you know?"

Father Gallagher and Mina exchanged worried glances. Arthur and Jonathan held a quick conference about strategic vantage points for his men. The front doorbell rang, but Van Helsing stopped Mrs. Hardman from answering it.

"Let a man answer for tonight," he cautioned. "Just to humor me. *Ja?*"

She looked from face to face, then noticed the rifles being pulled from long cases, and she nodded. Arthur hurried for the door.

"I'm expecting friends anyway. I'll go."

He returned with six more men, each carrying long rifle cases. Henry looked at the firepower in the small house in confusion.

"Shouldn't we just call the constables if this man is hurting women? Let them deal with him?"

"For now, we will protect Betsy, my friend," Van Helsing said. "Later, if need be, perhaps we call the authorities. In my experience, the law is not always the most eager to deal with complex problems of science. They need to see the exact cause and solution. This villain is much more devious. What he does is not so simple. Not so easy to explain to a court. Let us first make Miss Betsy well. *Ja?* Then we bring down her tormenter. Come, Henry. You and I will sit with the patient tonight, and hopefully, Mrs. Hardman will keep us supplied with tea. Father, you will come too?"

"Yes," Father Gallagher said. "In a moment." He paused with Mina and Jonathan. "Be careful. Whatever you are walking into, God is walking into it with you. Remember your training. You are ready. But remember to act as the Spirit leads; don't react, no matter what you see or hear."

"Do you have any idea what I'm going to see or hear, Father?" Mina asked, suddenly afraid.

"None whatsoever. But He knows." He made the sign of the cross. "Go with God, Mrs. Harker."

Jonathan pulled Mina into his arms and she leaned into his embrace. "That's the man who's been sending you home with bruises all over your body?"

"Just remember, my love," she chuckled, "I gave as good as I got." She tiptoed up and kissed him lightly. "We need to hurry if we're going to get dressed in time for this."

It took some whirlwind preparations to get her ready to leave. But within little over an hour, she and Jonathan were tucked into Arthur's carriage and the three friends were being whisked through London's foggy streets toward Leicester Street to the Alhambra Theatre.

The inside of the theatre was as amazing as it was garish. The central rotunda was ninety-four feet in diameter and ninety-four feet high, Arthur informed them. It had burned down a few years ago and had recently been rebuilt. They had been famous for their circus acts for a long time, which accounted for the Moorish décor and architecture. Their most recent addition was an equestrian ballet, which was deemed to be extraordinary.

"I had looked forward to seeing if anyone could really teach horses the ballet," Arthur mused. "But now I find myself wondering what on earth we're doing here, and why we aren't back there at your house."

"You have armed men crawling all over our house, Arthur," Mina murmured under her breath. "Betsy is safer than Queen Victoria tonight."

"Lucy had armed guards too, and look what happened to her," Arthur reminded her.

Mina paled. "But Betsy also has Father Gallagher. I have great confidence in that man."

"I hope you're right, Mina. I quite like that Henry Tunstall. I really don't want to see him following in my footsteps."

Jonathan groaned. Mina looked up sharply.

"What is it, Jonathan?"

"Don't look now —"

"Mr. Harker! Mrs. Harker! What a surprise to see you here!"

Mina cringed at the voice, knowing before she turned around. She pasted a smile on her lips, as she gave Arthur a careful eye roll before turning.

"Mrs. Drummond, I didn't know you liked equestrian ballet," she said brightly.

"Equestrian ballet? Good gracious, no!" Mrs. Drummond sniffed. "James, look who I found! Over here. No, Mrs. Harker, the divine Emma Palladino, the prima ballerina is performing tonight. Isn't that why you came?"

"Of course, but Arthur was just telling us about the equestrian ballet they've added to the program—"

"Oh, I do hope they'll drop that off the program for tonight," Mrs. Drummond fussed.

"Dorothea, we really must go find our seats. Did you find Maryanne and—" James Drummond pulled up short when he saw Arthur Holmwood with the Harkers. He greeted them all, but Mina could see him bristle in Arthur's presence. Jonathan wasn't kidding about Arthur's altercation with the older man! And he was still resentful, obviously. "Oh, Harker. Didn't think to see you here. Mrs. Harker. Bit below your station, isn't it, Lord Holmwood?"

"I enjoy Miss Palladino as much as the next man," Arthur quipped, nodding to Dorothea Drummond with a smile. "And I hear the horses are superb."

Mina thought Drummond's head might explode if Arthur teased him even one whit further.

"Did I hear you say that Maryanne is here tonight?" she asked brightly.

"Yes, she and her gentleman friend wanted us to attend with them. He's really quite charming. But we seem to have gotten separated in the crowds. Now we really must be finding our seats before the first act begins. Will you be sitting down front?"

"No," Arthur said. "I purchased one of the boxes for tonight."

"Would have preferred a box myself, but Maryanne's young man prefers to be down in the middle of the action. Talked her into it. She says it'll be more exciting to see it all up close." Drummond huffed in exasperation. "Where do these young people get such ridiculous ideas?"

"Mummy! There you are! We really should be getting to our seats. We—" Maryanne halted when she saw the Harkers and Lord Holmwood. "Oh! Fancy seeing you here."

Mina's smile faltered when she noticed Maryanne's pallor, and the brightness in her eyes, almost a feverishness. She heard Arthur's quick inhale and knew he had seen it too. Maryanne's hand seemed to automatically fly to the jewel-encrusted band around her throat. As she fidgeted with it nervously, the edge of a wound clearly became visible, though only for a fraction of a second, as Maryanne brought her hand away from her neck and raised her head in an imperious way.

"Lucas! Come, darling, I want you to meet my father's partner in the law firm."

But Mina had known before she even heard his name. She knew the minute she saw Maryanne. This was why she was here tonight. This was why God told her to come to the Alhambra.

The golden-haired man stepped up beside Maryanne and slid one hand possessively around her waist. His curls fell gracefully across his forehead as he bowed in their direction.

Mr. Drummond made the introductions with little ceremony. "Lucas Callan, may I present my newest partner, Mr. Harker and his wife, Mrs. Harker, and their friend, Lord Arthur Holmwood?"

"I am very pleased to meet you all, but if we don't get back to our seats, I'm afraid we may lose them. Perhaps we can meet again during the intermission?" He smiled, and Mina felt the wave wash against her and spill off. He was trying to mesmerize her! Her eyes narrowed, but she forced herself to smile.

"Perhaps, Mr. Callan," she said, before turning her full attention to Maryanne. "I would love to talk to you, Maryanne. I've been admiring your jewelry. Maybe you could tell me where you got it during the intermission." But Maryanne's attention was totally on Lucas. Mina's heart sank. Was it too late?

The Drummonds turned to follow Lucas and Maryanne into the main hall. Dorothea turned at the last minute and gushed to Mina. "Isn't he just too divine? Maryanne is smitten, absolutely smitten." Then she was gone.

"Well, I guess we know why we're here," Arthur muttered.

"Was that—" Jonathan asked.

"Yes," Mina and Arthur said in unison.

"And we've got to find a way to warn the Drummonds," Mina sighed. "I'm positive Maryanne has already been bitten at least once."

They climbed the stairs to Arthur's box, just in time to see the horses make their grand entrance. They were magnificent creatures, pure white, with plumes of blue feathers standing up from silver halters and headdresses. They entered in unison and reared on their hind legs to prance forward onto the stage. But as the three on the far left came closer to the edge of the stage where the Drummonds sat with Lucas, they reared back and broke ranks with frightened whinnies. Their trainer came out to coax them back into the line-up, but they refused to come nearer the place where Lucas sat. The audience front and center began to boo and hiss, which further confused and frightened the skittish animals. Mina watched as Drummond leaned over and said something that made Lucas throw back his head and laugh. When he did, the horses to the center of the stage reared back and retreated as well. They shook, visibly frightened by the presence of an evil they recognized even though the humans did not.

Frustrated by the animals' inability to perform, the trainer ushered his charges off the stage and the curtain came down quickly.

"What was that all about?" Jonathan asked with a sharp frown.

"The animals sensed a vampire's presence," Arthur murmured. "What's interesting is that he didn't even attempt to hide his nature from them. He's being very brazen. I wonder why."

"I think we may find out why tonight," Mina said. "Jonathan, please stay close to me tonight."

"Don't worry, darling," he said, reaching over to squeeze her hand. "I'll protect you from that man, even if it costs my life."

"That's not exactly what I meant," she said, and bit her lip. "I'm afraid he will try to attack you, to take you out of commission. I want you to stay close to me—"

"There's strength in numbers," Arthur cut in smoothly. "If we stick together, he can't separate us and pick us off one at a time."

Mina nodded while thanking Arthur with her eyes.

~~~

The ballet was exceptional, but Mina barely watched the prima ballerina. Her attention kept wandering to Maryanne and Lucas,
~~~

who were providing enough entertainment to hold her attention. Lucas seemed to keep one hand on Maryanne at all times, but he reached over to touch Mrs. Drummond's arm periodically as well. And she looked more dazed as the evening wore on. Mina worried for her mental well-being if this state of affairs continued. But what would she do when she found out her daughter was the victim of a vampire?

When the curtain came down and intermission was called, they rose from their seats.

"What is our plan of action?" Arthur asked.

"Aside from sticking together?" Jonathan added.

Mina bit her lip. "Maybe I can talk to Mrs. Drummond. Or the parents together. Tell them that I saw Lucas with Betsy. That *is* him, I swear it. Maybe they can get Maryanne away from him. I don't think Maryanne is going to listen to me. Goodness, I couldn't even get my own maid to listen to me when it came to this Lucas! But if we can convince the parents—"

"We're not exactly high on their list of favorite people, Mina," Jonathan said gently. "I'm not sure they're going to listen."

"But we have to try. That man is dangerous, far more dangerous than either of them can imagine. It's our responsibility to at least try." She gripped his hand tightly.

He squeezed back and smiled. "I'm right beside you, my dear."

They wound their way through the crowds and found Mr. and Mrs. Drummond looking about peevishly.

"Well, I don't know where they went, James. They were here just a minute ago," Dorothea Drummond said.

"Where did Maryanne and her friend go?" asked Mina.

"Well, I just don't know. They were here one minute, and now they're gone," Mrs. Drummond said, waving her hand about.

"I really wanted to talk to you about that young man," Mina began.

"Oh, isn't he just marvelous?" Mrs. Drummond gushed.

"No, he's not," snapped Mina.

"I beg your pardon?" Mr. Drummond interrupted.

"I apologize for being so abrupt," Mina said, and took a deep breath. "But I've seen that man before. You see my maid, Betsy, was attacked earlier this week. I saw the attack myself. It was that man, Lucas Callan. I believe your daughter, Maryanne, is in grave danger."

"Mrs. Harker, this is really most inappropriate!" Mrs. Drummond said.

"I'll handle this, my dear," James Drummond said, brushing his wife aside. "Harker, you may be a partner in my firm now, but I warn you, I will not tolerate slander in my company. Not from anyone."

"It's not slander when it's true, Mr. Drummond," Mina protested.

Drummond ignored her and pointed his finger at Jonathan. "I realize we just signed contracts, and I know you and Lord Holmwood may think you've got me over a barrel—"

"I did not put you over a barrel, Drummond, I simply offered my friend a position if you did not want to keep him on—" Arthur's voice rose, though he tried to keep the situation from escalating into a full-blown scene.

"—but I will not tolerate your interference in matters of my family which do not concern any of you. I don't know where you get the nerve to say something so outrageous about my daughter's beau, but you have no right, no right at all. Whoever attacked your maid was probably some reprobate. Or maybe some young man your maid flirted with. But it was not, I repeat *not*, Lucas Callan. He's a fine man. End of discussion."

Jonathan tried to reach out the Drummond. "Please just listen to her, James. She's trying to warn you about a serious situation."

"Harker, I'm beginning to think you should seek some medical attention for that wife of yours. But whether you do or don't, just keep her away from my family."

Drummond stalked away, talking his wife with him. Jonathan wanted to go after the man, to try one last time, but Mina stopped him. "It didn't work. Let it go, Jonathan. Maybe we're just here to witness what's going on. We tried."

"Tried and failed." The voice made them all jump. Lucas Callan stood behind them, smiling like he had not one care in the world. "I could have told you that. The Drummonds adore me. The already think of me quite like... well, like a son." He laughed.

"Until you drain Maryanne dry?" Mina hissed.

"Oh, Mrs. Harker." His voice caressed her senses. "You don't know what you're missing. The things I could show you."

"I have seen what you offer, Callan, and I don't want it," Mina hissed, her eyes flashing, but she held her anger in check. *Act, don't react.* The words echoed in her mind.

"Why are you resisting me?" His voice tickled her neck again, though he was nowhere near close to her.

"Stop now." Her command was clear and concise.

Lucas' eyes widened. "How are you doing this? How are you resisting me?" His eyes narrowed. "What are you?"

Mina smiled. "I'm the one who is going to destroy you, vampire."

"Been reading trashy novels lately, Mrs. Harker?" he asked, his confidence shaken, but his determination to succeed just as strong as ever.

"No, Mr. Callan. But I did follow my maid, Betsy, to the park two nights ago. Where she met you. And you bit her on the neck." Mina stared at him with a gaze that could frost windows.

Lucas stared at her, and the sensation of a wave rolled over her again, but without affecting her. He drew a step nearer and hissed, "I ask again. How are you resisting me?"

"Step back!" Jonathan commanded, his voice sharp.

Lucas eyed him, his head tilted to one side. "You are the snapping terrier, nipping at ankles." He turned his attention from Jonathan back to Mina, and her blood turned to ice water. "But I haven't quite figured out what you are yet."

He knows Jonathan is vulnerable! God help us. God, please protect Jonathan.

"Where is Maryanne, Mr. Callan? What have you done with her?" Mina asked coldly. "You see, we know who and what you are. Your tricks won't work here like they have with the Drummonds. But if you hurt their daughter —"

"He hasn't hurt me in the slightest," said a silky voice. Maryanne appeared beside Lucas and slide her arm through his, gazing up at him with eyes that sparkled anew in the candlelit rotunda. "And he won't. We're meant for one another, and if you know what's good for you, you'll keep your nose out of my affairs, Mrs. Harker." She smiled, and Mina felt the predatory vibration emanating from the girl.

"I bet that's what he told my maid, Betsy, when he met her in the park two nights ago, too," Mina said. "She's not doing very well tonight, Maryanne."

"He's mine, Mrs. Harker, and you can't possibly think he's interested in some little housemaid when he can have me." She laughed, then she rolled her eyes. "Go home and tend your little maid. The night belongs to the young, like us. You should be home in bed where you belong. Go home, Mrs. Harker, and mind your own business. I don't need your advice."

Lucas laughed as he led Maryanne away. Mina watched them walk away, while Arthur and Jonathan stuck close to her on each side. They gazed at her impassive face, then at one another in concern. After several moments, Mina blew out a huge sigh and sagged visibly.

"We might as well go home," she said. "I have what we came here for."

"What? We didn't accomplish anything tonight!" Arthur exploded. When he noticed several people turn to look their direction, he lowered his voice. "We didn't succeed in warning off Mr. or Mrs. Drummond. We couldn't get Maryanne away from that monster, and he obviously lured her outside and fed on her again during intermission. And now he knows that we know."

"Yes," Mina said. "We know his name. We know his plan to use Maryanne to gain entry into the Drummond family, and we know he's not being the least bit cautious about hiding his nature in public. Those are vital pieces of information, and Van Helsing and Father Gallagher need to be informed at once. God sent us here for this confrontation. I don't understand why, but I know it had to happen. Now we wait to see what God will lead us to do next."

Arthur frowned at her. "How are you so calm right now? I've never seen you behave like this, Mina."

A smile tugged at the corner of her lips as she looked up at him and quirked an eyebrow. "Father Gallagher is a good teacher," she said with a shrug.

CHAPTER 24

They returned to find Van Helsing at the kitchen table with Mrs. Hardman, who was making tea and sandwiches to take around to the men at their various stations in the house. Even Freddy was there, making his way through a thick roast beef sandwich. Van Helsing had a portfolio of papers and file folders scattered all over the long table as he read through each, then set it aside for the next. As he read the files, he placed them in one of three stacks to his right.

He looked up as they trooped into the kitchen.

"Back so soon? That cannot be good. Mrs. Hardman, perhaps you would be so good as to request the good Father to join us. *Ja?*" His gaze darted over the three of them in rapid succession, as they slumped wearily into seats at the table. Jonathan paused to take some cups from Mrs. Hardman for them, and he proceeded to pour them all fresh tea from the pot on the table.

"Freddy, those sandwiches that Mrs. Hardman just made." The professor motioned with one hand. "Perhaps you would be so good as to deliver them to the men."

"Sure, Professor. Just don' let the lady toss m' dinner," he whispered, staring down the hall at Mrs. Hardman's retreating back. Mina suppressed a giggle.

"I promise to guard your plate," the professor promised solemnly.

Father Gallagher strode into the kitchen just as Freddy headed for the stairway.

"What happened?"

"He was there." Mina's voice was flat. Her levity seemed to disappear with Freddy. She sighed. "His name is Lucas Callan. He's not even hiding himself. He's flaunting his power, to the point of almost causing a scene." She went on to describe the events of the entire evening.

"I've heard his name," Father Gallagher said with a nod. "In the confessional, so of course I can't go into detail—not that you would want to hear the details—but some of the 'fallen angels' or 'unfortunates,' as the Crown tends to call them, have told me about this man. They talk like he's the devil himself." Father Gallagher began to pace, his robe swishing back and forth with his agitated movements. "So, he's involved with your employer's daughter. That explains quite a lot, actually."

Van Helsing appeared to be lost in thought, his hands still flipping through his folders, though his thoughts seemed a million miles away.

"He's my law partner now," said Jonathan, "and what do you mean it explains a lot?"

Father Gallagher looked at Mina for a long minute.

"Say it, Father," she said. "We've made a promise. No more secrets between us. Whatever it is, we face it together." She looked up at Jonathan as she took his hand in hers and clasped it firmly.

"All right. I've wondered for quite a while about the concerted effort that Mr. and Mrs. Drummond seemed to be making to keep Mrs. Harker away from the church, away from me and the Sisters of the Maid. Away from the training we could provide her with. I had begun to feel that there was a definite plot to influence you into forcing her to change direction. This would make sense. Lucas Callan had to have been working behind the scenes. But why? And why pretend he didn't know about you?"

He paced some more, then abruptly stopped. "Or maybe he doesn't know about you. He just knows you are training with me. But he doesn't know the degree of your abilities yet. He doesn't know how much Dracula actually changed you in the process of trying to subject you. If he knew that, he might try to replicate the process with Maryanne."

Mina's stomach sank.

"Yes!" The professor's voice startled them all. He held a very old photo engraving in his hand, his eyes wide. Slowly he met Mina's gaze and held it out to her. "Tell me. Is this the man? Is this Lucas Callan?"

The man in the picture wore a very old Russian uniform, but the shock of blond curls and the arrogant, aristocratic profile were unmistakable.

"That's him exactly! But this picture is too old. Is this an ancestor? His grandfather perhaps or—?" Mina gasped as the implication hit her.

Van Helsing nodded, seeing the understanding on her face. "*Ja,* you see, I too thought that this must be one of Dracula's first converts here in London. Someone out for revenge on the woman who caused his destruction. We have been mistaken, my friends."

"Who is this man?" Arthur demanded.

"Dracula converted him, but not here in London. It was Austria about 120 years ago. His name is Frederick Von Bardenburg. At one time, he was a Russian cavalry officer until he fell under the Count's influence. He had a natural charisma, something that Dracula found amusing at the time, but it wore thin over the years. After a time, it became obvious, by the accounts I have read and heard, that if they remained in close proximity, one would destroy the other. They were too strong-willed, too powerful to co-exist. But Frederick still gravitated to Count Dracula's sphere of influence, though he learned to keep his distance, never living close enough to give the Count a reason to see him as a threat. I still wonder who would have destroyed whom in that battle."

"So he's much older than we thought," Father Gallagher whispered, fingering his rosary.

"Do not try to take him on alone, Mina," Van Helsing said, leaning over the table. His blue eyes pierced into her with a gaze that held her frozen. "He is much too strong for you."

"You'll need help, Mrs. Harker," Father Gallagher said. "From all of us."

She nodded, then she rose and went upstairs to change into daily clothes. She would not be sleeping tonight.

When she entered Betsy's room, Henry was seated on Betsy's bedside, holding the girl in his arms as she clung to him.

"I'm so sorry, Henry… so sorry… so very sorry…" she cried. "Please forgive me. You shouldn't … you know… You should walk away… and forget me. I'm a … terrible person."

"No, Betsy, I'm not walking away. I'm not going anywhere." Henry spoke in soft, soothing tones, but Mina could hear his voice faltering. "I'm right here. I'll stay with you, I promise. You're going to get better. And we're all going to keep you safe. I don't understand what's happening here, but whatever it is, I'm not going to let you go. Do you hear me? I'm not going to give up. And you can't give up either."

When he saw her, he started to move, but she motioned him to stay. "Keep talking, Henry. She needs to hear you. If anyone is going to pull her through this, it may well be you." She nodded, and he nodded back. Mrs. Hardman had brought more chairs into the room, and Mina took one in the corner. She prayed as she watched Henry plead with Betsy to fight for her life, while Betsy cried that her life was filled with shame. But Henry didn't care.

Yes, if Betsy had a hope in all the world, it might be Henry Tunstall's love that would help to turn the tide.

~~~

They kept watch for the next five days, and Van Helsing performed two more transfusions to replenish Betsy's blood supply and to hopefully dilute the destructive effect of Lucas' blood cells. They prayed and watched as the vampiric side effects seemed to abate in Betsy. The fangs disappeared, and color reappeared in her cheeks, Most of all, she stopped fighting their efforts, and she began to actively pray with them, reciting Scriptures with Mina, and hanging onto Sister Anne Marie's rosary when the pain was at its worst, something she had been unable to do in the beginning.

Miraculously, Lucas Callan left her alone. Mina remained at home during that time period and took over the bulk of her care. Henry still came daily and sat with her, though his father was furious at first.

"The girl threw you over for another man, and you go crawling over there to give her your very life blood? Are you daft, son?" the father had roared. But Henry was adamant. He loved Betsy, and he wanted to give her a fighting chance to live. If she still wanted to walk away, so be it. He would turn and walk away too. But he wanted her to be healthy when she made that decision.

When she began to eat again and sit up in bed, Henry returned to the store for a few hours in the mornings to run deliveries but was back well before mid-afternoon to sit by Betsy's bedside. Her mother feared it was indecent, but he assured her that Mrs. Harker or Mrs. Hardman, or even one of the nuns from the convent were always present as well, so they were never left unattended. When Mina stopped into the shop herself to leave a list for delivery, she made a point of telling them how invaluable Henry had been to Betsy's recovery, and that she was so pleased that it looked like Betsy had turned from her "foolish mistake." When the groceries came, they even contained a small sachet of lavender and a pot of violets with a note that said: "For Betsy — best wishes as you recover."

"You'll win them over, Betsy," Henry whispered to her gently. "My mother will love you as much as I do, my dear."
~~~

"How can you love me after I was so cruel —?"

"Hush now! We'll speak no more of that," he said. "You must get well. Then perhaps I can talk to Mrs. Harker about our engagement. How is that for an incentive for getting better, dearest?"

"Do you mean it, Henry?" Betsy asked. "Do you really mean it? You would marry me?"

"Of course I would, you silly girl," he chided her lovingly. "I've been in love with you since the very first time I saw you. I can't let you slip away from me again."

"Oh, Henry!" Betsy's arms slipped around his neck, and he held her gently in his arms.

Mina smiled from her chair in the back of the room. She always tried to remain unobtrusive, but it would never do to leave them alone. Henry's reputation, as well as Betsy's, must be protected. She owed his parents that much.

Father Gallagher still visited daily, usually in the evening, though he kept it brief. Father Matthew was on the warpath and felt that Gallagher was trying to "sneak around behind his back," so the pressure was on. Sister Joan came often though, and Sister Anne Marie carried messages back and forth. Mina was eager to return to the clinic and her duties. She missed the routine they had established, even though she knew her lessons would no longer be part of the regimen. But she feared leaving until she felt that Betsy had sufficiently recovered and would no longer be subject to Lucas Callan's influence.

For two weeks, they heard nothing of the mysterious Lucas Callan/Frederick Von Bardenburg. Mina knew he would not have left London. Whatever plan he had set in motion, he was not a man to walk away, of that she was certain. So why this silence?

The men at the house grew restless, and Arthur finally released all but two, keeping a rotating guard in the attic window at all times.

"Something else bothers me," Mina said during one of their frequent teas together. She met with Jonathan, Arthur, and Professor Van Helsing at least every other day to compare notes. More importantly, it was their way of touching base and assuring themselves that they were all still alive and breathing.

"What would that be?" Van Helsing asked with a smile.

"If this Frederick Von Bardenburg is so old and so powerful, and if he's the one calling the shots here in London right now, what about that vampire who was following me around? Mr. Top Hat? Who is he? Is he connected to Frederick? Older? Younger?"

"I'm still looking into that," Van Helsing said. "I have my suspicions. But I hope to know soon. Yes, I am certain they are connected. How, that we must ascertain."

"I'd like to get my hands on that one myself," Jonathan growled. "He caused enough trouble for Mina before this Michael or Frederick even showed up."

"Oh, I would guess that Frederick has been here all along. He is only now showing his hand." Van Helsing's voice was placid, but from the rigidness of his spine, they could tell he did not take the situation lightly.

"Well, my detectives have been trying to follow him around, and I can't say he's made their job difficult. In fact, he's been most cooperative." Arthur picked up a thick dossier from the chair beside him. "I have had reports of him all over London with a dozen different women. Sometimes, he's seen with Maryanne Drummond, but he's also been out on the town with Emma Palladino."

"The prima ballerina from the Alhambra?" gasped Mina.

"The very same," said Arthur. "And she's looking a little pale these days. One hopes he won't destroy such a gifted talent just for his own thirst, but restraint doesn't seem to be in his vocabulary."

"Who else?" Jonathan asked.

"There is a complete list. The daughters of Lords of the Realm and captains of industry, and several of our more notorious ladies of the night, a few actresses from the East End theatres. It's all in there. He's being very brazen about it, much like he was at the Alhambra the night we saw him. He's not hiding the fact that he's different. He's flaunting it. Whatever game he's playing, he either thinks he's just so powerful we can't stop him, or… he's so far out of control, he's completely insane."

"Is a vampire really sane?" asked Jonathan quietly.

Mina reached for his hand and gripped it firmly. She could tell by the look on his face that his thoughts were suddenly a thousand miles away in that castle with the females who had held him captive, and her heart ached for him.

"Dracula's grief was its own type of insanity. Who knows what drives each of them to do what they do?" she said. "Maybe it's different for each of them, just as it is for us."

"Are you feeling sorry for them, Mina?" Arthur asked, a frown creasing his features.

"No, not really. They are beings who have given themselves to evil impulses," she said, feeling her way carefully along paths she hadn't quite thought out yet. "But where was that point of no return? For me, there was a specific place and time. The professor and Jonathan pulled me back from that abyss and helped me recover. Henry helped to pull Betsy back. Jesus does the saving, but the loved ones around us provide us with a reason to turn to Him. What if there are no loved ones left to give that? What if everything is stripped away from you? As it was with Dracula after his wife was killed — then where is that line drawn? I'm just wondering."

"Perhaps a good question for Father Gallagher? *Ja?*" said Van Helsing with a sad smile. "But I will say this. God allowed everything to be stripped from a man named Job. Still he said, 'Though He slay me, yet will I trust Him.' Every man still has free will — a choice. Evil is a choice. It does not beat us over the head and say, 'Here I am — you have no choice.' Always God provides the way of escape."

"That we might be able to bear it," whispered Mina.

"Exactly."

CHAPTER 25

"Good night, Henry," Mina said, smiling at the young man who stood on the doorstep, poised to leave. "It's time you get some rest."

"Are you sure, Mrs. Harker?" Henry seemed unwilling to leave. "Maybe just one more night—"

"Your mother is going to think we've kidnapped you!"

"Your lady is on the mend, young man." Father Gallagher clapped him on the shoulder. "Come. I'll walk you back home, and we can talk along the way. I understand we have some wedding plans, so maybe a little bit of counseling would be in order about now."

Henry blushed, but his smile widened.

That'll distract him, Mina thought with a smile. *The poor boy needs some sleep for a change.*

It had been a full three weeks and Betsy was even beginning to move around a bit at a time. Henry had been helping her walk up and down the hallway every day. She was still weak but growing stronger every day. They had watched and waited, but no attacks had come. She had tried to leave, but they had been able to stop her. It all seemed too easy.

Mina looked up as the clouds shifted and a full moon shone through. She shivered and pulled her shawl around her shoulders a little more tightly. She slipped back inside and bolted the door. Had that shiver been a premonition or merely a chill? She went back to help Mrs. Hardman settle Betsy in for the night, then they both headed for the kitchen.

"Would you like a spot of tea before you go to bed? Or maybe an herbal tea for sleep?" Mrs. Hardman peered into Mina's face with kindly eyes. "You know you haven't been getting much rest yourself. A good night's sleep would do you some good too."

"Ow, that's not fair! Making me eat my own words now?" Mina laughed.

Suddenly they heard a crash and the sound of breaking glass from the second floor.

"Jonathan!" Mina raced up the stairs.

Wind blew through the broken window of their bedroom and Jonathan lay on the floor. He groaned as she half-lifted him. A scuffle at the doorway alerted Mina, and she whirled in a crouch, expecting to take on a vampire. She stopped short when she saw it was the guard from the attic, rifle at the ready.

"Help me!" she ordered tersely. Jonathan groaned as they lifted him to the bed. That was when she saw the brick, which had come through the window with enough force to hit Jonathan in the head and knock him down.

"Someone… on the balcony… outside the window… just before the window broke…" He pointed weakly.

Then screams from downstairs ripped through the house.

"Go!" Jonathan shouted hoarsely. "Leave me! Go!"

Mina led the charge down the stairs, her feet a blur as she hurled herself down to the servant's quarters. Mrs. Hardman lay in a heap on the kitchen floor. The back door was open.

Too late… Too late… Mina's heart sank, but she had to check anyway. As the guard knelt to help Mrs. Hardman to her feet, Mina flew down the hallway to Betsy's room.

Her bed was empty.

She came back to the kitchen and knelt before Mrs. Hardman. She was sitting in a chair, and her eyes were filled with tears. The guard stood at the back door, his gaze taking in every angle for clues. When he spied Freddy, he summoned the lad and sent him out with the messages that would bring help. Prearranged signals that something had gone terribly wrong. Signals they had all hoped would never be necessary.

"I'm so sorry, Mrs. Harker—" Mrs. Hardman moaned as she leaned her head against the old wooden table.

"Did you see him?"

"No. He hit me from behind before I knew he was there. Then I tried to get up. Betsy was screaming. I wanted to help her. She fought him. She didn't want to go, ma'am. She swas trying to stay here. He… laughed at her." She wept. "He just picked her up and hauled her out like a sack of potatoes."

Jonathan staggered into the room.

"Oh, Mr. Harker! You're hurt, sir."

He motioned her to sit still, as he sat beside her. He looked up at Mina.

"You're going after her, aren't you?"

"Yes," she whispered.

"Can you really do this, Mina? Are you really capable of this?" His expression held more pain than she could bear to witness.

"Yes."

And then she was out the door. She wandered through the streets, down alleys, her feet flying so fast she was almost a blur under the light of the full moon. She heard a strangled scream up ahead, and realized it came from the park.

I should have known.

She turned down the last alley that opened into the park and sped across the street. Her feet skidded to a stop. Father Gallagher knelt beside Betsy's body. He administered last rites while Freddy stood by, cap in hand, tears streaking his dirty face. They were half-hidden behind the bench where Mina had first seen Lucas Callan. Trees surrounded them on two sides. Just then, the moon slid behind the clouds again.

"She fought him, Father. Mrs. Hardman saw it. She fought him. She didn't want this." Mina felt tears cover her face. Weren't they ever going to win? Was it always going to be loss after loss after loss?

"I know," he whispered. "She still has this clutched in her hand." He pointed. In the girl's fingers, she clutched a crucifix, a bit of blackened crust still smoking along the bottom edge of it. "Vampiric 'blood,' if you will, or what they have in place of blood. She tried to stab him with it. She was fighting for her life. For her soul."

Father Gallagher stood up and withdrew his sword from beneath his robe. "We have to be quick. We don't want to risk it, Mina. You know he may have forced her to drink his own blood, just to make her rise again."

The blood drained from Mina's face, but she nodded. With one smooth stroke, Father Gallagher beheaded the girl, then he handed the sword and scabbard to Mina.

"Go. Quickly. Before the police get here."

Whistles sounded in the distance and voices shouted. Mina whirled and ran. She wanted to run until she reached the ocean, then swim until her arms gave out. But she knew the police would arrive soon to inform them of Betsy's death. She needed to be at home. Needed to be with Jonathan when they arrived. And she needed to clean and hide Father Gallagher's sword.

Where did this clarity of thinking come from?

You know where, child. The thought was a still, small Voice. *I'm still with you. Be not afraid.*

When she reached the back door, the guard was still there, rifle at the ready. One look at her face told him half the story. The bloody sword told the other half.

"Police coming?" he asked tersely.

She nodded. "Eventually."

"I'll take that." He nodded toward the sword.

"It belongs to Father Gallagher. He'll need it back at some point."

"I'll see that it's cleaned good and left with Lord Holmwood," he said solemnly. At some point, he had evidently retrieved his rifle case from upstairs, because he quickly packed the gun and the sword within it and he slipped out the back door into the night. Mina entered, then closed and bolted the door.

"Mina!" Jonathan enveloped her in his arms, and she inhaled his scent. Here was stability in her world. For just one moment, she needed to feel something solid in her life. He and Mrs. Hardman were still sitting in the kitchen where she had left them.

"Betsy?" Mrs. Hardman's voice behind them quavered.

Mina pulled back slightly. "I was too late. So was Father Gallagher. He got to her first and gave her last rites though. She died fighting, Mrs. Hardman. She didn't give in. He never took her humanity from her." Then she broke down and cried again.

~~~

Jonathan shook hands with Betsy's father and Mina hugged her mother gently. They watched as the grieving parents stumbled away from the cemetery, weeping inconsolably. Mina pressed Jonathan's arm for a moment then nodded toward the solitary figure still standing by the open grave. Men stood by with shovels at the ready, unable to proceed until the last of the mourners had departed. They shifted uncomfortably from one foot to the other.

Mina laid a gentle hand on Henry Tunstall's arm. They stood side by side at Betsy's grave. Mina and Jonathan had paid for the resting place and a lovely tombstone to mark the spot.

"I'm so sorry, Henry," Mina said. "But she did not go with him willingly. She fought him every step of the way. He had to use brute force to remove her from my house, and even then, there were signs she fought him off. She never betrayed you."
~~~

He nodded. "Father Gallagher told me. I just don't understand why God allowed this to happen."

"I wish I knew the answer to that, Henry. But I won't try to give you answers I don't have. I'll simply point you to someone else who was once in the same predicament. A worse one, actually. Job lost all of his children, his cattle, his property, his goods, everything."

"Ah, but Job got to keep his wife." Henry smiled bitterly through his tears. "God didn't even allow me that."

Mina laughed tearfully, as she nodded. "Well, yes, but she wasn't a very good wife either. She told Job to curse God and die. She railed at him and didn't do anything to comfort him in their grief. I don't think I'd consider that one of God's blessings at that particular moment in time."

Henry squeezed his eyes shut for a moment, then looked up at her. "So I should be thankful God didn't burn down the family store as well?"

"Ah now, I didn't say God did all those things, Henry. The Bible says that God allowed Job to be tested. He removed the hedge of protection, and the enemy did all those terrible things. God doesn't set out to hurt us. But the point is that when all was said and done, what did Job end up saying? Do you remember that Scripture?"

"Great minds must think alike, Mrs. Harker." Henry smiled sadly. "Father Gallagher gave me that passage to read this week, along with this." He pulled out a Bible just like the one the priest had given Mina to study. "Job said, 'Though He slay me, yet will I trust Him.'"

Tears filled Mina's eyes as she nodded. "And God must have somehow dealt with Job's wife too, because God blessed Job so abundantly, that he ended up with a whole new line of children, wealth, possessions, cattle, property, everything he'd lost and more. I don't know what God has in mind for you, Henry Tunstall, but I know He's going to do more than you ever bargained for."

Henry nodded. "I hope you're right, Mrs. Harker. I hope you're right."

"Will you still come by now and then?"

"I would like that. I truly would. But I'm leaving England."

Mina felt a sudden pang for the young man. "Where will you go, Henry?"

"My father owns a store in Canada. He'd like me to go there and take a look at the business from a new point of view. Maybe a change of scenery…" He stopped and cleared his throat a couple of times. "Quite frankly, I think my parents are afraid for me, Mrs. Harker. After the way … Betsy's body was found… Well… it was horrible what that man did to her. Bad enough that he bit her, but to cut off her head too. What kind of monster does that?"

Mina bit her lower lip. They'd been more than willing to let the police think that Betsy's attacker had kidnapped her, bitten her — causing the abrasions on her neck — and then beheaded her in the park when his capture seemed eminent. They were never going to believe in the vampire angle anyway. Belief in the supernatural just didn't happen unless it slapped people in the face, and even then, many would bend over backwards to rationalize it rather than accept the unbelievable.

Henry continued. "Anyway, I think they would rather send me out of the country than take the risk that he might come after me next for coaxing Betsy away from his influence."

"She did love you, Henry."

He smiled sadly. "I'll always love her, Mrs. Harker."

"Go with God, Henry Tunstall." She left him standing beside Betsy's grave. Who knew when the boy would make it back here again?

CHAPTER 26

An uneasy peace draped over London on Sunday morning. Jonathan and Mina had returned to their regular church services, though Mina had a hard time keeping her mind on the sermon this morning. Grief still clung to her spirit, clutching at her skirts. She felt they had failed Betsy by not keeping her safe.

"We did not fail Betsy," Father Gallagher had insisted over and over, his patience growing thin. He, too, felt anger for the girl's death. "Her soul was the most important part, and he did not gain that back. She fought him. That's a victory." He had spat out the last word and stalked out of the clinic without seeing the rest of the patients.

"He's in almost as much pain as you are, Mina," Sister Joan had said softly. "He spends hours at the altar in prayer. Even Father Matthew is steering clear of him right now. He's like a lion with a thorn in his paw. You both need time to heal."

"And is this Frederick going to give us that time?" Mina had asked.

"Probably not," Sister Joan had sighed, as they headed back to their duties on the ward. There were more and more casualties coming in every night. Obviously, his attacks were growing. Or was he turning more converts, and increasing the need for warm bodies to feed them? Mina had shuddered. At least Betsy had been spared that much.

She shuddered again as she sat beside Jonathan in church, and he reached over to grasp her hand.

Dear Jonathan. He is such a comfort. What would I do without him? She longed to lean her head on his shoulder, but that would not be appropriate in church. She sighed and wished for the service to end so they could retreat to the solace of their home.

Finally released into the rare sunshine, Mina breathed deeply.

"Luncheon out?" Jonathan asked lightly. "Or home?"

It was on her lips to say 'home,' but the day was perfect. It seemed a shame to spend it cooped up inside. London didn't see too many bright days like this. Luncheon at a small tea house and a walk in the sun with her handsome husband would be a blessing on a Sunday afternoon. Her lips curved into a smile.

"Mrs. Harker, how delightful to see you."

Her smile froze. The voice was laced with sarcasm and a trace of venom, and it felt like fingernails on a chalkboard.

"We had begun to think you might never return to church services here, since you seem to prefer hobnobbing with poor and unwashed masses in Whitechapel."

The second voice was equally unwelcome. Mina turned. "Good morning, Mrs. Drummond. Mr. Drummond. How are you?" She completely ignored their jibes.

Drummond nodded to Jonathan, who had stiffened at the way they were intentionally tossing barbs at his wife. Mina tightened her grip on his arm in a comforting way. *It's all right, Jonathan.* She tried to send the message through her touch.

"Is Maryanne with you this morning?" she asked brightly.

"No," Mrs. Drummond said in clipped tones. "She hasn't been feeling well the last few days, so she remained home in bed this morning."

"Too many late nights with Lucas. That's my opinion," Mr. Drummond grumbled. "They should both attend with us. It's the way things are done."

"Oh, you know these young people," Mrs. Drummond said, flapping her hands. "They have their own way of doing things. They'll settle down eventually. Besides, she was very pale. I do believe she might be coming down with something. I tried to send for a doctor, but Maryanne insisted that I leave her to rest."

"She's still seeing Lucas Callan?" Jonathan asked.

"Of course she's still seeing him," Drummond said, his brow lowering. "They have a serious relationship, Harker. We expect to be making an announcement any day now."

"Well, it's just that..." Jonathan looked at Mina and they traded a worried glance. "We've heard some worrisome reports about that young man. He's been seen escorting several young women around town recently —"

"Harker, I've warned your wife, and now I'm telling you. Watch what you say. Lucas Callan will soon join our family. I will not tolerate any slanderous rumors. Don't repeat them, don't bring them to me, and stay out of our family affairs. Good day."

The Drummonds both stalked away in a huff. Arthur

Holmwood sauntered up to them.

"My goodness. What put their noses out of joint so badly?" he asked.

"Maryanne is ill," Mina said softly.

Arthur sighed. "And Lucas is still their golden goose."

"They think he's going to be their son-in-law," Jonathan said with a derisive snort. "They don't realize they've let a viper into the hen house."

"I can put a couple of good men on their house. I've got some operatives who can be discreet. Let's see what happens over the next few days. If she's taken to her bed, it won't be long now. We need to know if he makes his move on the family."

Mina nodded and hugged Jonathan's arm. "You tried, Jonathan. We both have. We can't do more than that. We can't make them listen."

At that moment, a dark cloud covered the sun and the first drops of rain splashed Mina's upturned face.

~~~

It was only two days later when disaster hit. Mina sat in the study going over some Scriptures that Father Gallagher had slipped into her hand in clinic that day. She scribbled her thoughts in her notebook and paused to listen for guidance, as she had been learning to do lately.

The front door opened and closed. Mina frowned as she looked up at the clock. She reached into the drawer for a silver dagger she kept nearby. She had them scattered all over the house now. Too early for Jonathan. Who had walked into her home? She frowned as she half rose from her seat.

Jonathan stepped into the study. She sank back down into her seat with a sigh.

"Jonathan! You gave me such a start." She slipped the dagger back into the drawer. "What are you doing home so early?" Then she took a second look at his gaunt face. He looked positively gray. "What is it? What has happened?" She hurried around the desk to grasp his arm and walk with him to the small divan.

"Maryanne is … missing." His words were stiff.

"Missing? What do you mean? Missing?"

"She's gone. No note, no explanation. She's been ill for days. Today they went to her room to check on her. Her nurse was asleep, and Maryanne was gone without a trace. Her clothes are still there.
~~~

No luggage is missing, her jewelry is all still where she left it. Nothing else was taken. They think she was abducted. But they can't find Lucas Callan either."

"Surprise," Mina grumbled.

"Drummond sent me home. Now he wants to take us seriously. He's sending someone from Scotland Yard over to interview us. They're going to want to know everything we know about Lucas Callan. Mina, what are we going to tell them? How much can we tell them? Obviously, we can't tell them that he's a vampire and he's over a hundred years old."

Mina sighed. "How soon will that inspector be here?"

"I don't know. Knowing Drummond, it could be any time. He's furious. Mrs. Drummond is almost hoping that they've eloped. But she and Maryanne had been talking wedding dresses. From the sound of it, this was something they didn't think she would walk away from. It was going to be the event of the year." His head drooped, and he rubbed his eyes with a weary hand. "I should have pressed the issue. Should have shown him those reports before that monster took his only daughter. Now —"

"It wouldn't have made any difference, Jonathan," Mina said, embracing his shoulders. "You cannot make people see what they don't want to believe. Right now, the question is whether or not he has turned her. If he hasn't, maybe there's still time to get her back. But with an inspector on the way, I can't exactly go out looking for her." She bit her lip. "Do you think I can get to the professor and back before they arrive?"

"Perhaps," he said, looking up at her warily. "But why?"

"Well, I could get Van Helsing and the nuns to start watching the streets for Maryanne. They can get word to Arthur, too." Mina's mental gears were turning now, and she frowned in concentration. "And I think we might need a few of those reports in his files. But I'll need to choose them carefully. They can't contain any reference to his real identity or his purpose."

"How are we going to justify having those reports?" Jonathan asked. "It's going to look strange if we're shadowing Maryanne Drummond's fiancé, Mina."

"Betsy. We were concerned about the man who was dallying with our maid when we also saw him with Maryanne. We had a friend who followed him a few times, took a few notes, and let us know who he was seen with. Nothing more. Just enough to let us know this was a man of questionable character."

She kissed Jonathan and readied herself for a quick trip to the professor's lab. She made sure she had a dagger up each sleeve, and a crucifix in her coat pocket. Even the pin that held her hat in place was made of pure silver. Mina took no chances these days.

For the first time, she could honestly be thankful that Betsy was not here to be grilled by the police about her connection to Lucas Callan. She would have been mortified and further shamed by her own gullibility.

Mina slipped out the back door and hurried to the professor's house. It was relatively easy to pull several pages from Arthur's thick dossier and slip them into a worn file folder for use as a makeshift report from an "informant."

"As for looking for this Maryanne," Van Helsing shook his head sadly, "we can try, *mein liebling*, but I am afraid we will be too late. If he has taken her from her father's house, I fear he has turned her — or will turn her tonight."

"But if we could find her before nightfall—"

"Where do you suggest we look?" He laughed mirthlessly. "In all of London, do you have any idea where this man keeps his lair? We have only a few hours of daylight."

"We have to at least try!" Mina insisted. "I would search the city myself, but I have to get back to Jonathan. Please, Professor. Promise me you'll at least try."

"Yes, of course, I'll try. But you must not expect too much, Mina. It will be like finding the needle in the haystack. *Ja?*"

She scurried back through the streets to her own kitchen door. Mrs. Hardman unbolted the door and she slipped in.

"Oh, thank goodness, Mrs. Harker! That inspector just showed up. We made up a bit of housekeeping down here, and hoped you'd slip back in without him knowing you weren't in the house. Here, slip out of your coat and hat." She helped Mina shed her outerwear and her battle gear. Mina smoothed her hair and calmed her breathing.

"Where are they?"

"In the study."

"Bring tea into the parlor."

"The—?"

"Yes, the parlor. I'll suggest it and tell them that you are serving our tea there. Once we've moved, I want you to slip into the study and leave this file on the desk under some of my papers. Under them, mind you. If the inspector comes back to the room with me, for any reason, I don't want him to notice that something is there that wasn't there before."

Mina smoothed her skirt with both hands and pasted a smile on her face before heading to the study to greet the inspector.

~~~

The interview went better than Mina had hoped. The inspector was dubious at first as to why they would take such pains over a "mere maid," but their genuine affection for Betsy soon became apparent. They told him only as much as they could say from their limited encounters with the man. He appeared to be a womanizer, a scoundrel who used women for his own purposes, then abandoned them or killed them. They couldn't prove he had killed Betsy, but she had been found exactly where Mina had first seen him "wooing" Betsy. (They left out the part where he bit her and drank her blood, requiring her to have multiple transfusions.) The inspector had promised to look into the police reports from the night of the attack. Under the circumstances, this Lucas Callan did indeed look like a person of interest in Betsy's death, as abduction figured in both cases. It didn't bode well for Maryanne. He took their file and left them with a final tip of his derby hat.

They closed and locked the door behind him.

"I've got dinner ready," Mrs. Hardman said, coming into the hallway. "I'll clear the tea from the parlor and give you a few minutes, but then you really must eat something. You can't keep up this pace you're going at without decent meals in your stomachs."

Jonathan grinned over the top of Mina's head, as she buried herself into his vest, arms around his waist. "Whatever would we do without you, Mrs. Hardman?"

"You'd dry up and blow away, Mr. Harker, no doubt," she said with a wry smile, as she bustled from the room.

"I'm not very hungry," Mina mumbled.

"Mrs. Hardman will scold us both if we don't eat," Jonathan whispered. "Remember the blue war paint."

Mina burst into giggles. "Mrs. Hardman standing over us with a battle ax?"

"Aye. Eat yer veggies, else I'll be cleavin' yer head from yer boody." Jonathan tried for a Scottish accent and failed miserably.

Mina laughed harder. "I'll eat. I'll eat."
~~~

They walked to the dining room, their arms still wrapped around one another. Mrs. Hardman's fresh bread awakened Mina's taste buds, and she found she had an appetite after all. Delicately roasted chicken with asparagus tips and summer squash in herbs and butter made up a delightful dinner for the two of them, and they enjoyed every bite. Mina had just swallowed another bite of the fresh bread when someone pounded on the front door. She froze.

Jonathan rose, a frown etched on his handsome face. Mina reached toward the windowsill and found the silver dagger lying on the ledge. Then she heard a familiar voice in the foyer. Father Gallagher strode into the dining room before she was even halfway across the room.

"You're needed at the clinic immediately." His face was haggard in the dimly lit dining room, and every fiber of his body tensed. Mina braced herself.

"What happened?"

"Sister Anne Marie was attacked tonight. Sister Joan Phillippe asked me to come for you. We need all the help we can muster."

"Sister Anne Marie?" Mina felt her knees go weak. "She was looking for Maryanne, wasn't she?"

Father Gallagher grimaced. "Yes, but this is not your fault. Besides, Sister Anne Marie is asking for you. She won't calm down. Sister Joan was most insistent that I ask you to come right away."

"I'm coming with you," Jonathan said. He pulled a pistol from the cabinet in the corner and checked the ammunition, grabbing a handful of extra bullets and cramming them into his trouser pocket. He shoved the gun into a coat pocket and grabbed Mina's coat from Mrs. Hardman to hold for her.

"Be careful out there," Mrs. Hardman said, her voice thick with concern.

"Lock the doors behind us, and don't open them for anyone you don't know," Jonathan instructed.

Father Gallagher sighed. He looked like he wanted to argue, but knew it would be a waste of precious time.

"Come. We have to hurry."

Screams filled the night as they stepped out into the street. Two blocks away, they found a woman who sold flowers on the corner. She lay crumpled on the curb, clutching her throat and crying. Her grey hair hung in disheveled strings around her wrinkled face, and she stared up at Mina through glazed eyes.

"Don' hurt me, Miss…. Please…"

"We're not going to hurt you," she said soothingly. "We're going to take you somewhere safe." She gathered the elderly woman in her arms and held her close, feeling bird-like bones beneath layers of clothing that was clean but worn thin.

Father Gallagher quickly anointed the bite marks with holy water, which elicited a moan from the old woman, then Mina pressed her handkerchief to the woman's neck and they hoisted her to her feet. They hurried her along, as she stumbled to keep up with them. Mina and Jonathan held her up between them, almost carrying her in their haste. They could not protect her out here in the open street. They needed to get her to the protection of the church.

Only a few blocks later, they stumbled over a ginger-haired lad of about ten. He was barely coherent, as he lay among scattered newspapers. Father Gallagher once again treated the wounds on his neck, then he tossed the lad over his shoulder, and they pressed onward.

"We have to make it to the church," he said through gritted teeth. "It's Holy Ground, consecrated. It's the only place where these people will be safe."

They were within sight of the steeple when they spotted the third and fourth victims. The little girl sat on her mother's lap, weakly patting her cheeks and begging her to wake up. Both bore the marks of the vampire's bite.

"Take him," Father Gallagher said brusquely. He lowered the boy from his shoulders and Jonathan took his weight easily in his own arms. Mina lowered the old woman to the curb, but the woman clutched her skirts with trembling fists. The priest knelt and coaxed the little girl away from her mother. He lifted her into Mina's waiting arms, then examined the mother. "She's in bad shape. But we can't leave her here."

"Indeed, we can't."

Jonathan's gun came up in a flash. Thankfully, they all recognized Van Helsing and relaxed. They each took a victim and managed to stumble the last two blocks to the doors of the massive church. With a sigh of relief, they made their way to the clinic.

"*Mon Dieu!* You were supposed to come help me, not bring me more charges," admonished Sister Joan.

"Yes, well… it's such a lovely evening for a stroll. The more the merrier, isn't that right?" Mina's words fell flat. "I'm sorry, Sister. It's been a terrible day. I shouldn't even attempt humor at this point."

"We'll get them settled." She motioned for Sister Gertrude and three other nuns to step forward and help with the injured people. Then she grasped Mina by the elbow and propelled her down the hallway toward the nun's quarters. "I need you back here, Mina. Sister Anne Marie wants to speak to you." She ushered Mina to the sparse quarters the nuns used.

Mina gasped. Stripped to her shift, Sister Anne Marie looked like a tiny waif, her brown hair cut short as a boy. Her body was rail thin without the layers of clothing she normally wore. But it was her neck that shocked Mina the most. This was not a bite mark! Her throat had been viciously ripped, and she had bled copious amounts already.

She fell to her knees beside the nun's bed and grasped her hand, willing some of her strength into the girl. *No, God! Not another one!* Her heart cried out in pain.

"You… came…"

"Of course, I came. I came as quickly as I could. Your … uh, friend," she nodded toward the wound on Sister Anne Marie's neck, "left us a few other gifts along the way. We had to bring them along with us."

"Oh, no! No! She is … moving … too fast." Sister Anne Marie became agitated, but her words came out in gasps.

"She? Who?" Mina asked. Her heart was in her throat. "Is it Maryanne? Sister, did you find Maryanne Drummond?"

"Yes… I fear … she… is lost. But… the other one… helped her … to do these wicked things." Sister Anne Marie gripped Mina's hand frantically. She wheezed as the words came harder and harder. "We've … been… betrayed…"

"Who? Sister, what do you mean? Who betrayed us?" Mina could feel the Sister's life slipping away through her fingers. The hands clinging to her own slackened.

"One … of … us…" The hand fell. Sister Anne Marie's eyes stared lifelessly at the ceiling.

Sister Joan reached down and gently closed the girl's eyes with her fingertips. "Rest safely, little warrior. Your battle is finished."

"What did she mean, Sister Joan?" Mina whispered. "One of us?"

"I don't know, Mina. I don't know. I cannot believe that anyone in this Holy Order would betray their vows or would do anything to endanger the people beneath this roof. But that does seem to be what our sweet Sister was saying. We must be on guard."

Father Gallagher entered the cubicle. "How is sh—?" He stopped in his tracks and crossed himself. He sighed and pulled his stole and his rosary out and began the last rites. Mina listened, but her mind still sifted through the ramifications of what she had just heard.

Someone within our own ranks? Who among them? And if they began to look at one another with distrustful eyes, how long would they be able to stand in this battle for the people of London?

She rose stiffly from the floor and stepped away from the bed, whispering 'amen' with Father Gallagher and Sister Joan Phillippe. Sister Gertrude slipped into the room and saw Sister Joan folding Sister Anne Marie's arms across her chest.

"No! She cannot be dead!" Her outburst made Father Gallagher frown, but Sister Joan simply put motherly arms around the girl and led her from the room to counsel her privately.

"These girls are so young," Mina said. "They go to a convent, expecting to give a life of service to God and to die in their beds of old age. Is it any wonder they fall apart when confronted with evil of this magnitude?"

"Perhaps," he said thoughtfully. "They do seem to get younger and younger all the time, don't they?"

"I want to help with those people we brought in tonight," Mina said. She smiled sadly as some of the older nuns moved past her to tend to Sister Anne Marie's body. These were the women she had been working with for several months. Sister Julienne, Sister Annabeth, Sister Bernadette, and Sister Mary Margaret. They would wash the body and prepare it for burial.

Father Gallagher led her down the hallway to the clinic area.

"Where is Jonathan?" she asked as she kept pace with the priest.

"At the moment, he's staying pretty close to the young lad we brought in. Once we got him into the light, your husband recognized him as the boy he buys his newspaper from every day. He felt badly that he didn't see it sooner." Father Gallagher shrugged. "Dark streets, tension of the moment, not much wonder. But he seems to be taking it hard. I think it just hits too close to home. Again." He shook his head.

"I need to know, Mina. Is your husband going to be able to handle himself if things go downhill fast? Or will he fall to pieces and panic?" He stopped and stared into her eyes for a moment, worry creasing his forehead. "Can we count on him?"

"Yes," Mina said calmly. "Jonathan will do whatever needs to be done."

He gauged her answer for another moment, then nodded and resumed their walk through the old church building. They checked on the women first. The old flower lady was resting comfortably, her skin pale against the pillow beneath her cheek. Sister Martina, a young novice who had grown up with a dozen brothers and sisters, rocked the little girl in her arms and hummed softly as the child's sobs softened into hiccups. The mother was going to be touch and go.

"If she can make it through the night, we might have a fighting chance." The Professor stepped up behind them, wiping his hands on a towel. "The damage is significant. Even if we can replace the blood she has lost, I am not certain we can reverse the damage done to her." He looked back to the room where the mother lay, fighting for her life. He shook his head sadly. "Her life is not in my hands this night." He returned to watch over his patient.

Mina thought back to the room where the little girl lay curled in Sister Martina's arms, her hair a tangled mass of golden ringlets. So precious, so innocent. Was she to be an orphan now because of one vindictive vampire?

"You can't think about the child right now." Father Gallagher's voice brought her back to the present. "Focus on the battle before you. Don't be distracted."

She nodded.

Heels clicked angrily against the stone floors and Father Gallagher groaned. "God, please, not now. Please not now."

Mina knew the sound too and winced before she turned to face an angry Father Matthew.

"Mrs. Harker. I know we are supposed to be grateful for the fact that you graciously bestow so much of your precious time upon our lowly ministry here." His tone reeked of disdain, and Mina braced herself. "But I would remind you that I am not your personal lackey, and I do not appreciate being treated as such."

Jonathan came to join her in the hallway. Sister Joan Phillippe also bustled toward the commotion.

"Father Matthew, I really must protest," she hissed. Her voice was low but expressed her anger impressively. "This is a hospital, and we've just received four new patients tonight who are critical.

One might not make it through the night. If you wish to throw a fit, please do it elsewhere. It is not appropriate to do it here."

Father Matthew's jaw dropped open. "I beg your pardon?"

"As well you should," she snapped. "Furthermore, we've suffered a sudden death among the sisters and are mourning tonight. This is highly insensitive of you. So please lower your voice or take yourself back upstairs. If you wish to remonstrate me tomorrow, I will receive your discipline with a humble spirit. Upstairs. Away from the patients and the body of our dearly departed sister."

"Do you wish me to perform last rites, Sister Joan Phillippe?" he asked stiffly.

"Father Gallagher has already done so," she said. "But thank you for offering. Now if you have nothing else?"

"Mrs. Harker has a visitor who insists she come upstairs," he said, glaring daggers at Mina.

"A visitor? No one knows I'm—" She looked at Father Gallagher, then at Jonathan, and Sister Joan. Father Matthew turned and stalked back down the hallway, fury in every step.

"It's a trap," said Jonathan. "You can't go up there alone."

"But nothing can attack me inside the church, right?" She looked to Father Gallagher and Sister Joan for confirmation. They did not appear to be very reassuring.

Van Helsing was the one to say it first. "We all go up. Whatever this is, we face it together. *Ja?* Strength in numbers."

"And armed," Father Gallagher said grimly, slipping aside the slit in his robe to reveal the hilt of his sword. Mina had daggers up both sleeves. Jonathan had his gun, loaded and ready in his pocket. Sister Joan smiled and said she was prepared.

They headed for the church. Before they reached the sanctuary, they could hear raised voices. Father Matthew was trying to reason with a woman, but she screamed and railed at him.

"I told her you were here. They are very busy in the hospital tonight. You might have to wait for a bit. You could at least come in and sit down like a civilized young lady." Father Matthew's tone was not the least bit inviting, and Mina couldn't help feeling like she would rather wait in the foyer herself with an invitation like that.

"I'm not setting foot in there!" The voice shrieked. "I want to see her now!"

"Young woman, I am not the footman here. You cannot order me about. Now either come in and sit down or you can stand here by yourself and wait." Father Matthew almost turned his back on her.

Mina arrived just in time. "No!" she cried. Father Gallagher leapt forward and grabbed the older priest by the arm, propelling him safely into the confines of the sanctuary. Sister Joan scurried between the priests and the girl with her crucifix held high.

"What are you doing? Father Gallagher, let go of me. What…? Sister Joan, what is this?" He stared as the young visitor hissed at the crucifix, then laughed. It was a sound tinged with insanity.

Jonathan coaxed the older man into stepping back a few more steps. "Please, Father, let us handle this. I think you'll understand soon enough."

"Maryanne." Mina stepped forward cautiously. "I'm glad to see you. We've been worried about you."

"So. I. Hear." Maryanne's voice is scathing. "I go away with Lucas for two days and when I return, all of London is in an uproar. You've been lying about my Lucas, filling my parents' heads with crazy notions that he's been seeing other women. Well, no one is keeping me away from the man I love, Mrs. Harker. Not two stuffy old aristocrats from an era that's best forgotten, and certainly not some religious nut." As she spoke, she had inched toward Mina with menace in every step.

Father Gallagher spoke quietly. "Miss Drummond, we can help you. As we've helped many others here just like you."

"I don't need your help!" Maryanne exploded. She slammed a fist into Father Gallagher's chest, and he fell backward against the nearest pew. She hissed and, as she did, her fangs grew until they extended over her lips in long, curved arcs. Mina dipped both hands in the fount of holy water and splashed it liberally at Maryanne. It caught her full in the face and sizzled, as her face burned. She lashed out with elongated claws, but she missed. Maryanne turned to dash for the door just as it opened.

"Maryanne! What in God's name!"

Mr. Drummond and Arthur Holmwood stood in the doorway, staring in shock.

"I want no part of your God! Lucas is my only god!" She shrieked again and Arthur drew his pistol as she bared her fangs at her father. Drummond grabbed Arthur's gun hand.

"No, man, don't!"

But Maryanne was focused on her father. She knocked Arthur

aside and his body slammed against the edge of the open door. His pistol slid across the floor, and he scrambled to retrieve it.

Mina tackled the girl just as she leapt forward, her arms outstretched to grasp her father's shoulders. She rammed the silver dagger into Maryanne's back, straight through to her heart. Maryanne's head tilted back and an inhuman scream ripped from her throat as she turned to dust, leaving her handprints on her father's coat.

Drummond fell to his knees in shock. Arthur heaved himself to the old man's side.

"It's over now, sir. Come, sit down." Between Arthur and Jonathan, they managed to get Mr. Drummond to a pew.

"I think I'd better send for tea," Sister Joan said softly.

"I think we're going to need something stronger than tea tonight," Father Gallagher muttered, nodding to the elderly Father Matthew.

"What just happened here?" the old priest asked.

They spent the next half hour explaining about the people in the clinic, and finally showing Mr. Drummond his daughter's handiwork.

"The newsboy I took care of tonight, Danny, said that a lady bit him, not a man," Jonathan said. "I'm so sorry, James. I had hoped that Lucas was responsible for all this, but we believe it was Maryanne this time. Tonight was her first night as a vampire. She was supposed to draw us out. And she succeeded. We followed the trail of her victims all the way to the church."

"This still doesn't feel right," Father Gallagher said. "If it was a trap, was Maryanne the bait? Or did he think she could come in here and take us all out?"

"It doesn't feel like it's finished, does it?" Mina asked, shifting uncomfortably.

"Who is this Lucas Callan?" Drummond asked. Father Gallagher had pulled out the wine and it was beginning to take effect. Van Helsing took over and explained the origins of Lucas Callan or Frederick Von Bardenburg, all the while watching for signs that Drummond would call them all crazy and bolt from the room.

"I'm so sorry about Maryanne," Mina finally said softly, reaching out to touch his coat sleeve softly. "I truly had no choice. She would have killed you, Mr. Drummond. I couldn't stand by and allow that to happen."

"No, Mrs. Harker, it's I who owe you an apology. You see, it was Maryanne who pitted us against you in the first place. As I've been sitting here listening to everything you people have been saying, I realized that Dorothea never gave you a second thought until Lucas started suggesting to Maryanne that she and her mother should involve you in more of their activities. That you were stuck in your boring routines and needed some more stimulating company to occupy your time. That man led us around by the nose, and we let him. I'm the one who is sorry. You tried to warn us, and we didn't heed your words. Now our daughter is gone."

"What are you going to tell your wife, James?" Arthur asked quietly.

"I really don't know," the old man said. Mina thought he had aged ten years just sitting in this pew.

"The truth can never be told to the general public. There would be widespread panic." Arthur's voice was gentle. "There is no body, James. We can say whatever you want us to say. You tell us the version you wish to be told, and we will stick to it faithfully. We can always say she ran away."

"And this is how you lost your Lucy? Miss Westenra?" he asked without raising his head.

"Yes, it is."

"It wasn't a fever?"

"No, Dracula turned her. When she rose from her grave and tried to feed, we—" Arthur faltered.

"We were forced to do much as Mrs. Harker did tonight," Van Helsing stepped in.

"Arthur tells me you killed the man who did this to his Lucy, Mrs. Harker," Drummond said to Mina, finally raising his eyes above his glass.

"Yes, I did," she said. "I had a lot of help."

"Please. Kill this one too." His voice broke as his eyes filled with tears.

"If we have our way, he'll be dust before long, Mr. Drummond." Father Gallagher's voice was grim.

"That's murder, Michael!" Father Matthew exclaimed, rousing from his bewildered state.

"These are not human beings, Father Matthew," Gallagher explained. "They aren't living men or women. They are undead. They are Nosferatu, creatures of the night. Yes, they can navigate by day, but they thrive in the night. They feed off the living, drinking the blood of the innocent. We are not killing people. We are destroying monsters. There is a vast difference."

"We cannot murder. Can they not be saved?" the old man muttered.

"Father Matthew, did you not hear Maryanne tonight? She disavowed God." Mina tried to keep her voice soft and respectful. Father Matthew had suffered a shock that few could withstand. It would not do to challenge him too far.

Then they heard a series of screams from just outside the church.

"It's not over," Mina whispered. "I think that's the signal for the next round."

CHAPTER 27

"Father Matthew, it would be best if you remain inside," Van Helsing said. The elderly man bristled, and the professor raised a placating hand. "I am not dictating to you, mind you. I am simply suggesting that it is in the interest of your personal safety that you should remain inside the sanctuary. As should you, Mr. Drummond."

"Lord Holmwood, are you by any chance armed with silver bullets tonight?" Father Gallagher asked. He drew his sword from beneath his robe, and Father Matthew's jaw dropped in alarm.

"As a matter of fact, I am," Arthur said with a tilted eyebrow. "I've been loaded and ready for the past several weeks."

"As am I," added Jonathan, pulling his pistol and checking it carefully. Mina opened her mouth to ask him to remain behind in the sanctuary, then closed her lips abruptly. She would not do that. Jonathan had as much at stake here as everyone else, and as much right to fight for those he loved. She would not hold him back any more than she had wanted to be held back and caged by him. She owed him that respect, even though it frightened her to think of his life being in danger.

"We'll have a better chance if we fan out and surround him, but the guns need to stay in one place. If you start firing across all of us, you could hit someone you don't intend to. And if we know where to expect your line of fire, we can anticipate it and avoid getting in your way. So stay fairly near the church door. Incidentally, you are also the last line of defense for the people inside this building. He shouldn't be able to come inside, but just in case we're wrong… let's err on the side of caution. After all, he's very old." Father Gallagher's words were brisk, but calm enough to instill them with confidence.

Like a general before a battle, Mina thought.

"Mina, you might find this more useful than those daggers." Sister Joan Phillippe handed her a double-edged silver sword with a hilt perfectly sized for a woman's smaller hand. "You can keep a little more distance between this man and your own body. Don't let him draw you in too close, child. He's far too dangerous."

Mina held the sword up in one hand. The weight was perfectly balanced, and when she practiced a few moves to get the feel of it, she felt like the blade became an extension of her own arm. "How exquisite, Sister Joan. We must discuss where you got this and how I can obtain one later."

"Yes, later." Sister Joan smiled grimly. "First survive this battle, Mina Harker." She murmured a quick blessing over Mina. "I'm afraid my hands are not as strong as they used to be. I'll try to keep Father Matthew out of the way," she whispered when she drew near for a quick hug. "Go with God," she said to them all.

Father Matthew called out as they strode toward the door. "I really must protest this violence. If someone out there is in trouble, we should notify the constables. Or wait within the church. I'm sure the local police are already on their way here. There is no need to go out there with swords and guns!"

"Please, Father, trust us just this one night. We have dealt with this type of problem before."

Mina didn't hear the rest of Sister Joan's comments, but she knew that it would likely do very little good. Father Matthew had made up his mind that they were all crackpots. The ministry here was in God's hands now. And this could well be their last stand tonight.

Well, Lord, I'm stepping out in faith here. Did You really raise me up to fight these monsters in Your name? Or am I as crazy as Father Matthew thinks I am?

She and Father Gallagher moved out to the left and the right respectively while Arthur and Jonathan took position in front of the church door. Lucas Callan stood about fifteen feet away with a buxom young woman in his arms. He held her facing forward, and her expression was a mask of terror. Her brown eyes brimmed with tears, her thin painted lips trembled. Her clothing suggested she had been plying her "trade" on one of the many street corners down by the docks, and her hair hung in long, loose curls. Lucas brushed it back to one side to give himself a generous advantage, should he wish to dig a fang into her veins before their eyes.

"Let the girl go," Father Gallagher ordered.

"Give me Maryanne, and I might consider it." Lucas flashed his fangs and the girl shrieked in terror.

"Help me! Father, don't let 'im hurt me! Please, God! Don' let me die like this—"

"Shut up!" Lucas growled at her. "I want Maryanne. I know she came here. To see you, Mrs. Harker, though I told her it wasn't necessary." He grinned in her direction.

"You can't have her, Callan!"

Mina hadn't realized the door to the church was still open until she heard Drummond's voice from the doorway. Her heart sank. This would go so much better without the angry father getting into the mix. She didn't dare take her eyes from Lucas for a moment. She watched his every move, gauged his reactions, every blink of his eyes.

"You'll never have her now. She's dead, and it's all because of you." Drummond's voice was laced with grief, but it carried a savage war cry as well. The old lawyer was throwing down the gauntlet.

"She can't die, old man," Lucas laughed. "Not now. I made her mine. She's going to live forever. None of you can touch her. So you might as well let her come out to me. We belong together."

Drummond's voice exploded into the darkness of the city street. "She's *ash*!"

"What?" Lucas blinked. He stared at the old man.

Mina heard Sister Joan urging Mr. Drummond away, then she heard the sound of the heavy wooden door as it closed and locked. Lucas began to shake with rage.

"Noooooo!" His howl burst from his chest, then in one swift move, his hands twisted the girl's neck and she fell into a lifeless heap at his feet.

"She was mine. Which one of you pitiful humans took it upon yourself to touch my property?" His chest heaved. He watched Father Gallagher and Mina step off on opposite sides, saw them grip their swords, ready at any moment for the first lunge. He observed the two men still standing at the doorway with pistols aimed at him, and he laughed. It was a vile, wicked sound, a contemptuous dare. "You truly think you stand a chance against me? You have no idea who you are up against."

Mina shrugged. "I killed your maker. I think my odds are pretty good. I've been practicing since then."

"You don't know who my maker is," he sneered. "In fact, my dear Mrs. Harker, you have no idea who I really am." He laughed jeeringly at her, tossing his blond curls.

Mina tilted her head. "Really? Why, you're Frederick Von

Bardenburg, and you were created by Count Dracula. Do I win any prizes yet?"

"How did you—?" He drew himself up stiffly. "Then you are saying that *you* killed Lord Dracula? That's impossible!"

"Can't blame a girl for trying," she shrugged again, her eyes narrowing. "But I am telling the truth. I guess you'll have to learn the hard way."

"You whore!"

"Now!" Father Gallagher shouted. Jonathan and Arthur fired their weapons. Lucas bent his body backwards at an impossible angle and the bullets whistled past him as he twisted and spun in Father Gallagher's direction. The priest's blade slid beneath the vampire's arm, missing his body, but he brought the pommel up sharply to rap Lucas in the throat, snapping his neck back. The vampire flipped and spun again, and this time he kicked Father Gallagher in the ribs. Mina heard the crack from a few feet away, where she was waiting for an opening. As Father Gallagher's body flew ten feet across the cobblestone street and slammed against the stone steps of the church, Mina lunged, her sword catching Lucas in the side, but her blade glanced off his ribs, sizzling flesh and scorching his clothes. Lucas dove into a roll and came up a few feet away. As he lunged forward, intent on attacking, Mina slid to the pavement and drove her sword upward at an angle to pierce up through his rib cage. As she did so, Jonathan and Arthur fired again.

Ash rained down upon her. She lay back on the pavement, stunned, still clutching Sister Joan's sword. Feet pounded on the pavement and Jonathan was beside her, lifting her gently to her feet.

"Mina! Are you all right?"

"Yes," she stammered, "Yes, Jonathan. But Father Gallagher was hurt."

Jonathan helped her to rise and dusted her off, then they hurried over to the church steps. Arthur was assisting Father Gallagher to his feet. The priest leaned heavily on him and was having a hard time catching his breath.

"I'd say you cracked a few ribs, Father," Mina said.

"Nonsense." He frowned. "Just a few bruises."

"Bruises don't snap," she said. "I foresee a few days in the clinic, but as a patient this time."

"Not bloody likely." He scowled. "Good work. All of you. I'm not sure whether it was the sword or the bullets, but you three did it."

Mina frowned. "I don't think it was me. I didn't feel any resistance against my sword at all."

The church door opened and Sister Joan Phillippe came out, followed by Mr. Drummond and finally by Father Matthew.

"He's dead?" Drummond asked.

"Yes," Arthur said. "You can rest easy now, James."

"Rest easy? My daughter is dead, Arthur. I doubt I'll ever rest easy again." The old man shook his head, then he allowed his gaze to flow over each of them. "But I thank you all."

"And what of this child?" Father Matthew said, scowling. "Who is responsible for this… this heinous crime?"

"That was the work of Lucas Callan," Mina said. "He was the one behind everything. He was the one who made a monster out of Mr. Drummond's daughter, Maryanne. He killed my maid, Betsy. He's killed no telling how many all over London. But he's gone now, Father. We can't bring back this poor girl, but we may have just saved dozens more just like her."

Sister Gertrude slipped out of the church and stood beside Sister Joan, her eyes wide as she listened to the conversation, which quickly grew more and more acrimonious.

"Young woman, I've had enough of your insolence! Gunfire outside my church. A woman lying dead on my doorstep. Another one that you knifed right inside the door. This is going to stop right now. These activities are going to stop. I demand it."

Mina stared at him in disbelief. "It can't stop, Father Matthew. Evil is out there. If we don't put a stop to it, who will? What do you think will stem this tide? Do you think a handy sermon will make it all go away? There comes a time when we have to stand up and fight for what is right. You can't just close your eyes to what's going on in this city and hope it passes you by! The clinic is full of the products of this war."

"Well, I'm beginning to think that the clinic needs to go elsewhere too," he said with a jerk of his chin.

"You can't be serious," Mina exclaimed.

Father Gallagher and Sister Joan Phillippe tried to intervene, but Mina and Father Matthew were toe-to-toe and head-to-head.

"This is my church, young lady, and I will not allow these activities on sacred ground."

"Really? I thought this was God's church, Father. Don't you

serve God? You might want to consult Him before you go throwing His true servants out of *His* church." Mina's anger rose.

"You are far too impudent! I've half a mind to excommunicate you!"

"Maybe you're the evil one, Father Matthew. If you're not part of the solution, maybe you're the problem. Before you start cutting people out of the church, you should consult with your own Boss. He might have something to say about that. See, we *did* consult with Him before this little soiree tonight."

"I want you out of my church!" Father Matthew bellowed.

Father Gallagher stepped between them, stumbling as his breathing hitched. "Please, let's just calm down here." He wheezed, and gasped, as the breath wouldn't quite reach from nasal passages to his lungs.

"Let me help you, Father." Sister Gertrude stepped toward him and gripped his left arm. With a sharp tug, she yanked with her left hand and rammed a knife into his ribs with her right hand. "Finally!" she screamed. "Revenge for all whom you have destroyed!"

Mina screamed, "Nooooo!" and reached for Father Gallagher as he fell.

Sister Gertrude turned to Father Matthew. "You, Father Matthew, you are a blind fool." Fangs sprang out as she lunged for the old man. Mina leapt for her and ran the sword into her heart. Sister Gertrude turned to dust and covered Father Matthew head to toe.

Jonathan and Arthur carried Father Gallagher to the clinic and settled him into a bed, stripping him down to his underwear. Sister Joan worked with Van Helsing to deal with his injuries until at last she could report that the bleeding was under control, his ribs were taped, and Father Gallagher was finally resting comfortably.

"She would have killed me," Father Matthew murmured. "Why would she do that?"

Mina sighed. "Sister Anne Marie's last words tonight were that someone in our midst had betrayed us. Evidently it was Sister Gertrude."

"But why would she do that?" the bewildered priest asked.

"Evil is alluring," Mina said with a shrug. "It's … tempting. If it was ugly, who would desire it? Evil offers us what we long for, whether it's recognition, love, power. The list is endless."

"I--I'm going to have to think about all of this, Mrs. Harker."

Father Matthew's voice shook almost as much as his hands.

"I suggest you pray about it too," Mina said gently. "You'll know what to do. Oh, and have a nice long talk with Sister Joan Phillippe. I think she might be able to help you sort out a few things, if you'll just listen to her with an open mind."

CHAPTER 28

Arthur gave Mr. Drummond and the Harkers a ride home in his carriage. The sky was beginning to lighten up at the very edge of the horizon. Mina had never felt so tired in her life, as she leaned against Jonathan's shoulder. They arrived at the Harker home first.

As they pulled to the curb, Mina's stomach went into free fall. The front door stood wide open and fresh blood spattered the door frame. She stumbled from the carriage, but Jonathan grabbed her arm. He and Arthur pulled their guns and checked ammunition quickly. Mr. Drummond almost sobbed.

"I thought it was over," he whimpered.

They entered the house cautiously. Lucas bent over the form of Mrs. Hardman, feasting on the last of her blood, but her lifeless eyes told Mina she was clearly beyond all earthly help.

"Oh, back a little earlier than I expected," Lucas said, rising with an arrogant grin. "No matter. Your housekeeper kept me well entertained in your absence." His smile widened, and exposed bloody fangs.

Cease from anger and sin not. Cease from anger and sin not. Mina kept repeating it, but the sight of Mrs. Hardman was too much. She felt the fury rising. Dear, kind Mrs. Hardman.

Jonathan pushed Mina behind his body, shielding her from the sight, as if he knew the gruesome visage was too much for her overloaded emotions right now.

"How are you still alive?" Jonathan sputtered. "We saw you go up in a cloud of ash." He still pointed his pistol at Lucas, as did Arthur.

"I learned this lovely little trick several decades ago. A magician taught it to me. It has come in handy several times, though he didn't use it to quite the same purposes as I do." Lucas laughed. "Watch closely." He reached into his pocket and pulled out a handful of ash. "Soot from the fireplace. I always keep bags of it around. Then when I need to make a hasty exit, I toss it up in the air, and voila!" He tossed the ash and it descended in lazy sprinkles. In the blink of an eye, he darted forward, grabbed Jonathan by the lapels and hurled himself up to the second-floor landing, as black soot rained down on their heads. Jonathan's gun went off, the bullet shattering Mina's china cabinet in the corner, as it fell from his hand and hit the floor.

"Jonathan!" Mina screamed.

Arthur cursed and fired off a shot. Lucas laughed. "Careful there, Lord Holmwood. Are you sure you can hit me without hitting your good friend? He's terribly frail, you know."

Mr. Drummond picked up Jonathan's gun and fumbled to reload it. "How many times do you have to kill these creatures before it takes?" he growled in frustration as he rammed another silver bullet from Arthur's stash into the chamber.

Mina's heart pounded so hard, she thought it would break her ribs. *No, Lord, please. Not Jonathan!* Fear held her immobile. For the first time, her training deserted her. She couldn't think, couldn't reason, couldn't plan. All she could do was watch and pray, and hope for a miracle.

Lucas held Jonathan in a headlock, cutting off his air. Jonathan clawed at the arm around his throat. His face turned red as he choked. Lucas glared at Mina, his blonde hair dusted with black soot, but his features twisted with hatred.

"I did not always get along with Dracula, Mrs. Harker, but I respected him. So this is for the Count." He extended his fangs and ripped Jonathan's throat open. Blood spurted, spraying Lucas, the walls, and the railings in bright crimson.

"Noooooooo!" shrieked Mina, as she collapsed in a heap. Her eyes filled with tears as Jonathan's last heartbeats ebbed away.

"And this is for my Maryanne!" He tossed Jonathan's body over the railing as Arthur and Drummond both fired their pistols. Jonathan's body hit the floor with a thud, and Mina's heart broke into pieces at the sound.

"You think bullets can hurt me? Me? I can't be killed by your silly pieces of lead." His laughter faltered. "Silver? Well, well... aren't you full of surprises."

With a growl, he vaulted over the railing and grabbed Arthur by the throat with his left hand. With his right hand, he punched Drummond in the chest so hard, the older man slammed into the wall and slid to the floor in a heap. Arthur tried to break his grip. The silver was working. Lucas weakened, but every time he faltered, he redoubled his efforts to choke the life from Arthur.

Mina pulled herself to her knees and slammed one of her daggers under Lucas' arm and into his heart. She felt it slide in this time. Felt it enter muscle. Lucas looked down at her in disbelief.

"I told you I killed Dracula," she cried. "And I've killed you too. I'll take down every blood-sucker that crosses my path. I'd tell you to warn them, but you don't even have time to say your prayers." She twisted the blade, and Lucas screamed just before he disintegrated into ash.

Mina released the dagger, which fell to the floor. Arthur staggered backwards, coughing and heaving air back into his lungs. Mina collapsed back to her hands and knees and crawled over to Jonathan's body. She cradled him in her lap and cried until she fell over in a heap of exhaustion and grief.

~~~

Arthur had Mina removed to his own estate and given rooms and servants to attend to her needs. She saw no one except Arthur and Professor Van Helsing for the first two weeks, with the brief exception of Jonathan's funeral. Then finally Sister Joan was allowed into her sanctuary. After her initial outburst of grief, Mina retreated into silence for a time.

"Too much loss in such a short amount of time," Sister Joan told Arthur. "Jonathan was her world. It will take time for her to get her bearings now. But she will come around. Just give her time."

Arthur had dealt with Jonathan's body and all of the necessary arrangements. Between himself and Mr. Drummond, they said that Jonathan fell down the stairs and broke his neck. Arthur had the house cleaned up and repaired, and everyone was paid to keep silent. Van Helsing was sent for to attest to the state of the body for the inquest. He stitched up the mess Lucas Callan had created, then said that he had performed a type of autopsy to determine just how badly the neck was damaged by opening Jonathan up and looking at the condition of the spine. He came under some heavy criticism for what was considered butchery, but in the end, the story was accepted, and the case closed. Accidental death.

It was over.

~~~

Mina sat in Arthur's parlor. She was still very pale, and appeared more so, dressed in black from head to toe. Mrs. Drummond, too, wore black silk, and sipped tea from Arthur's best china.

"You know, you were so right, Mrs. Harker. I'm sorry we didn't take you more seriously. That wastrel has enticed our dear Maryanne away and God only knows when we 'll see her again." She sighed wistfully. "It's almost like losing her, though at least we know she's still out there somewhere. But it's just so terrible to not be able to see her, you understand? If we could just write to her, or send the occasional telegram, anything to let her know we still love her."

Mina nursed her tea and listened to Mrs. Drummond rattle on endlessly. Mr. Drummond stood by the window, distracted and withdrawn. Mina felt sorry for the old man. He'd aged twenty years since the night Jonathan died. The wrinkles across his jowls were far more pronounced, and he rarely smiled anymore.

"He just hasn't been himself since the night she ran away," Mrs. Drummond whispered. "I'm at my wit's end to know what to do to pull him out of it."

She rose and wandered over to the window to coax her husband with another cup of tea and a biscuit. She patted his arm gently.

Arthur came in and sat beside Mina. "How are you holding up?"

Mina sighed. "Are you sure we shouldn't try to tell her some version of the truth? How can he stand this? She goes on and on about Maryanne. It's almost unbearable."

Arthur took a sip of tea. "What version could he possibly contrive that would satisfy the thousands of questions she would come up with? No, it's better this way. But I agree with you. It's going to be hell for the poor man for the rest of his life."

"I don't know how he manages." She shook her head.

"Well, I happen to know he's getting a little help." Arthur smirked as he took another sip of tea.

"What?" asked Mina, her eyes widening. She dug an elbow into Arthur's ribs. "Tell me quickly before she comes back over here!"

"He's going to church," Arthur whispered, "at Father Gallagher's parish. And rumor has it they've had some counseling sessions. Something about the basement?"

Mina faked a cough to cover her sudden laugh. "Well, something good did come out of this! But Father Gallagher isn't up to training sessions yet, is he?"

Arthur shrugged. "I hear Sister Joan is substituting for the moment, with verbal sessions at Father Gallagher's bedside afterwards."

"Oh, my goodness! Don't make me laugh, Arthur! Mrs.

Drummond will make a scandal of it all!" Mina wiped her eyes with a handkerchief and covered her lips to keep her smile from being seen.

Arthur's expression turned serious. "Do you really believe that God always brings something good out of tragedies, Mina? Truthfully?"

She looked at Arthur and felt a shared grief. They had both lost their true loves.

"Always."

CHAPTER 29

Mina gazed up at the church façade. It was the first time she had returned since that fateful night. As she took in the view from the steps of the church, she could not tell that they had fought a life-and-death battle right here on this very street. She took a deep breath, mounted the stone steps, and opened the heavy wooden door.

She paused in the sanctuary and looked up at the heavy wooden cross over the altar. Everything looked the same, but how could it be? Her own world had altered so drastically. Jonathan was dead. And she felt cut adrift from her moorings.

"Mrs. Harker! I'm so pleased to see you!" Father Matthew hurried toward her, his face wreathed in a smile. Even though she had learned of the priest's change of heart through Sister Joan, it was still disconcerting to see it for herself. But his smile was warm and engaging, and he took her right hand between both of his own hands, pressing gently, affectionately. Mina was touched by his sincerity.

"Here to visit Father Gallagher? He'll be so glad to see you. I'm afraid he's proving to be a most difficult patient," he confided, as they walked briskly through the hallways toward the clinic.

"I expected nothing less," Mina said with her first real laugh.

"Yes, he is something of a character, isn't he?" said Father Matthew with a chuckle. "But you know, I've grown quite fond of him. I do hope I'll be able to convince him to stay in our parish for a long time to come. This is such a troubled area, and we need someone like Father Gallagher."

Mina felt very much like she'd fallen into a familiar children's book. She wondered if the good Father would grow long ears and whiskers and mutter about being late. Or if she should watch out for Mad Hatters or crazy queens. This was certainly a change of heart for the elderly priest.

"Let me make sure he's … erm… appropriate for visitors," the good Father suggested. He slipped into the small cubicle, and she soon heard a familiar voice raised in cranky grumblings.

Father Matthew finally let her in. "He's in a mood today." He grimaced.

"Good morning, Father Gallagher. How are you feeling?"

His eyebrows rose. "Well, well, well, look who's here!"

"You must be feeling better. I could hear you all the way out in the hall." Mina laughed.

"Yeah, well, it's going to take more than one little jab with a needle to do me in," grumbled Father Gallagher.

Mina cocked an amused eyebrow. "Yes. Well, Lucas Callan managed to crack two ribs and bruise your spine in that little tussle. Then Sister Gertrude nicked your lung with her 'little needle.' I think you'd better rest. Besides, I've heard a nasty rumor that the Professor is threatening to install some old-fashioned restraints in here if you don't cooperate."

"If he thinks he can keep me tied to this bed…" Father Gallagher pushed himself up with both arms, gasped, and collapsed back on the bed. "… he's probably entirely correct."

Mina chuckled and shook her head. "Would you like to be propped up a bit more, Father? I can help with that, and it will hurt a lot less with assistance."

He groaned and nodded his assent. The nuns had provided several extra pillows for this purpose, and Mina eased them behind Father Gallagher's back until he was propped up a bit better.

"I've seen so many of these creatures over the years," Father Gallagher confessed to her when he was finally settled comfortably. "But I don't think I've ever seen one so thoroughly manipulative. I mean, the way he worked to influence the Drummonds against you, using his minion to track you all over town. Did Van Helsing ever come up with an identity on that one?"

"Not yet, but he's still working on it. Arthur put a couple of detectives on it too, but he seems to have disappeared. Maybe the death of his master scared him off." She tried to pull off a hopeful smile, but it fell short. Neither of them believed it.

"Unless Lucas wasn't really the master in this situation," Father Gallagher added grimly.

"Thanks," Mina said. "I feel so much better." She rubbed her eyes wearily. "I've wondered about that lately, truth be told. But I've tried to tell myself not to be paranoid. You're not helping my cause."

"You have to be prepared," Father Gallagher said softly. "I am so sorry about Jonathan, Mina. He was a good man. And he loved you very much."

Tears filled her eyes, but she brushed them away, nodding her acknowledgement. They sat in silence for a few minutes.

"What will you do now?" he asked gently.

"Stay here, at least until you're back on your feet. I can't leave Whitechapel defenseless, can I?" Mina smiled sadly. "After that, I really don't know. I guess I'll take it one day at a time until God opens a door and shoves me through it."

Father Gallagher chuckled. "Good plan."

"Father—" Mina faltered.

"Ask it," he said. "Whatever the question, it always deserves an answer. If I can, that is."

"Are we always going to lose? Don't we ever get to win a battle?" The anguish her heart was palpable. "We lost Betsy, even when we got her back. We lost Maryanne, and now her parents are bereft of their only daughter. And Jonathan..." Her voice broke. She recovered her control and looked to Father Gallagher for answers. "Won't we ever get to win?"

"Mina, we did win great victories," Father Gallagher said, his eyes wide. "Betsy's soul was saved from damnation. That was a huge victory. Heaven rejoices over her now, and you made that possible. You never gave up on her. You fought for her; you protected her."

Father Gallagher held up a finger for Betsy, then brought up another finger. "Two, we found a spy in our midst. Gertrude could have done untold damage. She was serving in the clinic. Sister Joan thinks she was releasing many of our patients to go back to Lucas or whoever bit them at night. It's how we were losing some of our patients. When she checked the records, our losses occurred on nights when Gertrude worked alone. Or when Gertrude worked, but we were short-staffed, and spread thin. She was taking a chance and slipping one or two out when the other nun's back was turned. Gertrude presented a continual danger to our community. She could have started turning the other sisters too."

Mina's blood chilled. "What if—"

"Sister Joan Phillippe has already checked every nun. She did find one novitiate who had been bitten. It looks like it was only once. Van Helsing is treating her for the physical effects. Sister Joan is counseling the girl to help her through the emotional trauma. She'll be all right with time." He smiled wryly. "She's in the right Order."

"Might I ask which one?" Mina said.

He hesitated only a moment. "It was Sister Martina, but don't let on that I told you. She's very sensitive about it. Sister Joan has taken her on as her new assistant, so you'll see her often. She's replacing Sister Anne Marie now. That way we can keep an eye on her."

"And it keeps her out of the clinic for the moment." Mina nodded. "Wise move." She remembered the young novitiate rocking the child in the nursery on that awful night, and shuddered.

He raised a third finger. "We got Father Matthew on our side. And Mina, that's a ruddy miracle!" They both laughed. "He's practically sharpening the stakes these days. Sister Joan is undertaking some of his more strenuous training at the moment, and he comes in here constantly with questions. We've had some highly entertaining discussions." Father Gallagher's grin widened. Mina laughed outright for the first time.

"I do hope you've been behaving yourself," she said with a hint of mischief.

"*Moi?*" He put on an innocent act for all of ten seconds then laughed, until his ribs reminded him that was not a good idea just yet. He winced and gripped his sides. "Ow, don't do that!" He took a couple of shallow breaths. His face sobered a bit and when he looked up, his expression held peace. "I told him about my past. Do you know that crusty, angry old priest sat here and cried? He wept, Mina. He wept for the little boy who endured that. He wept that he had never even asked about my arms or my hands, or about the things that drove me."

"Does he know about Sister Joan as well?" she asked.

"Yes. She told him. It's changed his whole life to know that these things have been happening right under his nose to people around him while he's been oblivious to it. He's down here in the clinic every day now. He listens to people. Really listens, Mina, and he tries to help where he can. Don't you see what a victory that is? Father Matthew was the greatest stumbling block to this ministry and now he is becoming our biggest asset."

Mina felt her heart begin to shift.

"But fourth, and most importantly of all—" Father Gallagher nailed Mina with his stare. "We defeated Frederick Von Bardenburg, one of the most devious and heinous vampires of the last 120 years. That was a major victory, Mina Harker, and don't you ever forget it. Battles are rarely won without casualties. That's a fact of warfare. Ask any general in any army or navy in the world. And I'm not making light of our casualties, because we have paid dearly, you most of all. But we have won major victories. And you must never forget that."

"It's hard to see past these losses, Father Gallagher," she said softly, twisting her handkerchief.

"You know, I bet the disciples felt exactly the same way," he said with a smile. "Jesus' cause looked defeated too. Death on the cross is a pretty final blow. But the greatest victory mankind will ever know happened that day. Jesus took our sins onto His own body and gave us a way into God's family, if we only accept and believe. For those few days, the world looked grim." He let her digest that for a moment. "You will always face moments like this, Mina. Remember, you have to look for the victories. See things from God's perspective. You might lose one battle, but that doesn't mean the war is over. Keep going, keep moving forward, keep searching. And count those victories. God does. He rejoices over Betsy. He's pleased with Father Matthew's change of heart. And I believe He's pleased we stopped three evil beings and saved those who would have been their future victims."

Father Gallagher's face was becoming gaunt. Sister Joan Phillippe entered the room with a cup in her hand.

"Right on time," he sighed.

"I thought you might be starting to need this, but I hated to interrupt," she said, smiling at them both. "It is so good to see you back here, Mina."

"Long overdue, I know," Mina admitted.

"Nonsense, my dear," Sister Joan said. "Grief is work too, and must not be ignored." She handed Father Gallagher the cup, which he drank down in one gulp, grimacing.

"Must all of your medicines taste bitter, Sister Joan?" he groused.

Her chuckle was low and warm. "Does it help you, Father Gallagher?"

"Yes, it definitely does do that," he sighed.

"Then thank the Lord for His providence."

Sister Joan began removing the excess pillows and shifting him back to a prone position. Mina quickly rose and began to help her from the opposite side of the bed. Between the two of them, he was quickly repositioned and comfortable, his eyelids drifting shut almost immediately.

"I wore you out today," she whispered. "I'm sorry, Father

Gallagher."

"No," he mumbled. "Good… to see… you. Must… come … back."

"I will," she promised, as she quietly adjusted his cover, then followed Sister Joan from the room.

"He's been so anxious to see you," Sister Joan said. "We've had to almost tie him to the bed to keep him from heading to Lord Holmwood's house to see you. He's been so worried ever since your husband's death."

"I won't stay away any longer," Mina promised.

"You needed time. That's understandable, child. But now you are needed. I'm glad you've come back to us."

They walked briskly to the clinic.

"What's been happening in my absence?" Mina asked.

"Well, the flower lady, Annie, is almost fully recovered, and she has asked for you several times," Sister Joan said with a smile. "The newsboy too." Her smile faded. "Though he asked for Mr. Harker. Danny was most distressed when we had to tell him about his death. It seems your husband was kind to him every day when he bought his paper, and the child remembered that, even in the midst of the terror of that night."

"I'll see him today too, if he's still here," Mina said.

Sister Joan smiled. "I was hoping you would."

They had almost reached the clinic, and Sister Joan had not continued. Mina flinched.

"Sister Joan, you have not mentioned the little girl and her mother yet."

"The child is well," Sister Joan said gently.

"But the mother is not." Mina's voice was flat.

"No. The damage was just too great. The professor tried to save her, but she was beyond our help." Sister Joan laid a sympathetic hand on Mina's arm. "Remember, Mina. You destroyed the man responsible for all this grief. He is gone from this world. Be thankful for that. And be thankful for the three who survived the ordeal."

"But that child will now grow up without her mother." Mina gritted her teeth and pursed her lips.

"Yes, without her mother." Sister Joan's smile returned. "But God does work in mysterious ways. And He works all things to the good." She motioned to the doorway they had paused beside. Mina frowned and peeked inside.

Arthur Holmwood sat in the rocking chair with the child on his lap, a large storybook open.

"Look! What a wonderful garden. Isn't that lovely? And Alice is so tiny! Can you imagine being that tiny among all those huge flowers?" His smile was wide and gentle. She hadn't seen him like this in years.

The child wore a new dress of powder blue and her hair was neatly brushed and held back with a blue bow. Mina's breath caught. *She looks like Lucy when she was a child!* The resemblance was uncanny.

"Do you know, Mary, there is a garden very much like this where I live? Would you like to see it sometime?"

"Yes, I would," she said with a shy nod.

Mina slipped away without interrupting them.

"He comes almost every day," Sister Joan said. "He began to talk of adopting her last week, though for now he wants to see about making her his ward. Let her get used to the idea first. I wanted to ask for your opinion. Is this a good idea?"

"She could have been the child he and Lucy bore together, Sister Joan," Mina said, her eyes straying back to the room where Arthur sat with the little girl and the storybook. "Yes, I think it's a very good idea." She blinked back tears, as she smiled.

CHAPTER 30

Mr. Drummond and Arthur sat with Mina over tea. They had requested this audience, and she waited patiently for them to come to the point, as she poured tea and offered biscuits and scones.

"Mina, there is something we have to confess," Arthur said, hesitating to meet her gaze. "You see, Jonathan asked us not to at the time. Maybe we shouldn't have, but—"

"We felt that, as your husband, he really should have some say." Drummond picked up the narrative when Arthur faltered. "Whether that was wise or not is a moot point now."

"Gentlemen, whatever you have to say, just say it. I won't try to second-guess my husband at this late date," she said with a wry smile. "Besides, I'd say he's had the last word anyway, wouldn't you?"

They both chuckled and glanced shame-faced at one another.

"She has a point there," Arthur murmured.

"The woman has a good head on her shoulders." Drummond nodded.

"Here it is, Mina," Arthur said, looking her in the eye. "Lady Westenra left you a sizeable portion of her estate in her will."

Mina's teacup hit the saucer with a clatter.

"That's quite right," Drummond nodded. "Jonathan hesitated to let you know that. You two were going through a particularly rough patch at that time. I—er—I fear he suspected that you might strike out on your own if you had independent means at your disposal."

"Knowing Jonathan, he would have told you readily enough, had you truly wanted to leave him," Arthur added quickly. "But he wanted you to go or stay according to your heart, not the means available to you. I believe he may also have thought that, if he told you, you might feel he wanted you to go."

"He was always so insecure about their wealth," Mina said, rising to drift to the window. She stared out over the garden where Mary frolicked with a new puppy among the flowers, her governess watching over her. "He dreaded the time I spent with Lucy, thinking

I would not be content as a lawyer's wife after my visits with my wealthy friend. I just never thought of it that way. Lucy was Lucy and Jonathan was my beloved. I loved them, not the worlds they lived in."

"The point is, Mina, Jonathan had little to leave you in the way of physical wealth. There was a small life insurance policy, but it will not give you much. And I owe you a debt I can never repay." Mr. Drummond sighed. "You destroyed the man who took our daughter from us. And you saved my life in the process."

"But you are now a woman of independent means, Mina," Arthur said. "Thanks to Lady Westenra, you can go anywhere you wish. Your resources are large enough to last several lifetimes. And if Sister Joan's story is any indication, you might have a few lifetimes ahead of you. I think God has provided for you, my friend."

Mina stared at the child in the garden. She pictured the children in Whitechapel, hungry, dirty, living off scraps. Being hunted. Prey.

"Didn't you have my house cleaned, Arthur?" she asked suddenly.

"Yes, I did," he said, startled at her sudden change in subjects. "What are you thinking, Mina?"

"I think I want to redecorate."

~~~

For two weeks, Mina flitted in and out with new fabric samples. She couldn't bear to remain within the walls until it no longer resembled the house she shared with Jonathan. Workmen painted every room, carted away the furniture and brought in beds for every room. The study became her parlor and office, the upstairs rooms became dormitories, and the old parlor became a nursery. The dining room held a large, sturdy table, big enough for twenty little bodies. Mina took Mrs. Hardman's old room, though she rarely used it more than a few hours at a time. Soon, the beds began filling. Sister Joan and Father Gallagher brought her most of the little ones, often in the dead of night, after a vampire left their parents in the clinic with injuries. She cared for them, fed them, protected them.

Her first permanent boarders were Freddy Barnes and Danny Ford, the little newsboy. They considered themselves her personal messengers and errand boys. And though she often joked that they consumed their body weight in groceries, they became indispensable members of her household. They knew the risks and they stayed anyway, protecting the younger children willingly.
~~~

When she had six regular boarders, she hired a cook, coaxing Arthur out of one of his own undercooks, to make the savory meat pies the children all loved. Then she needed an assistant to watch the children, when she began to patrol the streets with Father Gallagher. At that point, Annie Hartford came to live in the big house. The old flower lady from the corner had reached a point where sitting out in London's weather was too much for her arthritic joints, but the children needed affection, and she had that in abundance.

Mina's household now ran efficiently with or without her, and she was free to chase down the predators that still infested their streets. There was no sign of the man in the top hat, though.

~~~

"You need this more than I do," Sister Joan said to her one crisp winter evening. She handed Mina the silver blade that she had used in the battle outside the church, the one that had slain Sister Gertrude.

"But Sister Joan! I couldn't!" Mina said, holding the blade reverently in her hands.

"I can no longer grasp the handle, my dear." The nun's hands had to be massaged daily with aromatic oils now to enable her to work with the sick. Her role was becoming more and more that of an instructor. "It must be wielded by a warrior. It is time to pass the proverbial torch. I want you to have it."

"Thank you, Sister Joan," Mina had whispered, hugging the nun gently, the sword held away from her body. "I promise to use it well."

That night had marked her first night patrolling London's streets. They cornered a female vampire trying to attack a young man coming from a tavern. Had the lad been a bit more intoxicated, she might have succeeded. She saw Mina run toward her, sword gleaming in the moonlight and shrieked.

The vampire crouched and hissed. "Master told me about you! He's coming back for you and when he does—"

Mina's sword whistled through the air as she swung and the vampire's head flipped twice before turning to ash and raining to the cobblestones with the rest of her body.

"What was that?" the man cried.

"You're safe now," Father Gallagher said, kneeling beside the lad.

"Father, I'll never drink again."
~~~

"I highly doubt that, young man, but it's a noble thought," the priest said, patting him on the shoulder. "Did she bite you?"

"D-did she what?"

"Bite your neck. Did she bite you, my son?"

The man felt his neck and his fingers came away smeared with blood. "What's this? What did she do to me? Father, what did that woman do to me?" His voice rose.

"Come on, lad," Father Gallagher hoisted him to his feet. "Let's get you to the clinic. You'll be fine. She didn't get more than a nibble."

"*What?*"

They led the young man back to the church, but Mina pondered the vampire's strange words. *What master?*

CHAPTER 31

Mina's life settled into a fairly predictable pattern for the next four years. She helped at the clinic, patrolled the streets with Father Gallagher, and destroyed vampires. No matter how many they dispatched, there always seemed to be more. But she had not seen the man in the top hat again. Van Helsing had not been able to identify him, and that was troubling. The longer they went without knowing more about him, the more convinced Mina became that he had been Frederick Von Bardenburg's master and not the other way around.

Then one day, she had a surprise visitor.

Ushering Mrs. Tunstall into her parlor, she had poured tea and offered her sandwiches and biscuits on a small tray. Mrs. Tunstall had accepted gratefully.

"Mrs. Harker, I am so sorry to intrude on you," Mrs. Tunstall began, toying nervously with the food on her plate. "But Henry thought so much of you. Valued your opinion. Well, my husband and I hoped… that is… "

"I was very fond of Henry, Mrs. Tunstall," Mina had said soothingly. "He's a fine young man. I was so sorry to see him leave London, though I do understand why that was the easiest course for him. Is there something I can help you with? Please don't hesitate to ask."

Mrs. Tunstall sighed in relief. Setting her plate on the small side table, she pulled a packet of letters from her purse. "We've been receiving letters from Henry.

"At first, he seemed to be more himself in Canada. He pulled himself together. Then he began to behave restlessly. Quite suddenly, he took off for some place on the far side of America called California. He had it in his mind that he was going to mine for silver!"

Mina kept her face neutral, betraying none of her surprise at such behavior.

"Then he met some man who convinced him to go into a

business venture with him. Some American. We know nothing of this man, Alexander McSween, other than he's a lawyer and wanted to set up a store. What if he's using our boy? Then we started getting these letters and they just sound… wrong." She thrust the letters into Mina's hand.

"Are you sure you wish me to read these?" she had asked.

"Yes, please." Mrs. Tunstall's lips had trembled, but she raised the teacup to her lips and sipped the brew until she had calmed enough to nibble at a sandwich.

Mina's brows had knitted as she read of the business venture in a place called New Mexico with Alex McSween. It was a rough town, but desperately in need of honest businessmen. There was only one store, run by an outfit called "The Company." A man named L.G. Murphy and his partner, James Dolan, were fleecing the whole county with inflated prices and terrible interest rates on loans. Small ranchers were going out of business at an alarming rate. Mina read the last couple of letters with raised eyebrows and widened eyes. She looked up and saw the confirming nod from Mrs. Tunstall.

"You see it too, don't you, Mrs. Harker?" she whispered.

"Henry thinks he's going to take over control of the county from these men, Murphy and Dolan?" Mina had asked incredulously. "This doesn't sound like Henry at all!"

"That's what my husband and I say too," Mrs. Tunstall said, her teacup clattering as she set it down abruptly. "I'm so afraid for my son, Mrs. Harker. I have this… this terrible… foreboding. Please, can you go to him? Talk to him? Try to get him to come home. He might listen to you. He always thought so highly of you."

"How old is Henry now?" Mina had asked thoughtfully.

"He's twenty-three years old. He'll be twenty-four next March."

"He may not listen to me either," she said ruefully. "Young men at that age don't like to feel like they're being 'instructed' — especially by women."

"I know." Mrs. Tunstall had nodded again. "But you're our only hope. We don't know of anyone else that Henry might listen to. We've tried to reason with him by letter. You've read his responses. At least, if you try…" she swallowed tears, "we'll know we did all we could."

Mina stood and walked to the window. She stared into the streets. Her streets. Who would patrol these streets if she left for America?

That Still Small Voice chuckled in her ear. *Do you think I am not able to handle the streets of London without the great Mina Harker? Do you not know that I can call down a legion of My angels, if need be, to help My other warriors in this city?*

Chagrined, Mina acknowledged her own hubris. God did not need her in London—especially if He was calling her to go help Henry Tunstall.

She turned back to Mrs. Tunstall, who had been sitting on the edge of her seat, all but holding her breath. "I'll make arrangements to leave as soon as I possibly can. Please allow me to copy down this address so I know where I'm going." She gave a wry smile and moved to Jonathan's desk as Mrs. Tunstall dropped her face into her hands in relief.

<div align="center">~~~</div>

First, she went to see Mr. Drummond in his office. With minimal fuss, she made legal arrangements for the house to be under the management of the Order of the Maids, with Arthur Holmwood as the executor. She left ample funds for its maintenance. Then she headed for the church.

Both Father Gallagher and Father Matthew greeted her warmly. They listened intently as she explained about Mrs. Tunstall's visit.

"I hate to see you go," Father Gallagher said with a wry smile. "You're the best partner I've had in years when it comes to taking these monsters out on the street. But if this is God's calling, you have to go where He leads."

"It may be nothing more than miscommunication, but I have a feeling…" She shook her head in frustration. "I hate leaving you here, especially with the extra responsibility of my house and the children. But I feel that Henry is in real trouble."

"Your instincts are good, Mina. Don't discount them. It might just be lawless men in a rugged country," he said with a sigh. "But I've heard some dark forces are at work in America. It's a country recently torn apart by a vicious war. You have no idea what you might be walking into. Be very careful."

Father Matthew abruptly left the room. Mina looked startled. "Did I upset him? Is he angry I'm leaving?"

Father Gallagher laughed. "If anything, he's going to take it harder than anyone else. You might not believe it, but that old man is very fond of you."

Mina shook her head. "I remember when he threatened to

excommunicate me," she mused.

"Yes, well, I think he'd enthusiastically stake anyone else who even suggested such a thing now." Father Gallagher laughed, then his tone became serious. "Don't let personal prejudice blind you, Mina. This is not a personal fight—it's a war against principalities and powers. Remember that. You won't be going to a country with a policeman on every corner either. It's a rough, new country, especially if you're headed to the western portion. That part isn't even recognized for statehood yet. The territories are wild, lawless places, and the men who go there answer to no one. Don't get sucked into someone else's bid for power."

Father Matthew returned with a small valise. He offered it to Mina with a gentle smile. "Just a little going away gift. You might need a few things, my child."

"Thank you, Father Matthew," she said, smiling. She set it on the desk nearby and opened it. "Holy water, stakes, knives, a small gun, a box of silver bullets, and a lovely silver dagger. Father, it's everything a girl could possibly need!"

"Well, it's everything **you** may need, at any rate," he said with a smirk. "You aren't exactly an average girl, Mina Harker."

He took out his own bottle of oil and blessed her. Mina felt the mantle of responsibility fall on her shoulders. Where it would take her, she didn't know, but the door had opened, and God was definitely shoving her through.

EPILOGUE

Mina strode along the deck of the *SS Bothnia*. Her passage from Liverpool to New York had been quickly arranged, and she was on her way to America. She had written to Henry to let him know she was coming, but she wasn't even sure he'd receive the letter before she got there herself. Arthur had advised her on travel arrangements. Trains should get her most of the way across the country. They'd made great progress with rail travel in the last decade. And with the end of the Civil War, the armies had stopped disrupting the tracks and tearing up each other's supply lines. Hopefully, she'd get most of the way across the vast expanse of territory before having to travel by stagecoach.

She enjoyed the fresh sea air on her face and the expanse of stars overhead. The night skies were peaceful, and she felt the waves roll beneath her feet. The ship was large enough that their voyage was relatively calm, but the first day or two had still rocked her enough to make her feel off balance. Now she understood the term 'sea legs'!

Mina frowned. A familiar scent floated her way, and she tensed. She waited one second, two—then she whirled, releasing her dagger from her sleeve in one smooth move as she rolled to the left and came up in a low crouch. The vampire turned, trying to follow her movements, but momentarily thrown off balance by her maneuver.

"Mrs. Harker?" He tilted his head to one side. "You are not what I expected." He lunged, but Mina was ready, and she drove the dagger home with pinpoint accuracy. Ash scattered in the sea breeze.

"Not even a few days respite to cross an ocean, Lord?" Mina asked, looking up at the sky with a smile on her lips.

She felt the brush of angel's wings in the breeze on her face.

END

About the Author

Deborah Cullins Smith has been writing stories ever since she could hold a pencil, but she came to her actual career in writing rather late in life. After dabbling in poetry and inspirational articles for several years, she dove into the deep end of the fantasy pool and found her true love in fiction writing.

In 2019, she published the trilogy, *The Last of the Long-Haired Hippies*, in a rapid release timed for the 50th anniversary of Woodstock, which she covered in great detail in the second volume. CWG Press released **Shroud of Darkness, The Birth of the Storm** and **Victoria's War** over a four-month period, a culmination of almost twenty years in development.

That same year, Ms. Cullins Smith joined forces with Michelle Levigne to create Ye Olde Dragon Books, a small publishing coop in Christian fantasy and science fiction. In their first year, they have co-edited two anthologies, and written a third one themselves. **When Your Beauty IS the Beast, Moonlight and Claws**, and **Two Olde Dragons Writing Wyrd Stories.**

Ms. Cullins Smith hopes to make this the first of many books about Mina Harker's adventures, featuring significant historical figures and events as time marches on. Her next story will continue the saga of Billy the Kid, which she began in the anthology **Moonlight and Claws** with the story *Habitations of Violence*. Her love of historical research makes these books challenging, as she is devoted to maintaining as much historical accuracy as possible while sliding things sideways to suggest that a few characters might be more than we gave them credit for! (No disrespect intended.)

Ms. Cullins Smith is the grandmother of twelve, avid dog lover, and still loves working with handicrafts of all sorts, from knitting and crocheting to cross-stitch and beadwork.

You can find her on Facebook, Goodreads, Amazon Author, and MeWe.

Ye Old Dragon Books Anthologies

WHEN YOUR BEAUTY IS THE BEAST
Fairytale Anthology Book 1

A marriage counselor who has never been in love...
A missing beauty queen with an oversized ego...
A hunter crippled by his own ambition...
Settlers on their way to a new home in the Rockies in 1848...
A jeweler's obsession...
A hero-tuber and a mystery man trapped in a haunted house...
Infatuation and ego aboard a space ship bound for a new world...
Curses, plants, and shapeshifters in a South American garden...
A gamers' quest with unconventional challenges...
A castle and a beast being strangled by roses --and a curse...
A princess' problematic seventeenth birthday and the curses surrounding it...
And a castle besieged by ice and basilisks!
What do all these things have in common? They are all variations on the Beauty and the Beast retelling. Fall in love with an old fairy tale in a whole new way as you enter their worlds and find enchantment!

MOONLIGHT AND CLAWS
Classic Monsters Anthology Book 1

The Wolfman.
Where does the Hollywood version end and folklore begin? What is the truth about the wolfman, the werewolf, the were, the lycan, the skinwalker and shapeshifter?
You know what? It doesn't matter!

Come explore and enjoy and shiver and cry and laugh and cheer and sigh and even fall in love with the amazing imaginations of seventeen authors, who explore their own particular twists and turns and reflections on just what it means -- or could mean -- to be the Wolf.

Just which version do you believe in? Lost soul -- cursed victim -- avenger -- motherless child -- star-crossed lover -- lonely heart -- healer -- music lover -- loyal friend -- hero?

Which version of the Wolfman most resonates with you?

Read, explore, and find out.

He could be someone you know. He could be the "boy next door." He could be you ...

Featuring the story that introduced readers to Mina Harker: ***Habitations of Violence.***

Mina journeys to the New Mexico Territory to help Henry Tunstall against the infamous Murphy and Dolan monopoly in Lincoln County. She finds that vampires aren't the only supernatural beings in existence when she meets Henry's hired hand, Billy the Kid.

TALES FROM THE TOWER
Fairytale Anthology Book 2

Consider Rapunzel, a woman locked in a tower all of her life.
Or was she?

Was she a prisoner? Or was she the jailer? Was she locked away, or was she hiding?

How does Rapunzel's story reflect what we've experienced over the last couple of years as we've locked ourselves away, then struggled to regain our lives again through the pandemic?

Check back in April 2022 and see what our authors have come up with!